The Least of These

William Price

537 Books

This work of fiction was human generated.

To my wife and sons for their unwavering support as I went on this journey and to my dogs who were my faithful writing companions

And the King will answer them, "Truly, I say to you as you did it to one of the least of these my brothers, you did it to me."

Matthew 25:40

An eye for an eye will only make the whole world blind

Mahatma Gandhi

1

February 10, 2022

Darkness evaporated into a flood of yellow, fluorescent light falling from the ceiling, accompanied by a slight hum.

"Hollins," a gruff voice called from behind the bars. "Get up. It's your graduation day."

Alex slowly sat up, squinting at the bright light, hung his legs over the bed as he tried to shake the inertia of sleep. The institutional smell of stale bleach hit his nose. Rubbing his eyes, he looked around the small six-by-eight room he had called home for the past twenty-five years. His brain trying to process that this was his last day here.

"Get your shower kit and stand back," the voice snapped.

Alex slipped his tattered prison grade shoes on and retrieved his shower kit.

A loud magnetic buzz filled the room and the metal bars slid back.

"Come on," the guard said, motioning him out of the cell.

Alex walked slowly, following the guard down the dimly lit hallway to the shower chambers.

Soon the cells erupted with celebratory yells and playful jeers.

"Free man walking!!!"

"Make sure you clean up nice!!"

The inmates used whatever object they could find to make noises across the iron prison bars.

Alex should have been happy. However, cold fingers of sadness and fear grabbed at his soul. He was leaving the only family he had known for the past quarter of a century. Some of these men would die here. He would never see any of them again. A moment of panic struck him as he fought the urge to dart back into his cell.

"Quiet down!!" the guard shouted at the inmates, "Keep it up and I'll knock twenty minutes off your yard time today."

Yard time was sacred and the hallway noise dropped to a murmur.

The guard approached the shower room and let Alex in.

"You got ten minutes."

Turning on the shower, he was met with the familiar low pressure lukewarm water he had grown accustomed to. This was the last shower he would take here; it was hard to absorb. Prison was the only life he had known for over two decades, returning back into the real world seemed daunting.

The rotten egg smell of sulfur water filled the stall as he desperately tried to clean his body with the cheap soap that barely lathered. After several minutes he turned off the water and stepped out of the shower, taking a moment to look at himself in the full-length mirror.

His body had grown lean and muscular thanks to spending hours every day in the yard or the weight room, not to mention all the work details he pulled. He had a few new scars thanks to some altercations in the yard. His black hair was buzzed tight to his scalp and his deep hazel eyes betrayed the sadness in his soul.

He grabbed a towel and dried off.

His clothes sat neatly in a pile. A prison issued pair of jeans and a white T-shirt. For the first time in twenty-five years, he was wearing something different than his standard orange monotone prison jumpsuit. A loud rap on the door brought him out of his thoughts.

"Two minutes Hollins...."

"Ok."

Tossing his jumpsuit into the laundry basket he turned and made his way out of the shower room. The guard led him down another hallway. The rough denim of the jeans rubbed against his legs in a distinctly different way than the comforting polyester blend of his prison jumpsuit. Another sign of the change awaiting him.

The guard led him into a small room with a faded sign that read "Office." It consisted of a small metal desk and a wooden chair. A stern looking deputy sitting behind the desk looked up.

"Mr. Hollins."

"Yes sir."

"Alright," the deputy said, pointing to the chair. "Take a seat."

Alex sat in the hard wooden chair.

The deputy slid a small wire basket toward him.

"Here are the contents of your person we cataloged when you were first brought in. They should include a wallet, twenty dollars, a pocketknife, and car keys." The deputy looked up at Alex, "I'll have you confirm it is all there."

Alex rifled through the meager contents which now represented his entire world.

"Looks good to me."

"Alright, just initial and sign here," the deputy said, handing Alex a clipboard with a tattered piece of paper on it.

"Per the State of Virginia, you are given a travel voucher and $100 cash to help get some of your affairs established." The deputy slid an envelope across the desk.

"You are still planning on staying with your mother in Pinehurst, is that correct?"

"Yes sir."

"Ok, I will go ahead and call a cab for you."

"Thank you."

This moment was surreal as the dull yellow, fluorescent light filled the room, bouncing off the white ceramic tile climbing the walls.

Was everyone who sat in this chair as scared and uncertain as he was?

He was thankful he still had his mother and at least had a place to go. He knew everyone was not that fortunate.

"Ok, Mr. Hollins, we will have you wait in the lounge until your ride is here." The deputy stood and extended a hand to Alex. "Best of luck. You have been a model prisoner and I'm sure you will have no problem landing on your feet."

For some reason, Alex doubted it.

2

Harper Layne shed her scrubs onto the tile floor of the bathroom and hopped in the shower. This had been her routine since starting in the emergency room over a year ago.

During a usual shift, she was exposed to more bodily fluids and germs than any normal person would have been in a lifetime. She remained even more cautious with a four-year-old, not want to bring anything home to him.

The hot water and lavender body soap washed away the stress of the last twelve hours. She enjoyed her job as a nurse, but she enjoyed being a mother more. Experiencing full-fledged mother's guilt every time she walked out the door leaving Landon in the capable hands of her older sister. Before the divorce, she only worked a few shifts a month. Now she was a single mom working full time plus overtime trying to support herself and Landon.

The shower ended much sooner than it should have. Grabbing her robe, she stepped out of the bathroom. Her sister's house was smaller than where she had lived. The wooden floors creaked and she made her way carefully down the hallway trying not to wake Landon. A dull glow came from the living room and she found her sister sitting in the recliner reading one of her trashy romance novels with a glass of wine in hand.

"Hey sis," Harper said, "How was Lando tonight?"

Vanessa Layne rolled her eyes, "You know he is always such a handful. It took two shots of Benadryl to get him down."

"You're awful!" Harper said sitting on the couch, "He is a perfect angel, just like his mother!"

"Oh my! It's getting deep in here," Vanessa said raising both feet off the floor, "How was work?"

"It wasn't bad, the usual, sore throats, vomit, strokes, heart attacks, level 1 traumas. The usual life of an ER nurse."

"Gross!!!"

"What's gross about that?"

"You said vomit, yuck!"

"This is why you are a teacher and not in the medical field."

"I know." Vanessa grinned. "I get squeamish handling lunch meat."

A quiet whimper came from the hallway. Both ladies turned to look.

"Guess who is up?" Vanessa laughed, "You are on deck!"

Harper was already down the hallway, her maternal instincts on full alert.

She stopped outside Landon's door, pausing to see if he was awake.

"Mommy!!" he cried.

She cracked open the door and stepped inside. "Mommy's here baby."

A Paw Patrol night light softly illuminated the room with a warm glow. Landon Layne sat up in bed hugging a tattered brown puppy dog tightly to his chest.

"What's wrong Lando baby?" Harper slid into the bed next to him.

"I had a bad dream," he whimpered, a lone tear running down his cheek. "The monster was back in the closet."

She put her arm around him and pulled him close to her side. Catching the faint scent of cherry scented baby shampoo.

"We scared the monsters away from your closet a couple of nights ago and they are not coming back, remember?"

"I don't think it worked," Landon whimpered, pulling the puppy closer to his face.

"Sure, it did, let me go check." When Harper stood a small hand grabbed her wrist

"No!" Landon's voice rose, "Call daddy! I want Daddy to check."

A knot formed in her stomach. The past year had been hard on both of them. Particularly Landon, who idolized his father. When the divorce was finalized, Patrick only had supervised visitation one weekend a month. This was best as the drugs had taken their toll on her ex-husband.

What started as an opioid addiction following back surgery led to a full-blown heroin addiction which, in Roanoke, was easier to get than Oxycontin. He had made a good living as a lineman for the power company, but when he didn't cooperate with the company's assistance with his addiction, it ultimately cost him his job.

Addicted, unemployed and no purpose, he became abusive. Initially taking it out on her, which she could handle, but he crossed the line when he struck Landon. He came home from an all-night binge. Landon was three, suffering from a horrible ear infection and was inconsolable.

"Shut the kid up or I'll do it for you," Patrick yelled from the couch.

She tried everything to keep Lando quiet, but nothing worked.

The door to the room burst open and he stormed in, yanking Landon out of her arms. He smacked him in the face and dropped him to the floor with a sickening thud.

"Patrick!!!"

She leapt towards Landon, a still mound on the floor where he'd been dropped.

"I said he needed to be quiet!"

A blinding flash of pain cut across her ribs as his boot connected with her side, knocking the wind out of her. She collapsed to the floor gasping for air.

A second later the front door slammed shut and the guttural growl of his motorcycle rumbled through the house and faded away as he drove off.

That was the last night she and Landon spent in the house. She left their home in Roanoke and returned to Pinehurst; her sister was gracious enough to have them stay with her.

"Baby you know daddy can't come." He is dealing with his own monsters, she wanted to say.

"I want Daddy!!" he cried, "I want Daddy!!"

She hugged him close, and he buried his face in her chest.

3

Lounge was a generous term.

It was a small room with two ugly orange plastic chairs and a brown plaid sofa that looked at least fifty years old. A vending machine stood in the corner appeared like it hadn't been stocked in years. On a small wooden table sat an old coffeemaker, the carafe empty and stained a permanent shade of brown, its digital clock blinking an eternal midnight.

Alex elected to sit on one of the plastic chairs, thinking it might be the most hygienic choice. A Sports Illustrated from 1997 and an old TV Guide decorated a small coffee table. There were some religious tracks laid out. Alex looked down at a yellow pamphlet lying on the corner of the table.

Not Sure Who to Turn To?
Lost with no Direction?
Find your Home with New Zion Ministries.

On the cover was a dated photo of Silas Weston, a practiced grin frozen on his face, surrounded by members of New Zion. Women and children smiled, trusting.

Alex's mouth went dry.

Grabbing the brochure, he balled it up and threw it in a nearby waste basket. The visceral reaction to seeing the pamphlet startled Alex.

"Hollins," a young female voice called from the door. He looked up.

"Rides here," she motioned him towards the door.

"Thanks." He stood picking up the box with his belongings and made his way outside.

The crisp February air turned his breath into a white cloud. A dingy orange Ford Taurus with Yellow Taxi Co. stenciled in bold black letters on the side idled in front of him. The trunk popped open and Alex laughed, looking at the small box in his hand.

I won't be needing that much space.

Placing his possessions in the trunk he walked around to the rear passenger door. He slid into the back seat and was hit with the smell of cigarettes and garlic. The fake leather seat felt cool on his legs this winter morning.

"Where to?" the driver said, keeping his gaze facing forward.

"Pinehurst."

"Gotcha, over in Bucks County, right?"

"Yes sir, I'll be going to 220 Wildwood Dr."

The driver typed something into his phone. Alex wasn't sure what he was doing.

"You got a map?" Alex asked.

The driver laughed and looked up in the rearview mirror. "No sir, got it all right here." He held up the phone.

The car moved forward. Alex had a lot of catching up to do.

"How does it feel to be a free man?" the cabbie asked.

Alex wasn't in the mood for small talk but figured he was a captive audience for at least an hour.

"Too early to tell," Alex laughed, "Being locked up is all I've known for the past twenty-five years. I think I have some adjusting to do."

"I'm sure."

An inquisitive silence hung in the air, like the cabbie wanted to ask, but knew better.

"Vehicular manslaughter," Alex said.

"What?" the cabbie sounded genuinely confused.

"What I was in for. I got drunk, made a bad choice, and killed someone."

"Aw man, that sucks. I'm sorry."

"No need to apologize, I learned my lesson," Alex said. "I wanted to let you know you weren't transporting a sexual predator back here."

The cabbie let out a cautious laugh.

They rode in silence for a while. The radio played some country music Alex recognized from the yard.

"You make this run a lot?" Alex asked, feeling uncomfortable in the silence.

"Not a whole lot. I've done it enough though. I usually take family members or significant others. A lot of tears have been shed in that back seat."

"No one is ever guilty though," the cabbie said, "at least according to their family."

"True, no one wants to believe their family member is a criminal. I don't think my mom has ever accepted this."

"Nothing like a mother's love," the cabbie said. "Miss my mom every day."

"I'm sorry. I can't imagine."

"Yeah, cancer is a bad actor. Don't take no prisoners."

The asphalt highway passed by as Alex's breath fogged up the window. The mountains were bare now in early February with patches of snow covering the forest floor. The morning sun had started to cut through the trees, casting fingers of light across the ground. Several houses tucked away in the mountains had smoke rising from their chimneys, a visual of how cold the winter morning was.

It seemed like forever before the familiar large green sign passed by.

Pinehurst one mile.

Almost home.

Had Pinehurst changed much or was it stuck in time?

Growing up there it always felt like time was frozen. Playing outside till the sun disappeared during the summer, having family dinners with everyone around the table, neighbors dropping in for long visits, Christmas parades, and Easter egg hunts.

His childhood was idyllic, yet he had still managed to screw up his life. The soft click of the turn signal and the car veering to the right brought him out of his nostalgic mood. Merging off the interstate and into the town of Pinehurst, Alex could see not much had changed and a lot had.

The road had one stop light, with the yellow light stuck on an infinite cycle of blinking. A Burger King and a local motel with the Vacancy sign lit up decorated the side of the road. There were also some older buildings with closed signs in the windows, one had a condemned sign and the front door was covered with bright yellow caution tape.

Soon they passed a large Walmart. The parking lot looked crowded.

"Pretty much the only thing to do around here anymore," the cabbie said. "Walmart is the new social club."

After a couple of turns, they made their way into a subdivision. Rows of brick ranch homes lined the street. Front yards were decorated with disabled cars on cinder blocks and children's toys strewn haphazardly on the lawns. An occasional dog wandered out to investigate the car as it made its way down the road.

The cab rolled up to the familiar single-story ranch home Alex grew up in. The front yard had turned brown in the winter weather. An older model Chevy Impala sat in the carport. Hollins 220 Wildwood Dr was crudely painted in white on the side of a black mailbox speckled with rust.

A sudden rush emotion hit him.

"This the place?" the cabbie asked.

"Yep, this is the place."

"The prison paid the fare, so you're good to go man."

"Thanks, appreciate the ride."

"Good luck out there, man. Hope things go well for you," the cabbie said.

"Thanks."

Alex slid out of the seat and walked to the back of the car. The trunk let out a dull click as the lock disengaged. Alex lifted the lid and got his box of belongings out. He shut the trunk and tapped on the back to let the cabbie know he could leave.

He turned and looked at the front door. He was home.

4

"Damnation is coming!!!!" the words spewed off Silas Weston's tongue in a venomous tirade, "Alcohol, tobacco, the lottery, fornication, marijuana, homosexuals!!!"

Scattered shouts and amens rose from the audience.

"Friends, these were once the scourge of large cities, places like Richmond or Washington DC." His round face turned bright red as spit flew out of his mouth. "But now...now...these diseases have found their way to our quiet little town!!!"

"Pinehurst is no longer the innocent place many of us grew up in!!!"

"No!!! The sinners and their liberal agenda have tainted our town!!" he shouted and then jumped, his large body barely leaving the floor.

"But you know what?"

"What pastor?" a voice came from the audience.

"Ha ha.... we have a secret weapon!!" he laughed, "Whooo!!!"

Shouts and screams went up from the congregation.

"He is bigger than any of this filth we are dealing with!! He is bigger than that liberal agenda."

"Amen!! Hallelujah!!"

"We don't need to be afraid!!" his voice thundered. "We need to take action!!"

- 19 -

The congregation erupted in a chorus of shouts, screams, and applause.

"Christ wants us to be active followers; he wants us to be the cure for the disease plaguing our town!!"

"Just like Christ drove the merchants out of the temple, we need to drive these vile sinners from our town!!! We need to make Pinehurst great again!!"

With the obvious political nod, the congregation all stood on their feet and cheered.

New Zion Road church was founded by Silas Weston Sr. in 1940. He was fresh out of seminary and on fire to change the world. When he died suddenly from a heart attack in 1980, Silas Jr. returned to Pinehurst and assumed control of the church.

Soon he grew more enamored with the power he could wield as a pastor instead of the true influence he could have for the Kingdom of God. Young, good-looking, and charismatic, he quickly established a large following.

The crowd now worked into a frenzy as Silas paced across the pulpit whooping and hollering, adding an occasional jump for flare.

"I don't believe Gawd intends us to sit back and watch our town go directly to hell!!" Silas waved a white handkerchief in the air, brought it down to his face wiping his sweat soaked brow.

"No, I believe God has called us into action!!"

More cheers and Amens.

"I know it's not convenient, not popular, but neither was hanging on a cross!" he shouted. "If the Son of God can do that for us, this is the least we can do for him!"

The congregation erupted into a fervor with shouts, crying, and laughter. Some men and women began running laps around the sanctuary.

Silas stepped back with a slight smile and admired the results of his performance of a lifetime.

5

The cab rolled slowly away from the small brick ranch home, leaving a plume of exhaust in its wake. Overgrown dead shrubbery lined the front of the house; a faded Merry Christmas sign still hung on the front door.

The sight of smoke rolling from chimneys hit Alex with a wave of nostalgia at being back at his childhood home.

Despite being away for twenty-five years the street, he had grown up on looked remarkably the same. A series of cookie cutter homes lined the street with slight design differences attempting to make them look unique.

Making his way up the cracked concrete sidewalk to the front door, he hesitated then stuck out a finger pressing the doorbell. After a few seconds there was some shuffling inside and a female voice called out, "I'm coming."

The red wooden front door cracked open to reveal an elderly lady with faded silver hair who stood about to Alex's chest. Nancy Hollins threw the door open and wrapped her arms around her son.

"Oh, my baby!!! My baby's home!" She hugged him tightly, her body shook, "I missed you so much."

Alex squeezed her tightly to his chest. "I love you Ma!"

Alex caught the faint scent of coffee and buttery toast, whisking him back to winter mornings at home as a child. Warm air from the gas heat spilled out of the door.

"I was so afraid I would be dead before I got to see my baby home again!!" she sobbed.

"Come on Mom, that's a depressing way to greet your son." Alex laughed, giving her an extra hard squeeze. "Let's get inside before I freeze to death!"

Stepping back, she raised her wrinkled, leathery hands and placed them on his cheeks. "Come here," she said as she pulled him down to her and gave him a big kiss. "Let's get you some breakfast."

"It will be the first homecooked breakfast I've had in a long time." He grinned.

The kitchen was just as he remembered it. A faded yellowed linoleum floor ran the length of it. The dark green refrigerator sat against the wall humming loudly. There were still faded photos of him and his mom hanging on the refrigerator. Some newspaper clippings still hung announcing his achieving the AB honor roll his senior year of high school and getting hired into the apprentice program at the mill.

One clipping caught his eye:

Pinehurst man sentenced to twenty-five years in state prison for vehicular manslaughter.

A grainy black and white mugshot of Alex was under the headline.

"Justice was served today for the Grayson family. Nothing will ever bring Heather back but knowing this drunk maniac is off the street for a while will help the healing process." - Dwyane Lakes District Attorney

Alex's stomach dropped as he tried to process the tangible reminder of his past.

"Mom."

"Yes, sweetie," she said, scrambling some eggs.

"Why did you keep this?" he said, pulling the paper off the refrigerator.

"What dear?" Her back was still to him.

He stepped beside her and held the piece of paper up.

She grew quiet but kept working the eggs with a plastic spatula.

"Mom?"

"Oh dear, it's just…. it's just, for better or worse, it is part of our history now. I will never forget that day."

"Neither will I, but I don't want a constant reminder of it either."

"Dear…." her voice quivered. "I should have taken it down."

"I'm trying to move on from my past, not dwell in it."

Alex balled the paper up and threw it in a nearby wastebasket.

"Here's to starting over."

• • •

The day went by quietly. They spent most of it sitting in the living room drinking coffee and getting caught up on the past twenty-five years. There is only so much you can learn from thirty-minute visits each week.

It was odd just sitting. The drone of constant noise from the prison was absent. He could sit on the couch and not worry about meeting the curfew to be back at his cell. No guards making rounds every fifteen minutes. It was him, his mother, and the steady metronome of the large wooden grandfather clock.

She filled him in on the latest gossip in Pinehurst, all her friends who had died, and her various health ailments. Alex listened as he slowly drank his coffee.

"I really can't believe you are actually home." His mother grinned and another tear welled up in her eye, "Has it been twenty-five years already?"

"I know. It felt much longer to me. Time slows down on the inside." He sipped his coffee. "The same surroundings, same people, same activities every day for twenty-five years. Gets old fast."

"Well, we need to go out tomorrow and get you back into civilization. That means getting you a phone and you can start looking for a job."

"I know Mom but I was hoping to have a few days to adjust before hitting the real world."

She laughed which triggered a paroxysm of violent coughing. Alex got concerned, but she held up one finger, indicating for him to stay put. Eventually, the coughing subsided.

"Sorry," she grinned. "Didn't do my lungs any favors with all those years of smoking."

"That was pretty scary sounding," Alex said. "Maybe you should see a doctor."

"I have an appointment soon." She grinned again. "Don't go worrying about me."

They spent the rest of the day clearing out a spare bedroom Alex could use for his own. His mother continued to bring him up to speed on all the gossip and family drama he had missed over the past twenty-five years, which happened to be a lot.

Supper consisted of Campbell's chicken noodle soup, grilled cheese sandwiches, and a Little Debbie oatmeal creme pie. It was probably the best meal he'd had in years.

Around eight that night his mother walked into his room wearing her robe and had a glass of milk in her hand.

"Dear, I can't stay up late like I used to so I am going to sleep." She smiled and placed a hand on his shoulder. The strong smell of menthol floated past his nose. "You stay up as late as you want."

"Ok, Ma. It's been a great first day back home." Alex stood and wrapped his arms around his mother, giving her a big hug. Her surprisingly frail body hidden under the thick fabric of her gown. "I love you."

"I love you dear." Her voice cracked.

"What's wrong?"

"I'm just sad." She stepped back wiping the tears from her eyes. "Sad, I lost twenty-five years with my boy. It was hard seeing my friends go to weddings, have grandkids, and do the normal family things with their children."

Alex's mouth fell open in disbelief.

Like this had been a choice. He had not planned on killing Heather Grayson.

His chest tightened and he turned his back to his mother, "Well I'm sorry your son disappointed you. Spending twenty-five years in prison was not part of my long-term plan."

"Oh dear, I'm sorry. I know that sounded awful. I'm not trying to place a guilt trip on you. This is an adjustment for both of us. I have a lot of emotions to work through. I shouldn't have said that."

Alex kept his back to her, the soft sounds of footsteps leaving his room followed.

"I'll pull your door shut. Good night, dear."

The sounds of sobbing came from outside his door.

• • •

Alex woke to the smoky aroma of bacon cooking. He didn't even remember getting in bed last night. Compared to the meager cot in prison, the twin bed in his old room slept like a cloud. He lay motionless for a moment enjoying the warmth of the gas heat on a cold winter morning. The alarm clock on his nightstand read 9:00. This was the latest he had slept in twenty-five years.

A deep rattling cough interrupted the quiet. The wooden floor creaked in the hallway and there was a soft knock at his door.

"Alex, dear. Are you awake?"

He remembered last night and how he had made his mother cry on his first night home from prison. Guilt tightened in his chest.

"Just woke up Mom."

Another deep cough and the door cracked open.

His mother peeked into the room, "I made you breakfast when you're ready."

"Thanks, Mom."

"Do you drink coffee?"

"Yes, but I'm not sure you can make it as strong as prison coffee." He laughed.

His mom grinned and brought her hand up to her mouth as she started another spasm of coughing.

"You ok?"

"I'm fine dear." She sounded winded. "Just need to move my appointment with Dr. Wilson up sooner. Probably got a simple cold or bronchitis."

As if on cue, a wet rattly cough escaped her lips.

"Well, don't you go and get sick on me as soon as I get home." Alex grinned.

"At eighty, nothing works like it used to.

"Well, you take care of yourself," he said. "You were coughing a lot last night."

"Yes sir," she grinned. "Throw some clothes on and come into the kitchen, I'll be getting your plate together."

"Mom," he said, "I'm sorry about last night."

"No problem sweety." His mom grinned.

"Thanks. I love you."

"I love you too."

It was good to be back home. Of course, it was good to be anywhere other than prison. He sat at the old wooden kitchen table with his mother. The breakfast was good. They talked as he drank his coffee.

"We need to get you one of those cellular phones."

"I'm not even sure how to use one," he said, "I'm used to the pay phones in prison, they weren't exactly high tech."

"I won't be much help," she laughed, "but I understand they have cameras, music and video on them now."

She pointed to the old rotary phone on the wall, "Nothing beats old faithful."

6

Silas stared at the twelve men seated around the large mahogany table. This was the core of his leadership team, Jesus had twelve, so he figured he would follow suit.

The room was lit with the pale-yellow glow of several incandescent lamps. The stagnant smell of cheap cologne and sweat hung in the air.

Only a close few knew his secret; a secret he had paid a large price over the years to keep quiet. He couldn't risk it getting out. That would spell the end of his kingdom.

"I am calling to order this emergency meeting," Silas said with the authority of a Fortune 500 CEO.

The room grew quiet as all twelve men focused on Silas.

"You are probably also aware of the return of the convicted murderer Alex Hollins to our quiet community," Silas said.

More mumbles.

"Our pansy liberal legal system did not see fit to punish him as our Lord and Christ would have wanted." Silas's face grew red. "Heather Grayson lost her life, and Alex Hollins got twenty-five years in jail, a mere slap on the wrist."

Silas took a sip from a glass of water in front of him, sweat pouring off his forehead.

"The sixth commandment clearly states thou shalt not kill!" Silas slammed his hand on the table. "Alex Hollins, whether intentional or not, clearly broke this commandment."

Several Amens went up.

"Now he has brought his sinful nature back to Pinehurst," Silas said. "Our small town is already on the verge of moral collapse and now we have welcomed a convicted murderer back into our town. My friends, this could be the final straw that pushes Pinehurst over the brink."

The room became rowdy.

Silas taught forgiveness, however, rarely practiced it. In his view this was the problem with modern Christianity, it had become soft, and he felt the nation needed to return to the Old Testament philosophy of justice. Christians nowadays are too accommodating.

"We need to act. We need to drive the demons out of this town." Silas stood, the leather chair squeaking with relief as he leaned forward and placed his pudgy hands on the table.

"We are called to be the hands and feet for God's judgment. We need to start with Alex Hollins."

7

The first few days of Alex's return home were refreshingly boring. Riding to Walmart with his mom constituted the most exciting thing in his life. Being the passenger of an eighty-year-old driver evoked a special type of fear in him.

One morning Alex sat in the living room watching television when his mom walked in. She had her hair done and was dressed in what looked like church clothes.

"Wow, what's the special occasion?" Alex asked.

"I have my appointment with Dr. Wilson today," she said.

"That's right," Alex remembered.

He was worried about her. The cough had gotten worse and she seemed to be more short of breath.

"I am only doing this for you, "she grinned. "I'm fine and I'm sure Dr. Wilson will agree."

"Well, I appreciate you humoring me."

"Emory will be here soon," she said.

"Who is Emory?"

"You remember Emory Smith, don't you?"

"The same guy that owned the Pinehurst Pub?"

"Yes! That's him. I was close friends with his wife Ellie. She died a few years ago. Emory and I have stayed close."

"I gave him my fair share of business back in the day," Alex said.

"I remember staying up late waiting for you to come home while you got rid of all the money you earned," she said shaking her head.

Alex had a lot of regrets in life, the biggest was how much he had put his mother through.

"I was young and dumb," he said. "I'm sorry, Mom."

She grinned and hugged him.

"Do you need me to go with you?"

"Nope. You stay here and I'll be back before too long. Be thinking of what you want me to fix you for supper."

"Yes, Ma'am."

She shuffled slowly back down the hallway.

Shortly, the doorbell rang.

"Alex, would you mind getting the door," his mom called from the back, "It's probably Emory."

Alex opened the front door. An older man with thinning silver hair and a slight hunch stood there.

"Hello, you must be Emory?"

"And you must be Alex."

"That's me," Alex said. "Come on in, Mom is getting ready."

The man stepped inside and Alex caught a faint whiff of hair cream and Old Spice.

"I've heard a lot about you," Emory said. "I know your mom is glad to have you home."

"It's great to be home," Alex said. "Particularly eating real food and sleeping on a decent mattress."

"I can imagine. Your mom is one heck of a cook."

"You boys talking about me?"

Nancy Hollins appeared at the end of the hallway, dressed in her Sunday best with a big grin across her face. A pleasant floral scent filled the living room. Alex figured the older you got the bigger deal you had to make about going out, even if it was a doctor's appointment.

"You look nice Mom."

"Thanks, sweetie."

- 30 -

"We better get rolling so we aren't late," Emory said, stepping towards the door, "Nice to meet you Alex, and hopefully I'll be seeing more of you."

"Same here," Alex said. "I appreciate you looking out for my mom."

"Not a problem."

"Bye honey," his mom said, planting a gentle kiss on his cheek.

8

Luther Evans was one of the charter members of New Zion Road Baptist Church. His family had been one of the first families through the door when the church met at a vacant grocery store each Sunday.

Many considered Luther the heir apparent to New Zion when and if Silas ever retired. In contrast to Silas, Luther was a slim man with mousy features, a balding head, and a large mustache.

"Silas, we did confirm Alex Hollins is staying with his mother," he said. "One of our men saw a cab drop him off at her house in Wildwood a couple of days ago."

"Great news!" Silas leaned back in his chair, "So now we know where to focus our efforts."

Silas could not tolerate the fact that Alex Hollins was back in town. It placed too much risk on Silas and his ministry.

"Correct." Luther grinned, "I have the ladies working on some signs and we have plenty of volunteers."

"Excellent work Luther." A wide grin spread across Silas's face. "When do you think we can do this?"

"Hopefully soon."

"Perfect!" Silas raised a hand in the air. "The Lord does work in mysterious ways."

"Amen!"

"Ok, you can go, just keep me updated on the progress."

"Yes sir."

Luther turned and walked out of the office, pulling the door shut behind him.

Silas leaned back in his large leather chair. He wanted Alex gone for good and was going to make his life in Pinehurst miserable. He couldn't risk the truth getting out. As much as he preached against fornication from the pulpit, the hypocrisy might be enough to end his career.

This town did not need a drunkard and a murderer roaming the streets. Silas knew what happened in prison. For all he knew Alex was also some type of sexual deviant.

An eye for an eye is something Silas believed firmly in. He would keep turning up the heat until he made it so uncomfortable for Alex that he was forced to leave, or even better, do something stupid putting him back in jail.

9

Alex spent the day doing odd jobs around his mom's house and starting to fill out some paperwork to get reestablished in the community. It was tricky doing it the old-fashioned way with pen and paper.

His mom did not have the internet. She didn't even have cable and her antique television only picked up three channels with the rabbit ears antenna. At least the prison library had internet access and inmates could schedule some heavily monitored time there.

However, he wouldn't trade his current situation to go back to prison for the convenience of internet access. He was deep in thought working on the paperwork when the phone in the kitchen rang, startling him.

"Hello"

"Hello, Alex?" a gentle older voice said.

"Yes, who is this?"

"Um...yes...this is Emory. Your mom wanted me to let you know Doc Wilson is sending her to the emergency room at Pinehurst Memorial."

Alex's mouth went dry.

"Is it serious?"

"He doesn't think so. He called it an exasperation of her COPD, or something like that. Said she would need a few nights in the hospital and some antibiotics and she should be fine."

"Ok," he said, feeling relieved. "That's good news. What do I need to do? I'm sure you know my situation. I don't have a driver's license."

"No problem. Your mom gave me direct orders to come get you and take you to the emergency room."

"Thank you so much."

"I'll be there in fifteen minutes. Your mom also wanted you to grab a few things for her as well."

"Sure." Alex listened as Emory went down the list of items.

"Ok, I'll see you soon."

Alex placed the receiver back in the cradle. He stared blankly at the yellowed kitchen floor. The true realization of how alone he was in the world poured over him. Without his mother, he would have no reason to be here. He might just as well be back in jail.

Alex pulled himself together and got dressed. He found an old green suitcase in the closet and packed the necessities for his mother.

He sat in the living room and soon a large tan Oldsmobile Cutlass pulled in front of the house and gave a quick chirp of the horn. Alex made his way down the sidewalk, slid the suitcase in the back, and got in the passenger side.

Emory looked at Alex. "Nice seeing you again, but I'm sorry it is under these circumstances."

"I know, thanks again for picking me up."

"Oh, your mom is a special lady. I would do anything for her."

Soon they were moving at a slow rate of speed toward Pinehurst Memorial

"She took wonderful care of my Ellie when she was dying of cancer. We've been good friends since then."

"Sorry about your loss," Alex said.

"Thank you. Cancer is a beast. My poor Ellie suffered awful. Your mom though, she was a true angel. I could not have made it without her."

"Once a nurse always a nurse," Alex laughed.

"Ain't that the truth!"

Alex smiled. His mom had been a medical surgical nurse her entire life. Even after she retired, she spent her time volunteering and helping families out. From what he understood, med-surg nursing was not the most glamorous, but it was where his mom felt like she made the biggest impact.

They drove in silence for a bit, the radio playing the familiar notes of "Blessed Assurance." Emory hummed along as the homes and trees passed him by.

The music stopped and a fiery voice filled the car.

"Damnation is coming to Pinehurst!" The voice thundered through the static on the radio, "My friends, our little town is sliding into darkness. The election was almost stolen by those who mock God. Outsiders have crept into our community, bringing their corruption with them. Many stores are now open seven days a week desecrating the Sabbath. The theater filling our children's minds with the wickedness of Disney. Alcohol flows through our town. And…and…the sin our Lord called an abomination is now openly practiced in our small town. What are we going to do?"

Alex cringed.

"Silas Weston is still going strong," Emory chuckled. "He is a force of nature and is more emboldened since Trump won. You would think he thought more of Trump than Jesus Christ."

"Yup!" Alex laughed.

The voice continued, "My friends we can do something. We have the most powerful weapon in the world. Prayer!"

"My name is Silas Weston and I am the executive pastor at New Zion Road Baptist Church. I am inviting you to join my congregation as we surround City Hall in prayer. We will be praying for the mayor and our town leaders to turn from their iniquity and lead Pinehurst back to the family friendly, community it once was."

"Executive pastor?" Alex said. "Sounds fancy."

"Yep, pastors these days can't tolerate just being called pastor. I'm sure they're working on being called Chief Spiritual Officer next."

Alex laughed.

"So, my friends, join us on February fifteenth at noon in front of city hall as we pray for our city."

Emory reached down and turned off the radio.

"It's folks like him that are driving people away from church," Emory said. "Some folks trade the relationship for rules and call it faith. Then they wonder why people are walking away from the church."

Alex hadn't even thought about church since he left prison. After hearing Silas, he wasn't sure he wanted to start.

Soon a large brick building rose from the bend of the road. Pinehurst Memorial looked about the same as Alex had remembered it. He had spent a couple of nights in the emergency room with broken bones and asthma flares.

Emory turned the car left and followed the signs to the emergency room.

He pulled the large Oldsmobile around in front of the patient drop-off.

"I'll let you off here." Emory put the car in park. "Hope your mom feels better. Let me know when she gets to a room so I can swing by and visit."

"Sure thing." Alex opened the door and the crisp winter air hit him in the face. "I appreciate the ride and all you do for Mom. She's lucky to have you."

"It is my pleasure and I don't mind a bit. Us senior citizens have to stick together." Emory laughed.

Alex smiled, grabbed the suitcase from the back and shut the door. He walked quickly to the automatic doors that led into the emergency room.

10

Harper stepped out of the employee lounge and into the emergency room. She could tell by the chaos it was already busy. Trauma alerts rang out overhead, patients lined the hallways, the general background noise of yelling and profanity was strangely comforting.

She made her way to the charge nurse station, walking past one of the major bays where the team was actively working a resuscitation.

Nia Jones sat stoically behind the charge desk. Nia was a long-term fixture in the department, going on twenty-five years as an emergency room nurse. The staff loved her, the doctors feared her and the patients were lucky to have her. She was one of the few African American nurses in the department and had bootstrapped her way from a CNA to a Registered Nurse. Harper always enjoyed it when she was in charge because Nia had her back.

"There's my favorite white girl," Nia yelled out from behind the desk.

Harper laughed, "Nee! I am so glad you are in charge!!"

"Don't say that just yet I haven't given you your assignment." Nia laughed as Harper moved in for a big side hug, catching a faint whiff of tobacco.

"Nee! I thought you quit smoking?"

"Baby, you got to have at least one vice to survive this place."

"Alright, but I worry about you."

"I know, but I still ain't changing your assignment."

Harper laughed, "OK, what's the damage?"

"You're down Pod A with Devon." Nia pointed to her left, "Doc Wilson is sending a patient over from his office by ambulance, COPD exacerbation. I'm putting her in room 4."

"Yes Ma'am!" Harper feigned a mock salute, "Heading that way."

"Yell if you need anything."

Harper made her way through the busy ER to the Nurse's Station on Pod A. It looked like room four was the only one open.

Mandy Smith, a fellow ER nurse anxiously waited to give her report.

"It's been a day, girl!" Mandy said.

"Looks that way."

"I'm going to need three margaritas to recover from this one."

Harper laughed as she listened to Mandy's report of the patients. Typical ED stuff, chest pain, shortness of breath, a gastrointestinal bleed.

"Do you know anything about the one coming to four?" Harper asked.

"No. EMS hasn't gotten here with her yet," Mandy said turning quickly to Harper. "Total gossip, but I heard she is the mother of that Hollins guy."

Harper must have looked confused.

"You know he just got out of prison, spent twenty-five years behind bars for killing the Grayson girl while he was driving drunk."

The story sounded vaguely familiar to Harper, but the past year was a blur with the divorce and move; she barely had a chance to even watch the news, much less keep up on the happenings in Pinehurst.

"Yikes," Harper said. "Hope he doesn't show up. It would be awkward."

"You got a VIP patient, girl!"

"Great!"

Mandy grabbed her Hydro Flask and clipboard, "See you later gator, I got to get some sleep!"

"Thanks, have a great day!"

Harper turned to her computer to log in when a paramedic approached the nursing station.

"You getting number four?"

"Yep, that's me."

Harper got a report from the paramedic who looked like he had just graduated high school. She walked into bay four and stood at the foot of the stretcher watching the elderly lady struggle to breathe with a non-rebreather oxygen mask on.

"Mrs. Hollins," Harper raised her voice over the background noise of the monitors and chaos in the hallway, "I am Harper. I will be your nurse today until eleven. Ok?"

The old lady nodded; it took too much effort to talk.

Harper glanced up at the vital signs monitor, her oxygen levels were hanging around eighty-five percent.

Still too low.

"Are you hurting anywhere?"

The lady kept her eyes closed and shook her head no.

Harper stepped to the bedside. "I'm going to take a listen to you and then we will get you feeling better."

Harper placed the stethoscope on her patients back. She was frail, her bony spiny protruding through her skin. Her lung sounds were distant as Harper listened methodically across her back. As she got to the bottom of her lungs there was the familiar coarse rattle typically accompanying pneumonia.

Harper had been an ER nurse for years and at this point had a pretty good grasp on what was going on and what the patient needed.

"Alright, you're not moving much air and you might be working on pneumonia." She patted the patient's shoulder gently. "I'm going to see what doctor you are assigned to and I need to get some orders to start making you more comfortable."

The lady forced a smile, nodded her head and started trying to say something through the thick plastic of the face mask.

Harper leaned closer to her, "What honey?"

"My...son...."

"Ok dear, don't worry about him right now."

"Let...him...know...I'm...okay..."

She was far from ok but Harper wasn't going to tell her that.

"I'll make sure we get in touch with him and have the doctor call him after he sees you."

The lady smiled and closed her eyes.

11

Alex approached the clear plexiglass window where a large man in green scrubs sat looking down at his phone. Without looking up the man pointed to a clipboard in front of him. "Sign in and we will call you up when you are ready for triage."

"I'm not a patient," Alex said. "My mother was just brought in by ambulance."

"Name?" the man sounded increasingly frustrated.

"Mine or hers?"

The man looked up at Alex, his large jowls shaking with laughter. "What do you think?"

Alex repressed a smarter comment, "Nancy Hollins."

The man typed something and without looking up said, "She is in bay four."

He grabbed a sticker with the word 'Visitor' printed in bold black ink and quickly scribbled Hollins on a blank line beneath it.

"You will need to wear this at all times back there."

"Thanks."

The door to the left of the station magically opened.

Alex made his way through the door and stepped into the maze of the emergency room. Constant sound and movement surrounded him.

Sensory overload.

He looked for some signage to help him find bay four, but the signs were equally confusing.

He slowly made his way further into the department and was hit with a strong odor of disinfectant and vomit. An elderly gentleman with wiry silver hair wearing a red vest approached him.

"You look lost." The man grinned.

"That is an understatement," Alex said. "I'm looking for bay four."

"I can help you," the man said. "Follow me and stay close. If we get separated, they may never find you."

Alex laughed.

He followed the man through the corridors of the Pinehurst Memorial Hospital emergency room. It looked like every room was full and patients were collecting along the hallways.

"Looks pretty busy today," Alex said.

"Oh no, this is a slow day," the man said. "Sometimes we have patients in bunk beds and in the broom closet."

Alex appreciated the man's sense of humor. He supposed even a volunteer in the ED needed to have some type of gallows humor.

They rounded a corner to a hallway with patient bays on each side. The number four stuck out from the ceiling of one in the back corner.

The man led Alex to the curtain and partially pulled it back, "Is this Ms. Hollins?"

"It sure is, Jerry." a female voice responded.

"I have her son, is this a good time?"

"It's great! She has been asking for him."

Jerry turned around to Alex as he pulled the curtain back, motioning him to go on in.

"Thank you," Alex said.

"As they say at Chick-fil-A, my pleasure."

Alex didn't quite get the reference but grinned.

Stepping into the room his mother was sitting straight up on a gurney, an oxygen mask across her face. Her chest labored with each breath. Her eyes were closed. A wall of monitors hung beside her bed intermittently beeping and alarming.

A nurse typing on a computer stood next to his mother's bed. She had on navy blue scrubs with a floral headband pushing back her auburn hair. Alex could sense her tensing up as he walked into the room.

"So, you are her son?" she asked through a light blue surgical mask augmenting her deep blue eyes.

"Yes, I'm Alex."

"I'm Harper. I'll be your mom's nurse until eleven tonight." A strand of hair fell across her eye and she brought her forearm up to push it out of the way.

"Nice to meet you…" he said. "How is she doing?"

"Right now, she is struggling a little, but I'm going to change that. She has a lung condition called COPD and right now she likely has pneumonia which is making it harder for her to breathe."

"Is it serious?" Alex grew worried.

"It could be," Harper said. "But I just gave her a dose of steroids in her vein and I am about to give her some strong antibiotics. Between those two things, she should start to feel better."

Alex relaxed.

Something about the nurse's calming demeanor and confidence set him at ease. She moved effortlessly between the pumps and monitors like she had done this a million times in the past. The fact she was beautiful helped as well.

"Will she have to go on a breathing machine?"

"Our goal is to avoid that," Harper said, hanging a clear IV bag on a pole and adjusting some settings on the pump. "She has Dr. Grady as her physician and he is one of our best. If anyone can turn her around, he can."

"She may spend tonight in the intensive care unit as a precaution, but that shouldn't alarm you."

Alex smiled. "Thanks for the heads up."

"OK, I'm going to step out and get some charting done. I'll be down the hall." Harper smiled and walked toward the door. "She seems stable now, which is good. If you need anything, just let me know. The respiratory therapist will be coming in shortly to give her another breathing treatment."

"Thanks," Alex said. "You are good at what you do."

Harper's cheeks turned bright red.

"You're too kind," Harper said. "I love my job!"

She turned and left the room.

Alex stepped beside the gurney. He tried to find his mother's hand beneath the tape and IV tubing. He grabbed her limp cool hand and gave it a gentle squeeze.

"I'm right here Mom." He brushed some hair out of her face. "No need to say anything. You're doing great."

A slight smile came across his mother's face.

"You're probably going to be here for a couple of days. I'll take care of everything around the house."

She gave him a slight nod.

"I promise, no wild parties."

He stared at the withered body of his mother. Twenty-five years had taken a toll on her, and he was sure his situation hadn't helped.

He was scared. He had been looking forward to coming back home since he went to jail.

What if he lost his mother?

He didn't know what he would do.

A slight grip of panic squeezed his chest.

The harsh sound of the curtain being ripped aside interrupted his thinking.

"Ms. Hollins," a voice too chipper for this situation yelled.

"This is her," Alex turned, "I'm her son."

"I'm Andy, one of the respiratory therapists. I need to give her a breathing treatment."

"Sure." Alex stepped away from the stretcher.

The young man stepped behind the stretcher and fiddled with the oxygen tank. He switched her mask with another and soon the room was filled with a hissing sound as a plume of vapor poured out around his mother's face.

"This should take around five minutes," Andy said. "I'll be back shortly."

"Thank you," Alex said. "Hey, do you know where I can get some coffee?"

"Sure, just head back to the waiting room." Andy pointed. "The volunteer's man the coffee station for visitors. Not the greatest stuff, but hey, caffeine is caffeine."

Alex thanked the man. He stepped over to his mother. "Mom, I'll be right back. I'm going to grab a cup of coffee."

She nodded.

• • •

Alex stepped out of the room into the hallway, he could navigate his way back to the waiting room.

"Everything ok?" a voice from the end of the hall called out.

He turned to see Harper at the nurse's station looking at him.

"Yes, the respiratory therapist just started her treatment, I'm going to go grab a cup of coffee."

"Alright, sounds like a plan." Harper smiled.

Alex smiled back and headed out of the department.

By some stroke of luck, he found his way back to the waiting room. In the far corner, there was an elderly woman in a red vest sitting behind a table with a coffee pot and some cups. Alex approached the lady and asked for a cup of coffee.

She offered him a kind smile and poured him a cup of thick, black liquid looked like it could eat through the Styrofoam.

He had been standing a while he and decided to take a seat in one of the hard molded plastic chairs in the waiting room. He now understood why the chairs were uncomfortable in the waiting rooms. Probably figure if you wait long enough the pain would make you want to leave.

As he sipped his coffee, he overheard his mother's name.

"Nancy Hollins is in bay four," the man behind the Plexiglass said.

Alex turned slowly. Two pudgy men in matching black suits stood in front of the plexiglass. They both looked to be in their late forties. One held a large Bible the size of a small suitcase.

"We are deacons from her church. We would like to go visit, you know, say a prayer with her," one of the men said. "She is such a dear lady."

"I'll need to check with the nurse. It looks like she already has someone back with her. Our policy is one visitor."

"I understand, but I'm sure you could make an exception for the Lord," the other man said, hefting the Bible up.

Alex sat his coffee cup on the chair beside him and made his way toward the men.

"Hey fellas," he said.

The two men turned around in unison.

"I'm Nancy's son. Can I help you?"

The men paused.

"We were just telling the gentleman behind the counter we would like to go say a quick prayer for your mother," the man with the Bible said. A thin bead of sweat had formed across his forehead.

The other man chimed in. "We are deacons at her church."

Alex paused.

"Unfortunately, she is not feeling too well," Alex said. "I'll be sure and let her know you came by. I know she will appreciate your prayers."

"We would like to see her, but understand she needs her rest," one of the men said. "Fortunately, we can pray from anywhere."

They both grinned.

"I'm sure there's a lot of stress on her right now," the man who held the Bible said.

Alex grew confused.

"I mean, having you move back into her house," the man said. "Poor thing, these are the years she is supposed to be enjoying life, not having to justify to the community why she welcomed a murderer into her home."

The air left the room.

His heart pounded in his chest and his ears burned. He clenched his fists until his knuckles threatened to pop through his skin.

"I'm surprised they don't have extra security out here," the other man said.

"You should leave," Alex said through a clenched jaw and stepped towards the men. "I don't know who you are, but you have no right to talk to me this way."

"You, sir, have no right coming back to our community," the man with the Bible said. "We are a family community and have no place for a murderer. You should consider your mom's condition, an act of retribution from the Lord. Maybe that is a sign for you to leave."

A surge of rage flooded him and he stepped in closer to the men.

"We will be going now."

The two men walked past him. The slight hiss of the automatic doors opening as he stood in the middle of the waiting room, shaking.

12

Harper sat at her computer to begin charting. While she loved nursing, charting was the worst. Particularly now with the electronic medical record. Every service had its own metric that needed to be tracked and all the work fell back on the nursing staff.

"So, how was he?"

The voice caught Harper by surprise. She turned as Devon walked towards her.

"Who?"

"Alex Hollins, Pinehurst's famous convict." He laughed.

"Oh, him. He was nice." She grinned." You can tell he loves his mom."

"He better, she was the only one that visited him while he was in prison." Devon laughed.

"You don't know that."

"I do know. I have a friend who is a guard up there. Said no one ever came. Guess it serves him right for getting hammered and killing an innocent person."

"Well, he served his time. I'm sure he will carry that guilt forever though," She grew defensive. "He was very kind to his mom."

"Sorry!" Devon laughed, "Just be sure and invite me to the wedding."

"Shut up!" Harper laughed, tossing a pack of Post-it notes at him.

Harper wrapped up her shift. The intensive care unit was full so Nancy Hollins would be staying in the Emergency Department until they found a bed for her. Harper gave report to the oncoming nurse and clocked out.

• • •

On the drive home, Harper could not stop thinking about Nancy Hollins and particularly Alex. He had such a kind face, but his eyes looked like they had seen so much more for his age.

She couldn't imagine having a son in jail for anything, particularly something so horrible. Landon was only four, but her mother's love was already incredibly fierce.

Could she be as loyal as Nancy Hollins if something like that happened to Lando?

She shuddered.

She couldn't help but feel sympathy for Alex.

Was that weird?

He must be lonely, home from jail and his mother ends up in the hospital. She pulled into her sister's driveway, placed the car in park and sat for a moment, processing the last twelve hours.

Sometimes she had too much compassion, which was hard as a nurse. She often brought her work home with her, worrying about her patients. Maybe that made her a good nurse, she wasn't sure.

Grabbing her backpack, she stepped out into the cold winter night and made her way into her sister's house.

"Honey, I'm home," she laughed walking into the kitchen.

Vanessa sat at the table with her laptop and a glass of wine.

"Hey girl, how was work?" she closed her laptop and looked up at Harper.

"It was good. Busy as usual," she said, plopping down in an empty chair.

"Any good stories?" Her sister leaned forward. "Anyone put something strange in an orifice? Did anyone have any good sex related injuries?"

Harper laughed. Her sister loved her ER stories and the more R-rated the better. "Sorry. It was a pretty G-rated shift."

"Oh well, there is always the next shift."

"Hey, what do you remember about Alex Hollins?"

"That's random. You mean the guy who killed Heather Grayson?" Vanessa said, "That was about 20-30 years ago. Why?"

"No reason."

"Oh no. You don't get off that easy! I saw where he just got released," Vanessa paused, a wave of realization crossed her face, "Wait, he was your patient! That is why you asked!! You need to tell me everything and none of this patient privacy business."

"Vanessa!" Harper laughed, "You know I can't talk about my patients."

"Harper Layne, when has that ever stopped you?"

Harper laughed. Well, technically, he wasn't her patient.

"Let's just say I met him tonight. The details aren't important."

"Cool! What was he like? I've always wanted to meet a murderer." Vanessa gushed. Her love for true crime podcasts was showing.

"Well, not as exciting as you might imagine," Harper said, letting her sister down gently. "He was very sweet, kind, and concerned."

"That does not sound like a murderer to me."

"I believe it was vehicular manslaughter and not premeditated so there may be a difference."

"Whatever." Vanessa finished off her glass of wine, "He still killed someone."

"Anyway, he was kind of.... I don't know.... cute."

Vanessa stood up and grabbed Harper's water bottle off the table, opening the lid and sniffing it. "What are you drinking?!?! Does my baby sister have a crush on a murderer?"

Harpers face flushed, "No!! I just said he was cute."

"Ted Bundy was a lady's man also," Vanessa said. "I'm sure some of his victims thought he was cute."

"Is it a crime to call someone cute?"

"No, but it is a crime to get drunk and take out someone with your car." Vanessa raised her voice. "Harper, listen to yourself. You need to get to bed and sleep this off."

"Sorry!" Harper said, "I was making a general observation, didn't say I wanted to marry the guy."

"I know, I'm being the protective older sibling."

"Which I love you for," Harper said, "I was being stupid anyway. I'll find a man."

"Yes, you will. Go pour yourself a glass of wine and cool off in the bathtub. I got some new citrus bath oil."

"Yes, Mother!" Harper laughed, "I'll pass on the wine, I have to be back in there again tomorrow."

13

Harper stepped out into the busy hustle of the Pinehurst Memorial Hospital emergency room. The night went by fast and her day would be long.

It was only seven a.m. and people were already flying all around. She made her way to the charge nurses station where Nia Andres sat with her familiar smiling face.

"There's my girl!"

"I'm here, not sure if I am all here." Harper grinned and took a sip of her coffee.

"Well, good news. You have the same assignment as yesterday."

"Great!" she said. "Did number four get a room?"

"Nope, she is still here." Nia glanced at her report sheet. "I think she is doing better so we may be able to get her to a regular room today."

"That's good news."

"Did you see her son?" Nia winked. "Mmmm.... fine..."

Harper blushed. "I didn't notice, too busy taking care of his mom."

"Girl, I know you aren't blind to a fine man," Nia laughed, "May need to get your eyes checked."

"Nia!"

"Alright skinny, have a good shift!"

"Thanks!"

Harper was still blushing as she made her way down the hall. She did hope Alex would be back to visit his mom today.

After she got report she started her morning rounds saving Mrs. Hollins for last. Fortunately, her pod had not gotten busy yet but would inevitably change as people started waking up.

"Good morning Mrs. Hollins," she said, peeking around the curtain, "It's Harper. I'll be taking care of you again today."

Nancy Hollins looked much better than yesterday. Overnight, they had been able to wean her off the face mask and she now had a nasal cannula on for oxygen. Her respirations were much more relaxed.

Harper walked up to her bed and reached down stroking the older woman's fine gray hair. "You look much better than when I left yesterday."

Nancy opened her eyes, those deep blue eyes. Harper couldn't imagine the years of sadness kept behind them. She kept thinking of Landon and how much love she had for him at four years old. She couldn't imagine him being out of her life for twenty-five years. Just knowing he was alive, but away. A place where she could not hug him, tussle his hair, or smell his scent.

"Yes dear, I feel much better," Nancy said, "I actually slept some last night."

"Wonderful!" Harper said, "Maybe we can get you to a proper bed today instead of these uncomfortable stretchers."

"That would be nice."

Harper stepped over to the computer in the room and started scrolling through her meds and charting vital signs.

"Dear, have you heard from my son?"

Harper stopped typing and looked over at her. "Not today. I did get a chance to meet him yesterday. He seems like a very nice man."

Nancy smiled, the reflexive smile every parent has when someone says something kind about their child.

"I must have been out of it yesterday," Nancy said, "I don't remember him visiting."

"He was here, I can vouch for him," Harper said. "I can also vouch you were very sick yesterday, so I understand if you don't remember."

"I'd like to see him today."

"We can arrange that," Harper said. "Do you have his number?"

"Well, unfortunately, he doesn't have a phone. He just came back home recently." she paused.

Harper could tell she was trying to choose her words carefully.

"I'm sure you've heard. He's been in jail for some time. We were supposed to go yesterday and…"

She lowered her head.

Harper walked over and rubbed her shoulder. "It's ok. I can't imagine what you've been through. I know you must be glad to have him home."

"It's been awful." Nancy reached up and grabbed Harper's wrist, tears formed in her eyes, "He is not a monster. I feel like everyone sees him that way."

Harper continued to rub her shoulder.

"He is still my son and I love him."

Harper remained silent for moment and then said, "Alex is fortunate to have a mother like you. I'll find a way to get in touch with him. A visit would do you good."

"Thank you, sweetie." Nancy patted Harper's hand. "If he doesn't answer the home line, you could maybe try to call Emory Smith. He is a close friend. He should be listed on my contacts."

"Ok, I'll do that," Harper said. "Why don't you try to get some rest? Breakfast should be here soon."

14

Alex lay in the comfort of the warm bed, trying to motivate himself to get up. The encounter with the men at the hospital had shaken him and his mother's health was still heavy on his mind.

One of his biggest fears about returning to Pinehurst had been that his mother would continue to pay the price for his past. She had been through enough and he didn't want to make things worse.

He poured a cup of coffee left over from yesterday, put it in the microwave and threw a couple pieces of bread in the toaster. Since being out of jail, he was still trying to establish a 'normal' routine to replace the rigid cadence of prison. The microwave chirped and he retrieved the cup of coffee. Taking a slow sip of the black liquid, wincing as the hot liquid scalded his tongue.

"Yikes!" he shouted to no one in particular.   A   thin column of smoke rose from the top of the toaster, the distinct smell of burning bread filled the room. He ran over and ejected the two pieces of bread which were now black bricks. They hit the counter with a dull thud.

Well, I have got some time to go before I get fully domesticated.

He thought back to his mom's nurse, Harper. She was beautiful. He knew he didn't have a chance with her, but a man can dream.

He needed to call and check on his mom. No one had called last night which he assumed was good news. As if on cue the telephone on the wall vibrated with a shrill ring, Alex lay his burnt toast down and picked the receiver off the cradle.

"Hello."

"Umm...hello...is this, Alex Hollins?" a female voice came over the line.

"Yes...yes, it is, who is calling?"

"Hi Alex, this is Harper. I'm the nurse taking care of your mother. We met yesterday."

Alex was now instantly awake, "Oh, hi, is everything ok?"

"Your mom is doing a lot better today. They didn't have a room in the unit for her so she stayed down here overnight. She wanted me to call and check on you."

Alex grinned. No matter how old he got he would always be his mother's little boy.

"Let her know I am fine, and she needs to focus on herself and getting better."

Harper laughed, "I will, just knowing you are okay will go a long way."

"Let her know I'll see if Emory can bring me by today to visit."

"I will give her the message."

Alex said goodbye and hung up the phone. He had a giddy feeling like he was in middle school and had hung up with his crush.

He needed to call Emory and see if he could give him a ride. He also needed a shower in a bad way as well.

Alex spoke with Emory who said he would be happy to give him a ride. Emory said he needed to stop by city hall to take care of some business if Alex didn't mind tagging along.

Alex grabbed a quick shower. Afterward, he threw his clothes on and stood in front of the mirror primping like he was going on a first date. A big smile on his face.

15

Emory and Alex walked into the crowded waiting room in the emergency department. Alex was relieved to see a young female sitting behind the check-in counter, he was in no mood to deal with the man from last night.

Walking up to the counter, she greeted him with a welcoming smile, "May I help you?"

"Yes, I would like to visit my mother, Nancy Hollins."

"Sure, one second," the lady typed on her keyboard, "OK, she is in Bay Four and looks like she can have a visitor."

The lady handed him the familiar visitor sticker, "Our policy is only one visitor."

Emory grinned catching the hint, "No problem, I'll stay out here and do some people watching. It's my favorite pastime."

"Thanks, Emory," Alex said.

The automatic door opened and Alex walked back into the department. Not much had changed since last night, there was still a lot of activity. Luckily, he remembered his way back to his mother's room.

The sliding glass door was partially open and the curtain was pulled shut. Tapping gently on the glass he made his way into the bay.

"Hello," he said announcing himself as he slid the curtain back and walked into the room. His mother lay on the gurney, her upper body elevated at a ninety-degree angle. Her eyes were closed, and clear plastic oxygen tubing ran under her nose.

Her breathing was much easier compared to when he had seen her yesterday. He wasn't sure if it was the lighting or the fact she didn't have any makeup on, but it looked like she had aged ten years.

A twinge of fear knocked at his heart.

What if she doesn't make it out of here?

The sound of the curtain sliding open snapped him back to reality.

"Well, hello there," a cheerful female voice called out behind him.

Harper walked into the room, holding a clear medicine cup with some pills in it. Her hair was pulled back into a ponytail with a surgical mask partially covering her face. She was wearing maroon scrubs and a black jacket.

"Good morning," Alex said, "Looks like the patient is sleeping well."

"Yes, she is," Harper said walking over to her bedside and tinkering with the monitor suspended beside her stretcher, "It's amazing how easy you can rest when you don't have to worry about breathing."

"That's true," Alex said.

"Well, I need to wake her, I have to give her some medications."

Alex stepped up to bed and took one of his mom's hands in his.

"Mrs. Hollins," Harper said while gently shaking her shoulder, "You have a visitor."

His mom's eyes fluttered open. For a moment she looked panicked her eyes darting around the room, becoming restless like she may try to get out of bed.

"Mrs. Hollins, you're fine. Remember you are in the hospital."

"Mom, it's me, Alex."

Nancy Hollins settled down, turned her head and looked up at Alex. A smile spread across her lips.

"My baby," she said, her voice weak and raspy, "My baby is home."

"Yes, Mom, I'm back home, but we have to get you feeling better."

Alex's mom's cool hand wrapped around his fingers.

"Ok, Mrs. Hollins, I need to give you some medicine," Harper said reaching behind the gurney and gently raising the head of the bead, "We need you sitting up so these don't go down the wrong pipe."

Harper gently helped his mom lean forward.

"Here you go," Harper handed the medicine cup to Nancy, watching closely as her trembling hand brought the cup to her lips, dumping the pills on her tongue. She grabbed a cup of water from the bedside table bringing the straw to her lips.

"Alright take a few sips and I'll be out your hair then you can visit with your son."

Nancy grinned, took a few sips of water and swallowed the pills.

"Hopefully, we can get you a room today and into a more comfortable bed."

Harper looked up and Alex, "Any questions for me?"

Are you single was the obvious one that popped into his mind, but he knew better.

"No, I am happy you are her nurse again,"

"Well, she is a sweetie and I am glad I get to take care of her."

Harper cleaned some items off the bedside table and walked out of the room; Alex detected a faint hint of vanilla as she left.

"How did you sleep?" Alex asked.

"Better, but these beds are not very comfortable," his mom replied.

"Well hopefully you will have a short stay," Alex said, "I slept great, the bed at home is way more comfortable than a prison bunk."

His mom's face brightened, "I am so glad dear, I worried about you."

"Don't worry about me, you need to focus on yourself and get better."

"Did Emory drive you over?"

"Yes, he is in the waiting room 'people watching',"

His mom grinned, "Well then he is perfectly content, I'm sure there is no shortage of interesting characters out there."

Pulling up a chair, Alex scooted next to his mom's bed. They chatted for a while longer, but his mom kept nodding off. She was tired and probably trying to stay awake for his sake.

"Alright, Mom I'm going to step out so you can get some rest," he said, "I don't want to hold Emory up, since he is taking me home. I'm glad you're feeling better."

"Thank you dear."

She didn't protest.

He stepped out into the hallway. Harper was sitting at the nurse's station. She looked up and smiled.

"You leaving?" she asked.

"Yes," he said, "She fell asleep, my ride is waiting on me so I am going to head home."

"That is fine, she has been stable," Harper said, "Hopefully we can get her a room today and move her out of here. I'll give you a call if we move her or anything changes."

She gave him a big grin.

"Thanks!"

Alex face flushed as he turned and started walking toward the exit, acutely aware of his surroundings, his heart pounding away in his chest. He was a little embarrassed with himself.

He hit the silver button on the wall opening the door to the waiting room. Emory was sitting in a row of chairs at the far end of the waiting room. He raised his hand waving at Alex.

Alex made his way over to him.

"Well, how's the patient?" Emory asked.

"Sleeping comfortably," Alex grinned, "She looked much better, the nurse said she had a good night."

"Wonderful," Emory said.

"How was your people watching experience?"

"Fascinating!" Emory said, "Did you know people can get their eyebrows pierced?"

Alex laughed.

"Hey, would you mind if I ran by city hall before I took you back home?" Emory asked, "I have some papers I need to drop off."

"Not a problem," Alex said, "I am thankful for your help."

16

Silas stood on the granite stairs in front of Pinehurst City Hall. Built in 1851, it was an iconic structure in Pinehurst with its brick facade and arched entryways. The building portrayed the story of a simpler, more elegant time. A time when men feared God.

He was sure the town founders would be rolling over in their graves at the depravity that had descended on Pinehurst. He scanned the small crowd of church members and people from the community who had gathered to protest the direction the city was going. A small group of onlookers had gathered off to the side.

Sure, he wished there had been more. Back in its prime, New Zion Road had boasted a congregation of five hundred easily, every Sunday. However, much like Sodom, many of those congregants had listened to the siren song of more modern churches with electric guitars and drums. Where pastors wore jeans and sneakers and women were allowed to speak from the pulpit. Most damning was they espoused heretical translations of the Bible.

Glancing at his watch, it was about a quarter after twelve. He figured this was as many participants as he was going to get, standing he raised a large megaphone to his mouth.

"Believers!! Thank you for coming here today. Just by showing up, you have already shown a strong commitment to making Pinehurst great again!"

A series of whoops and hand claps sounded.

"We are here to pray for our leaders. We are here to pray for a change of heart as they lead our city down a path of destruction and damnation." His voice swelled. "Over the past year, in this very building, our leaders have adopted a policy that allows gambling in this beautiful town. They adopted a policy allowing stores and restaurants to sell alcohol on Sunday, God's Day!"

Boos and jeers went up.

"They issued the first same sex marriage license in our town."

The boos and jeer grew louder and someone in the crowd hoisted a sign that read:

God Hates Homos, how about you?

"We need to take our city back. We can't rely on our local government or law enforcement. We may be small in number, but we have God on our side. There is no stopping the power of prayer!"

The cheers grew louder.

"In a few moments, we are all going to join hands on these steps and pray for our great city. Today marks the start of a change. God has made us vessels for his work. Vessels for his vengeance."

The small crowd erupted into cheers.

Someone in the crowd waved a Make Pinehurst Great Again sign.

Silas motioned and the crowd formed a small circle on the steps of city hall. After a few moments of silence, he started.

"Father, I come to you today as your humble servant. The people of Pinehurst have fallen far away from you Lord. Your vengeance is close. Lord, I ask you spare your people as we work to release the jaws of evil from this great city. I ask you give us courage as we rise against the demonic forces that have descended on the town. I ask that you give us supernatural strength and wisdom as we aim to take your town back."

Amens and hallelujahs rippled through the circle.

"In your name, Amen."

Silas kept his head bowed for a moment. He grinned at how he had these folks wrapped around his finger. Power is intoxicating, power wielded in the name of Christ is otherworldly.

Luther Evans stepped up beside Silas and led the crowd in an impromptu round of "Amazing Grace."

The crowd sang while hoisting their protest signs high.

John 3:16

No Homos in Heaven only Hell!!

God Made Them Male & Female!

TRUTH! GUNS! JESUS!!

TRUMP 2024

Silas scanned the crowd, a satisfied smile on his face.

Stopping for a second, there were two men making their way toward the building.

Was he seeing things?

No this was divine intervention, Alex Hollins was coming to him.

His jaws clenched as the prodigal son started to climb the steps.

Silas grabbed the megaphone and gave Luther a signal to stop the singing.

"Children of God, I am also sure you are aware of the latest insult to the moral fabric of our town." Spittle flew from his mouth. "A convicted murderer has been released from the liberal prison system back into our community."

Some boos went up.

"Granted, he was inebriated when it occurred, but who is to say it won't happen again?"

"Amen!!"

"Like a shark getting the first taste of human blood, that is what it's like being an alcoholic. Once you taste the Devil's brew you never lose the desire."

The two men stopped and were looking up at the crowd.

"Who is to say your son, daughter, husband, or wife won't be the next victim when he decides to drive while drunk again?" Silas grinned. "As they say, it's not a matter of if, but when."

"Drunkards are not welcome here, drunkards who kill are even more so disdained in the eyes of God," Silas shouted. "To paraphrase Revelations 21:8. The cowardly murderers will be sent straight to the lake of fire!"

Fire sounded more like far with his heavy southern drawl.

Shouts rose from the crowd.

The men stopped and turned around walking away from the building.

He paused, pointing his finger out above the crowd.

"Do my eyes deceive me? Or is that our local drunkard and murderer right there, Mr. Alex Hollins?!"

Gasps went through the crowd as everyone turned, straining their necks to see.

Silas walked down the steps and made his way through the crowd, parting them like Moses had the Red Sea.

He kept his megaphone to his mouth.

"Pinehurst is not a haven for drunks or for murderers, Mr. Hollins," Silas screamed as the megaphone cracked with feedback. "Go back to prison where you belong."

The crowd erupted in cheers behind him as he soon caught up with the men.

The elderly man turned and stepped toward him.

"Silas Weston, you are an evil man. He served his time. He has to live with the guilt of what he did for the rest of his life. He doesn't need cowards like you making his life more miserable."

"Well, if it isn't Emory Smith," Silas yelled into the megaphone, inches away from the man's face. "Former proprietor of the den of iniquity known as the Pinehurst Pub. I wonder how many families your establishment destroyed?"

"You're a disgrace to Christianity," the older man said and turned away.

The vessels in Silas's neck surged with anger. His face became red and he threw the megaphone to the ground where it shattered into pieces, letting out a loud squeal as it died. He charged straight toward the older man.

He got within several feet of the man when Alex stepped in front of him.

Alex held out his hand, pressing into Silas's chest.

"How dare you touch me you unclean heathen!" Silas slapped Alex's hand away.

Alex's face grew red, his jaws clenched, "I served my time. I don't need some egotistical minister reminding the whole city."

Silas laughed. "You may have paid your price in man's eyes, but you have not paid your price in God's eyes."

"Why don't we have a look in your closet?" Alex shot back.

Silas leaned closer and pointed a finger within inches of Alex's nose. "Whoever sheds the blood of man, by man shall his blood be shed.... Genesis 9:6. You should not even be standing here according to scripture. You are the beneficiary of a liberal justice system."

Emory laughed. "Alex let's go. You don't have to put up with this."

Alex turned around.

Silas grabbed Alex by his shoulder. "Remember, by man shall his blood be shed."

Alex jerked his shoulder free and stormed off. Silas grinned as the coward walked away.

17

Alex's knuckles turned white as he gripped the door handle waiting for Emory to unlock the car. His pulse pounded in his ears as adrenaline coursed through his body.

"One second," Emory said as he turned the key, the subtle click of the locks disengaging. "Ok."

Alex pulled the door open and slid into the passenger side of the car. He dropped his back against the seat and let out a loud breath.

"I'm sorry," Emory said, "that guy is a real jackass."

Alex kept his eyes closed.

"The worst part is he calls himself a 'servant of the Lord,'" Emory continued. "I don't think this was quite what God had in mind when he told us to forgive."

"What the...." Emory said looking in his rearview mirror.

Alex opened his eyes and looked behind him. The crowd of protestors had followed them to the car.

"Are you serious?" Alex said. "Let's go."

Emory locked the doors and started up the car, but it was too late. Protestors quickly surrounded the car.

They were chanting, "Keep Pinehurst safe!"

Some of the protestors began banging on the roof of the car. The noise reverberated inside like a chaotic thunderstorm.

"Just go!" Alex shouted.

"I'll hit someone," Emory said, his voice shaking.

"Well, that will make two of us. Silas will love that," Alex said.

The car was now shaking between the shouts and the thunderous clapping on the roof.

Alex partially rolled his window down, "Move or we are going to run over you!"

"Go ahead!!" someone yelled, "Not the first time you've killed someone!"

The crowd intensified. The car began to rock as they pushed it back and forth.

"Where are the police?" Alex asked.

"Oh, they're no help," Emory laughed. "The sheriff is a member of Silas's church."

"Great!" Alex said, "So much for separation of church and state."

Emory honked the horn.

No one moved.

He shifted the car into drive and slowly eased off the brakes. The big Oldsmobile inched slowly forward.

Some screams went out as the crowd contracted around the front of the car.

Emory laid on the horn with little effect.

The crowd was in a frenzy.

Alex looked out as women were laying hands on the car praying, angry men were pounding the roof of the car. The whole scene was surreal.

As the crowd separated, Silas stood directly in front of the car. Stepping to the side he dropped his arms motioning the car forward.

The large car began to move. As they passed Silas on the passenger side, he motioned for Alex to roll down the window.

"I'm not rolling down the window for this crackpot," Alex said.

"I agree," Emory said, easing his foot down a little more on the gas pedal. Two large goons stepped in front of the car. "Great! I knew it was too good to be true."

Silas stepped toward the passenger window.

Defeated, Alex cracked the window about an inch.

"Mr. Hollins," Silas said. "Consider today a warning. The body of Christ is a powerful weapon. Maybe Pinehurst is not the safest place for you, or your mother."

Alex grew angrier gripping the armrest until his fingers hurt, "Thanks Dad, I'll keep that in mind."

Alex's voice carried over the crowd and it fell silent.

The color drained from Silas's face.

"But if I survived twenty-five years in prison, I can handle an overweight deadbeat like yourself."

Silas stood speechless as Alex rolled up the window.

The goons stepped aside and Emory took the chance to floor the Oldsmobile and get out of there.

Emory laughed.

"What's so funny?"

"I think that was the first time I've ever seen Silas Weston speechless!'

Alex grinned, "Yeah, but as they say around here. Don't poke a skunk! Well, I think I just poked a big one."

"For sure." Emory kept his eyes on the road. "Did you call him Dad?"

18

The men all sat silently around the table. Their eyes focused intently on Silas.

Beads of sweat formed across Silas' forehead. "No one!" he pounded the table, "I mean no one, disrespects a servant of the Lord." His voice trembled.

Silas should have known that harlot of a mother he had couldn't keep a secret, despite what was a fair amount of hush money. Alex had insulted him in front of his flock, which was unacceptable. The fact he was a murderous drunkard made it much worse.

"We have to send a message that this will not be tolerated!" Silas shouted, "The Lord has made it clear to me we must act quickly and decisively."

Some amens went up around the table.

Luther leaned in, "Do you have any thoughts on how we do that?"

"I think it's time to engage the Boone brothers, for their…services," Silas said.

The Boone brothers were fixtures in Pinehurst. A pair of undomesticated brothers living well off the beaten path down Mill Creek. They were known for violence and made a living off selling meth and oxycodone. No charges ever stuck because the Pinehurst police chief was on Silas's payroll. Silas used their services when he needed some dirty work done which you wouldn't want to be associated with a man of God.

Luther grinned, "I agree."

"Luther, let's you and I take a field trip to Mill Creek."

• • •

The Lincoln Town Car shook as Luther turned onto a small dirt road. Dust flew up as the car found every pothole. Silas's jowls bounced as they hit a rock in the road.

"Luther!" he shouted, "You're going to kill us before we even get to their home."

"Sorry boss!" Luther said, "Not exactly an ideal road for a luxury vehicle."

"Next time the church buys you a vehicle, maybe consider something with four-wheel drive."

"Yes sir."

They rode on in silence. As they rounded a curve, a large black Rottweiler with a metal studded black leather collar stood in the middle of the road. It looked to be the size of a small horse. Strands of drool dripped from its jaws.

"Holy..." Luther said. "Look at the size of the dog."

As if on cue the dog let out a vicious series of deep guttural barks vibrating the windshield. Thick strands of saliva flew from its mouth.

Luther laid on the horn. The dog did not budge.

"Great!" Luther said, slapping the steering wheel, "What do we do?"

Silas laughed. "Get out and throw a rock at it or something."

Luther turned pale and looked at Silas. "You serious, boss?"

"Of course I'm serious. Their house is another half mile up the road," Silas said. "I would say run the dog over, but I know how much the Boone brothers love their dogs. That wouldn't end well for either of us."

"Boss, I ain't going to get out of the car." Luther's voice shook. "That dog would kill me."

"Luther, that dog is probably all bark and no bite."

"Boss, that dog is all bark and all bite. They didn't train him to be a cuddly lap dog. They want him to keep people off their land."

"Luther, just do what I say!" Silas shouted. "Do you not have faith that the Lord who called us out to do His work is not going to protect you? Think of Daniel in the lion's den!"

Luther looked straight ahead. Questioning bravery was one thing, questioning your faith was another.

He slowly pulled the door handle out until it clicked open. The dog unleashed another series of barks, causing Luther to reflexively pull the door shut.

Silas howled with laughter. "Luther you are such a pussy!!"

Silas grabbed the door handle and pulled it open, stepping out of the car.

"Get out of here you mutt!!" he yelled. The dog answered with a deep growl. Scanning the ground, Silas found a large rock. Keeping his eyes on the dog, he slowly lowered himself down to retrieve it.

A loud bang echoed through the air, the dog turned, tucking its tail and ran. In the distance, a large figure lumbered down the road with a rifle resting over his shoulder.

Silas's throat tightened, forgetting how imposing a figure Zeke Boone was.

"Silas Weston!" Zeke shouted. "Been a while since I've seen you or your associates."

He pointed the rifle toward the driver's side, causing Luther to drop in fear.

"Well, the Lord works in mysterious ways," Silas said.

"What brings you away from your kingdom?"

"I'd like to talk about securing you and your brother's services again."

"Well, we've upped our prices since the last time you used us."

Silas grinned. The last time he needed them involved burning the parsonage of a competing church in town. The pastor had openly defied Silas from the pulpit. Calling him a heretic and false prophet.

Unfortunately, the pastor and his family lost most of their possessions in the fire. Shortly after, they moved out of town and the small church shut down. New Zion purchased the building and let it sit vacant.

Silas couldn't stand competition.

"That's fine, I'm willing to pay what the market calls for."

"If you say so." The large man made his way to the car. "Let's go up to the house then."

Zeke opened the rear passenger door and slid into the backseat. The car was instantly enveloped in a distinct odor of marijuana and body odor.

"God bless," Silas said rolling down his window, "You ever take a shower."

"Ain't Wednesday yet," Zeke said

The Boone residence was everything you would envision a bachelor pad for rednecks would be. A double wide with a rusted metal exterior and a stream of smoke coming from a makeshift chimney in the back.

The Rottweiler that had held Silas and Luther hostage reappeared. The front yard was strewn with empty cases of Budweiser and Coors and four vehicles in various stages of decay.

Silas looked at the rusty shed behind the trailer where a modern ventilation system was attached to the side. He could only guess what they made in there.

Pulling up to the house, another large man stepped onto the small stoop off the front door. He was shirtless, with a large but solid belly hanging over his pants. Tattoos lined his arms, A joint hung from his mouth. His hand reached for the 9 mm pistol holstered in his jeans as Luther put the car in park.

Zeke hopped out of the car. "Eddie, it's just me. "Don't shoot. Get back inside, you're high as a kite. I can tell by your eyes."

Sweat rolled down Luther's back. Silas stepped out of the car.

"Eddie!!" Silas yelled, "It's Silas and Luther."

The man gave a vague nod of acknowledgment toward Silas and stepped back inside.

"Alright fellas, what you say we talk business," Zeke said as the men followed him into the trailer.

19

Over the next couple of days, Alex's mom continued to make slow, but steady improvement. She had made it to a regular room and Emory had been faithful in making sure Alex was able to get over there daily.

He got updates from her nurses. None of them could top Harper, but he was a little biased. The days were boring, but a welcome change from the structure of prison.

He had gotten out of bed and was rifling through the drawers in the kitchen hopeful to find one remaining coffee filter, when there was a knock at the door.

Another knock. This one louder.

"Coming!" he yelled, irritated. Walking to the front door he looked out the side window. Two large, bearded men in bibbed overalls stood on the front porch. Both looked like they had stepped fresh off the set of Deliverance.

A beat-up Chevy pickup sat parked in front of the house.

If prison had taught him anything it was a healthy dose of caution. The last thing you want to do in prison is find yourself somewhere isolated with folks bigger than you.

"Can I help you?" he yelled through the door.

"Yeah, we need a phone to call our friend," one of the men said. "Our truck broke down."

Alex eased a bit. Looking at the rusted-out vehicle, he could imagine it wasn't the most reliable form of transportation. He turned the deadbolt and unlocked the door, opening it wide to allow the men in.

"Sorry about your tru...."

The words were barely out of his mouth when a fist connected squarely with his chin, knocking him off his feet onto the carpeted floor of the living room. His ears rang as the metallic taste of blood filled his mouth. The room turned gray as he looked up, two figures towered over him.

His breath exited his lungs as a foot connected with his abdomen. A spray of maroon blood misted the air as a wave of nausea rushed over him. He could taste the bile mixing with the blood in the back of his throat.

"Eddie, why did you go and do that?" the man with a faded tear drop tattoo below his right eye said, "We were just supposed to scare him."

"Well, I think it worked," the other man said.

One of the men kneeled next to him, grabbing him by the back of the head. A large grin exposed his yellowed teeth and the smell of sulfur and tobacco filled Alex's nose. His head spun as he tried to balance the pain while trying to grasp what was going on.

"Who.... are....you?" Alex managed to say, his mind clearing a little as a brutal headache was forming.

"You might call us the Pinehurst welcome committee," the man with the teardrop tattoo said. "But in this case, we wanted to let you know that you ain't exactly welcome here."

His vision blurred under the pounding force of a headache creeping along his head.

"Of course, this is a free country," he continued, "but if you decide to stay, then you may want to get used to periodic visits like this."

"And I guess if you're not home, your mother would have sympathy for some men stranded in front of her house," the other man called Eddie chimed in.

Both men laughed.

"Don't...you...do anything...to my....mother....or..." Alex fought to push back the bile rising in the back of his throat.

"Or what?" the man standing spoke up. "You'll call the cops?"

Both men laughed again.

"Good one!" the man kneeling in front of Alex said. "Maybe we should have him call the cops and see what happens!"

Alex turned his head to look up at the bearded man and spat directly into his face.

Everything went silent. The man's face was speckled with blood and saliva.

"Now I wished you hadn't gone and done that," The man said, his voice measured with an undercurrent of rage. He slowly brought an arm up and wiped his face against the flannel sleeve of his shirt.

The man called Eddie grabbed Alex's leg and wrenched sharply until a sickening pop filled the room.

Alex screamed in pain as fire shot through his leg. "Please.... please....stop!!"

"Oh, you started this," the man kneeling in front of him said. His face still held traces of blood.

Alex's head was now searing with pain as if it was trying to compete with the pain in his leg. The room spun.

"Just remember you are not welcome here," the man said as he stood. "Your mother is not welcome here."

He drew back his large steel toed boot and Alex's world went black.

20

Waves of heat shimmered across the asphalt in the yard. Alex sat on the weight bench after finishing a set of biceps curls. He wiped his face off with the t-shirt he had shed early on and took a drink from his water bottle. The contents were warm already. Sweat stung his eyes.

The guards walked across the wall making their rounds. One of the worst things about prison was the absolute lack of privacy. Even in your cell, someone was always checking in on you.

"Well, look who it is." The voice came from behind him.

"Guys, it looks like a killer here was working on his arms."

Laughter followed as three large men towered in front of Alex, eclipsing the sun.

"Got to have strong arms to knock back all that booze and still be able to control a car when he gets out of here."

"Knock it off, Deion," Alex said as he went to stand. Two large hands met him square in the chest pushing him back onto the weight bench.

"Where you going, killer?" Deion laughed. "We still got fifteen minutes left."

Alex looked at the large man standing in front of him, his dark skin glistening in the sun. Sweat beaded up on his bald head. His whole body was one large muscle with arms easily the size of one of Alex's legs. Tattoos covered his chest and arms.

Deion was doing life for first-degree murder, in addition to several gang related charges, and had been a thorn in Alex's side from day one. He and his thugs were well known agitators and their focus was mainly on inmates doing time for what they felt were morally repulsive charges. Typically, the child molesters, pornographers, and their likes.

Unfortunately, for whatever reason, they targeted Alex as well. There were plenty of folks locked up for worse crimes however, Alex had landed on their bad side.

"Come on Deion, I don't want trouble," Alex said. "Just let me finish my workout."

"Oh man, I'm sorry!" Deion laughed. "Don't want to stop you from getting all ripped or whatnot."

The other two men laughed.

"Marques, grab one of those one hundred pound dumbbells and give them to our friend here so he can finish his workout." Deion laughed, "Actually, grab both of them."

Marques stood an inch or two taller than Deion. The muscles in his arms bulged in a continuous state of flexion. Large veins roped across his biceps. He walked to the rack of weights and effortlessly lifted two one-hundred-pound dumbbells, like he was grabbing two bags of groceries out of the back of a truck.

"Stand up," Deion said.

"Come on man. I was minding my own business, Deion," Alex protested.

"Yep, so was that young girl when you plowed into the front of her car."

Deion reached into some tape around his wrist and pulled out a razor blade. "Stand up. I don't want this to get ugly."

Alex's mouth went dry. Prison politics were tricky, but someone who was in for life without parole rarely had much to lose. Alex was trying to bide his time to get out of here and he certainly could not do that dead.

Alex slowly stood.

"Marques, put those weights in front of our boy here."

Marques placed the weights down with a gentle thud.

"Now Alex," Deion stepped closer, "we will leave you alone, maybe even for good. All you gotta do is give me a set of biceps curls with these weights."

Alex laughed. "Are you serious?"

"Dead serious."

Deion stepped in closer and Alex felt the heat radiating off his body. By now a small crowd had gathered around and some hoops and laughter were going on. Alex saw the guards had started to notice the crowd and were beginning to make their way over.

"I can barely curl fifty pounds once," Alex said.

"Such a pussy!" Marques laughed.

"Why don't you shut up? I'm talking to your daddy!" Alex shot back.

Silence fell over the crowd.

"Boy, what did you say?" Marques asked, stepping in front of Deion.

"I said mind your own business; I'm talking to Deion."

Some heckles and laughter went up from the crowd. Rarely did anyone disrespect Deion or his crew and when they did it wasn't pretty. Marques looked over at Deion who nodded his head. Marques stepped forward and with both hands pushed Alex hard into the weight bench. Alex fell back and landed on the asphalt, catching his head on a dumbbell with a dull thud.

Everything went black.

• • •

A chirp woke him. His head locked in a vice cranked as tight as it would go. A sharp pain shot through the middle of his skull like someone was exploring his brain with a hot poker.

Chirp

Chirp

Chirp

Every muscle in his body was sore. He tried to open his eyes as a flood of fluorescent light nearly blinded him. He raised his hand to block the light.

"No, Mr. Hollins," a familiar voice said as a soft hand guided his arm back to his side. "You need to lie still. You have an IV in your arm."

Squinting, he looked around. He was in a hospital room. The sterile environment, the sounds, and the lights all made sense. His vision was blurry but he could make out the image of someone sitting in the corner, it looked like an older man.

"Emory?" his tongue was thick from the pain medication.

The female voice spoke up. "Yes. If it wasn't for him, you might not be here."

The nurse stepped into his field of vision to adjust an IV pump. He recognized the familiar kind face and auburn hair as the nurse who took care of his mother.

"Harper?"

"It's me," she said. "You are in the emergency room. You're not getting a family discount in case you're wondering."

Mom! What happened to her?

"My mom!"

She patted his shoulder, "Don't worry about her. She is doing much better and has all the nurses wrapped around her finger."

Alex grinned as much as his swollen face would allow.

Emory walked up to the stretcher.

"You are a lucky man, Alex."

"What happened?"

He remembered opening the door for the two bearded men.

"You got the tar beat out of you." Emory laughed. "Sheriff thinks it was a smash and grab robbery. The house was turned upside down, can't tell if anything is missing until your mom has a chance to go through the place."

"How did I get here?"

"I tried to call you to see about visiting your mom," Emory said. "You never answered and I got a little concerned and drove over to check on you. Thank God I did. The front door was busted wide open and you were lying in a puddle of blood on the living room floor."

Alex closed his eyes as the throbbing in his head intensified.

"Unusual for Pinehurst," Emory said. "Not much crime around here."

Harper stepped to the bedside with a syringe. "Let's try not to talk about that right now. Alex, your heart rate and blood pressure are sky high. Are you hurting?"

Alex nodded his head.

"On a scale of one to ten how bad?"

"Eleven."

"Alright, I'm going to give you some pain medication, but it will make you sleepy."

Reaching down she flushed some saline through the IV tubing and followed it with the medication. A warm, pleasant sensation soon coursed through his body.

Euphoria.

He was only able to enjoy the high for a few seconds before he was out cold.

21

Zeke & Eddie Boone made their way into the luxurious office space of Silas. Rich, dark mahogany paneling covered the walls, a deep purple carpet cushioned the floor. The sounds of instrumental hymns piped through speakers in the ceiling.

At the large wooden desk in front of them sat an attractive, young blonde lady with the "right dimensions" Zeke liked. A name plate on her desk read Anna Justice Executive Administrative Assistant.

Zeke approached the desk, startling the lady.

"Um…may I help you?"

Zeke looked at her name plate, trying to get a view of her chest as well, "Fancy title for a pretty little thing like yourself."

She remained silent. Her face started to turn red.

Zeke grinned, "Me & my brother here need to speak with Silas."

"Um, I'm sorry. The pastor is in a meeting," Anna said, shifting in her seat.

"We understand ma'am," Eddie said. He smiled and exposed a row of yellow teeth. "It will only take a minute and I believe he is expecting us."

"I'm sorry, I can't interrupt him now. I am happy to take your names and have him contact you when he is free."

"You see ma'am, that won't work with our schedule." Zeke stepped forward, his large hands swallowing the desktop, "Either you go and get the pastor now, or we will just make our way back there."

"Let me make a quick call." Her voice shook as she picked up the phone and dialed some numbers.

"I'm sorry…he is not picking up."

"Well, that's too bad, isn't it," Zeke said. "Eddie, looks like we will have to make a surprise visit."

They both made their way past Anna's desk toward the hallway that led to Silas' office.

"Stop!" Anna shouted. "I'll call the police!"

Zeke turned and looked back at her with a crooked grin. "Go right ahead, let's see how that works for you."

They made their way back towards Silas' office. Anna followed closely behind, trying unsuccessfully to make them stop. They reached a large mahogany door. A golden plaque hanging off to the side said:

Senior Pastoral Executive

Silas Weston

"Fancy title for a preacher man," Eddie said as he tried to open the door. "Locked."

Zeke stepped up and pounded on the wooden door with his large hand. "Silas, open up! We know you're in there!"

"I tried to stop them!" Anna chimed in from the back.

Zeke rattled the door.

"Hold your horses," a voice called out from the other side. "I'm coming."

A couple of minutes later the door opened and two ladies sheepishly stepped out, heads hung low.

"Thank you, ladies, why don't you work with Anna to schedule our next session? I think we have made some real breakthroughs today."

The two ladies made their way briskly down the hallway as Anna followed.

"Eddie, Zeke!!" Silas threw his arms out wide. "To what do I owe this unexpected visit?"

"You know why we are here," Zeke said, stepping into Silas's office. "Your fly is down, by the way."

Silas's face went red as his hands went to his pants. "No, it's...."

"Ha ha...made you look." Zeke and Eddie howled with laughter.

Silas remained silent, his face beet red.

"This is quite a place you have here," Eddie said, looking around the large office. "This is the brain center for the Lord's work I suppose?"

The office had deep plush eggplant colored carpet with furniture as large as Silas' ego. Photos of Silas with local and state officials and politicians covered the walls. A 72-inch flatscreen TV hung against the far wall. A large leather couch sat opposite it.

"You got anything to drink in this place?" Eddie asked. "Like maybe a bottle of communion wine?"

"Communion wine?" Zeke laughed, "That's good Eddie!!"

"We use grape juice for communion. You're thinking of Catholics," Silas said, sounding increasingly frustrated.

"Oh, so sorry," Eddie said. "I'm a little rusty on my knowledge of world religions."

"I have some water or Diet Coke."

"Do we look like a couple of Diet Coke boys?" Zeke laughed.

"Why don't you boys have a seat?" Silas motioned to two large chairs in front of his desk.

"Sure, I need to take a load off anyway," Zeke said.

They made their way to the chairs as Silas slipped behind his large desk.

Eddie kicked his muddy, steel toed boots up on the desk.

"How can I help you, boys?"

"Well, we need to discuss the matter of payment," Zeke said. "Eddie and I feel like we took care of our end, however, we have yet to get paid, and it is chafing us a bit."

Silas leaned back; a wide grin spread across his face. "Well, why didn't you just say so from the beginning? I can explain."

"That would be real nice," Eddie said.

"Boys, I appreciate your work, but I asked you to scare Alex a little, let him know he was not welcome here."

"I would say we succeeded," Zeke said.

"Well, I agree, but I didn't say to nearly kill him and have him end up in the hospital." Silas' voice grew strained. "Do you realize the level of attention that is now on this? Pinehurst is a small town. A home invasion with assault is a big deal. They will have news teams from Roanoke and Lynchburg down here snooping around!"

"Whoa there, boss!" Eddie kicked his feet off the desk and leaned forward, "You never gave us any guidelines. Looking at my brother and me, you can probably see we are not exactly the best with the kid gloves approach."

"Also, you never said our payment was contingent on keeping this on the down low," Zeke piped in.

"I'm sorry," Silas said in a terse voice. "Are you able to show me where you signed an agreement outlining your pay?"

"We ain't never had to sign anything in the past," Zeke said.

"You have always done good work in the past," Silas said. "Now we have a crime on our hands and, to be honest, you and your brother aren't exactly the type that blend in easily. Once Alex is out of the hospital and gives a description to the police, anyone who has lived here for any amount of time will know it was you two."

"I'm sorry you were not very clear in your instructions." Zeke leaned forward. "Just pay us what we are owed and we can lay low for a while."

Silas laughed. "The problem is I am going to have to send some of what you are due to Sheriff Blackwood to assist with the investigation so none of this can be tied back to you two or myself."

Zeke remained silent.

"I would hate for the three of us to end up in jail," Silas said.

"I would hate to see what happens to a preacher man in jail," Eddie said. "Particularly one with an affinity for younger types."

"You shut your mouth," Silas stood, his hands shaking, "I think we are done here."

22

Harper sat at the nurse's station catching up on her charting and eating a protein bar as a makeshift lunch. It had been one of those shifts.

As a nurse, the times you could actually sit and eat your lunch undisturbed were few and far between. She was thinking about Alex. Such a random event to have a mother one day and her son the next day. However, that was life in a smalltown emergency room.

"How is your guy in two?" Evan Wilson asked. "Sounds like he got jacked up pretty good."

Harper looked up from her computer. "Yep, home invasion gone bad. He got a concussion, nasal fracture, and they messed up his right leg. He is lucky he did not get hurt worse."

"For sure. Pretty violent attack for this area."

"Yep. Makes you wonder if some buddies from a former life paid him a visit." Harper frowned.

"That's a possibility," Evan said, taking a sip from his Yeti, "small town drama. You might make the local news!"

Harper laughed. "Let's hope not. The only time I want to make the news is if I win the lottery."

"Uh oh!" Evan said, looking down the hall.

The rotund figure of Sheriff Dalton Blackwood made its way toward the nursing station. His girth engulfing the entire hallway, almost eclipsing the light.

"Great!" Harper pushed her hair back behind her ears and started typing away on the computer, hoping to look too busy to be disturbed.

A large shadow gradually overtook the nurse's station with the heavy smell of cheap cologne.

"Excuse me, ma'am."

Harper looked up to see Sheriff Blackwood looking down at her. His forehead was damp with sweat and his pudgy fingers drummed on the counter.

"I understand you are the nurse caring for Mr. Hollins," he said, breathless.

Harper looked up at him, concerned she may have another patient on her hands. The walk from the main entrance to her station wasn't long.

"Yes, sir," she said, "I am the nurse assigned to his care."

"I was wondering if I could talk with him for a few minutes. I need to get a statement from him regarding the events that occurred earlier today."

Harper had just given him a generous dose of Dilaudid so he probably was in no state to talk.

"I recently gave him some pain medication; he probably is sleeping." She stood up from her chair. "Let me go check."

"Thank you kindly, miss."

Harper made her way to bay two. She had the uncomfortable feeling of being watched. Looking up in the reflection of the glass door, she Sheriff Blackwood staring intently at her.

Turning quickly, she caught him in the act. His face went bright red and he quickly developed an interest in the ceiling tile.

"I'll be back in a second."

She slowly slid the glass door open. Alex remained sound asleep in the darkened room. His face was swollen and disfigured from the attack earlier. The subtle beep of the pulse oximeter filled the room. She stepped beside the bed and gently shook his chest.

"Mr. Hollins."

A grunt and he turned his head away from her.

That was enough for her. She made her way out of the room and back to the nurse's station.

"I'm sorry, sheriff, he is still sedated. I am not sure he would be able to stay awake long enough to give you a statement."

"Well, ain't that a shame." He grunted. "I guess I should have called before I drove over here. Tell you what."

He reached into his front pants pocket and pulled out a crumpled business card.

"Here is my card. When he wakes up and is alert enough to talk, you give me a call."

She took the damp, wrinkled card, and immediately felt the need to wash her hands.

"Yes sir," she said.

"You call me anytime. I mean it," he said with a wink, then turned and walked back down the hall.

"That was creepy," Harper said.

"Yeah, he was totally checking you out."

"Gross!"

"You still got it, Harper!" Evan laughed.

Harper threw the business card at him and laughed along with him.

23

The leather office chair creaked in submission as Silas's large body leaned back. A long plume of cigar smoke rose above his head.

"Dalton, you always knew how to pick 'em," he said, savoring the cigar.

"Yes sir," Dalton Blackwood said, taking a puff of his and releasing a slow, satisfying breath. The room was filled with a cloud of smoke.

"So, you couldn't get in to see him?" Silas asked.

"Nope. He was drugged up and out cold," Dalton said. "Had some fine young thing taking care of him though. Wouldn't mind going back a second time, to get a good look at her."

"I'll bet she was at least twenty years younger than you, too." Silas laughed.

"You know I like 'em young."

Silas laughed uneasily, coughing a little on the cigar smoke. "I'd be careful how you say that around here."

"You know what I mean. I'm not that much of a pervert."

"I know." Silas crossed his fingers over his large belly and stared at a ring of smoke fading against the ceiling. "We have to get to him before he starts blabbing to the staff."

"I agree. It's not like the Boone brothers are the most inconspicuous characters in Pinehurst."

Silas grinned. "They also ain't the most intelligent boys either. Who assaults someone in their home in broad daylight?"

"Well, that's true. Probably won't go down as their best career decision."

"So, the nurse is going to call you when he wakes up?"

"I left her my card," Dalton said. "I'm probably going to wander back over there in a couple of hours if I don't hear from her. Just to take in the scenery one more time."

"Sounds like a plan," Silas said. "Let me know if you need someone to come pray with the poor guy. I know he is scared."

They both laughed.

24

The creaking of his cell door brought him out of a deep sleep and a pleasant dream. Both of which were rare in prison. The pungent smell of bleach and body odor met his nose.

Opening his eyes trying to adjust to the dim light of the room. The cell was never completely dark thanks to the bright fluorescent glow of the hall lights in the central yard that stayed on twenty-four/seven.

A dark shadow briefly blocked out the light, causing Alex to sit straight up.

A hard object struck him across the bridge of his nose, sending waves of blinding pain across his face. The room exploded into stars as his head rocketed back and struck the metal headboard of the cot.

"Drunk driving piece of shit," a gruff voice said, "Let's just say you ain't walking out of here."

His world went dark when a cloth sack was pulled over his head. He could hardly breathe. In a matter of seconds, a flurry of fists and other objects was unleashed on his body.

He blacked out from the excruciating pain.

Beep…beep…beep…

The steady beeping slowly brought him out of a stupor.

His face throbbed like a swollen balloon ready to burst.

Feeling hungover for the first time in years. His head ached like he had been on an all-night bender.

Blinking his eyes open, he was not in a jail cell, but the hospital. A pole off to the right of him was beeping. It held an IV pump that looked like something out of a science fiction novel. A bright red message flashed across its screen.

Air in Line

Had he been more lucid this would have panicked him. However, he probably had bigger things to worry about. His memory began to clear as he remembered the two large men who had played kickball with his face.

"Mr. Hollins."

A soft voice came from the foot of the bed. Looking down there was a figure of someone standing there.

"I need to fix your IV pump. I am going to need to turn on a light."

The figure made her way to the head of his bed. The overhead exam lamp turned on and the subtle darkness of the room partially washed away with a bright light. He groaned as the light hit his eyes.

"I'm going to adjust it so I can look at your IV," the voice said, "How is your pain?"

"Still there."

"I'm sorry. You're about due for some more pain medication."

"I'll take it on the rocks."

The voice laughed. "I'll see what the bartender can do."

There was some tugging around the IV tubing at his arm. Soon the beeping stopped.

"There we go," the voice said as the exam light turned off. "That should stop the beeping."

"Thanks."

"I'll go draw up your pain medication and be right back."

"Hey," he called as she was walking out of the room.

Harper stopped and turned back towards him.

"Do you think I could see my mom?"

Harper paused, "I'm not sure in your current condition that would be the best idea."

"I know she is worried about me," Alex said, "I really would like to see her."

Harper stepped to the bed and put her hand on his shoulder.

"I think if she saw you now, she would worry more."

Alex nodded; he was in too much pain to keep arguing.

"Alright," Harper said, "let me go get that medicine."

Harper left the room, pulling the sliding glass door closed on her way out.

25

Dalton Blackwood made it past the locked door into the busy emergency room without a question. He was amazed at the power a three-point-five-inch metal badge had. He had gone from being bullied in high school to having the power to put the bullies behind bars. It was intoxicating and he sometimes let it go to his head.

He made his way down the hallway toward bay two. The smell of bleach, urine, and feces filled his nostrils. He gagged. The thought of coming into this every day revulsed him.

Harper sat at the nurse's station down the hall, a smile automatically spread across his face. He passed room two and through the side window caught a glimpse of Alex Hollins sitting up with his eyes open and looking much more alert than earlier.

He approached the nurse's station. "Good evening Mrs...." he glanced at her name badge which was conveniently located on her chest, "Layne... I hadn't heard from you and was coming back by to make sure something hadn't happened to our patient."

The nurse looked up at him. "I'm sorry Sheriff, it's been a busy shift and I just forgot to call."

"Not a problem, I understand all about being busy."

"He has had a good day. I checked on him and he was still in some pain, but his last dose of meds was a couple of hours ago so you should be good to go in."

"Thank you kindly, Miss." Dalton tipped his large police hat towards her. "I shouldn't be long."

His large body made its way to room two.

He tapped on the sliding glass door and opened it before he got a response.

The room was dark and Alex was sitting up in bed, his head resting back against a pillow.

"Mr. Hollins?"

"Yes..."

"My name is Sheriff Blackwood. On behalf of the town of Pinehurst, I want to express my deepest apologies for the incident. I can say as a lifelong native of this great town, Pinehurst in general is a peaceful place."

Alex grunted, closing his eyes.

"No matter what your past transgressions were, violence is never condoned in my jurisdiction," he said. "Anyway, I realize this may not be an ideal time, however, there is some time sensitivity to solving crimes like these. I wanted to get a quick statement from you about what happened."

Alex nodded.

"Would it be alright if I asked you a few questions?"

Alex tried to talk, then tilted his head toward a white Styrofoam cup of ice water. The sheriff picked up on the cue and retrieved the cup from the bedside table and gently placed the straw to the swollen lips of Alex.

Alex took a few sips of the ice-cold water.

"Thanks," Alex said.

"No problem," Dalton said, placing the cup back on the bedside table. "So, as I was saying I wanted to ask you a couple of questions about this horrible random act of violence you were a victim of."

"Sure."

"I understand you were recently released from prison. Was there anyone from that time who may have wanted to harm you?"

Alex paused.

"No one I can think of."

Dalton scribbled something down in a ratty spiral notebook. "Ok. Did you recognize the two men who did this to you?"

"How did you know there were two of them?" Alex sounded surprised.

Dalton cheeks turned red as he tried to recover from his obvious misstep.

"Um...I....well.......just an....assumption." He struggled. "You look like a man who could take care of himself and I assumed it would take more than one person to do that much damage."

"Gotcha....and no." Alex wasn't convinced.

"No?"

"No, I didn't recognize them. There were two of them though, so your detective skills are on point."

Dalton cheeks flushed, "I'm curious why would you let two strangers in your house?"

"I didn't let them in; they let themselves in."

"Well, that's interesting because the team at your house did not see any signs of forced entry."

"I know." Alex was growing tired. "They knocked on the door and I thought they may have been friends of my mom's. I opened the door. The next thing you know I'm lying face up on the floor."

"I'm sorry. I guess you can never be too careful." Dalton went back to scribbling in the notebook, his forehead beaded with sweat. "Did they say anything to you? Or did they have any defining characteristics?"

"They told me I was not welcome in Pinehurst," Alex said. "Both of them looked like they had seen better days. One of them had a rough tattoo of a teardrop under his right eye, and not a very good one at that."

"Good...good...that is very helpful. Pinehurst is not a big town." Dalton continued writing in his notebook.

"Also...." Alex said, "One of their names was Eddie."

Dalton stopped writing and looked up at Alex, "How…do you know that?"

"The one with the tattoo said, 'Eddie, we weren't supposed to hurt him.'"

Dalton stood abruptly.

"Well…Mr. Hollins," he stammered. "I do appreciate your time and I know you must be exhausted. I think I have all I need. I will be getting back to you to update you on the progress of our investigation."

Dalton turned and quickly exited the room.

26

A doctor who looked like he had just crested over the peak of puberty came in and told Alex the good news that everything looked ok.

He had sustained a pretty good blow to the head with a concussion and would probably have a nice set of matching black eyes tomorrow. The doctor told him he had to staple a large gash in the back of his head and needed to come back to the emergency department in about seven days to have them removed.

They could refer him to the concussion clinic in Roanoke, but Alex declined. He was ready to get out of there. His headache had gone from a steady ice pick in his brain to more of a routine ache behind his eyes.

The doctor told him he had a significant knee sprain, and walking would be painful for the next couple of weeks. He should try to stay off his feet as much as possible.

Alex nodded. Shouldn't be that hard since he didn't have much to do anyway.

"You're lucky it wasn't a lot worse," the doctor said, stepping out of the room.

Alex sat in silence for a while trying to process what had transpired. He had only been back home less than a week and already his past was coming back to haunt him.

"Knock, knock," a cheerful female voice came from behind the curtain, "Dr. Andrews said you could go."

Alex sat up straighter as Harper rounded the corner and stopped at the foot of his bed. Her auburn hair was up in a messy bun and her blue eyes were accentuated by the light blue surgical mask.

"I'm going to get that IV out of your arm and go over your discharge instructions," she said, moving to a wall of cabinets and getting some supplies out.

"Thanks," he said, his mouth full of cotton from the pain meds.

"After what you've been through, getting the IV out is the easy part, although the tape can be a bear sometimes." She laughed, sliding up a rolling stool with a black seat.

"Here give me your arm." Her gloved hands were cool on his skin. "Alright, this is not fun."

She began pulling the tape off his arm from around the IV catheter.

He grimaced.

"I'm sorry."

"No, I'm just being a wimp." He laughed. "I know how us men can be when it comes to pain."

Her eyes lifted as she grinned under her mask. "Well, after what you have been through you may be the exception to that long held medical belief."

He relaxed some.

"There, all done." There was some pressure in the bend of his arm as she flexed it up, "Hold your arm like that for a bit."

"You did a great job."

"Well, I was nervous because it was my first time." She laughed.

Soon he had a stack of papers and some hospital-issued paper scrubs.

"Don't forget you need to get those staples out in about seven days."

"Thanks," he said. "I don't have a doctor yet. Can I come by here and get them out?"

"Sure," she said. "They would need to check you in and you may have to wait." She paused. "If I'm working when you come back, I may be able to help you out."

"Thanks. I don't have insurance or a lot of extra money for another visit."

"Understood. Alright, you're all set," she said. "Do you have a ride?"

A ride, he had forgotten all about that.

She sensed his hesitancy. "Do you need me to call someone?"

"I'm sorry, it's that I'm...." he paused," I've just relocated back here so I don't have anyone to call."

Emory popped into his mind, if he had his number he could give him a call.

"Come to think of it," he said, "my mom's friend could probably give me a ride. I need his number. Do you know how I could talk with my mom?"

"Sure, she is on the third floor," Harper said, "let me call the charge nurse up there."

"Thanks," Alex said. "Would be possible for me to see her?"

Harper looked at him. "I still think it is not the best idea right now. It might hard for her to see you like this."

Alex nodded.

"I'll talk with the charge nurse upstairs and see what we can do," Harper said. "What was your mom's friend's name?"

"Emory Wright."

27

"Get them down here now!" Silas said, red-faced, as he pounded a large fist on his sturdy mahogany desk.

Dalton Blackwood sat across from him, his face pale. "Ok, I'll need to have one of my boys drive up there. No cell reception near the creek."

"I don't care if you have to walk through the national forest to get them, I want those two inbred rednecks in my office."

Luther Evans stood quietly in the corner.

"Luther, how in the world did you mess this up so badly?"

"Sorry, Sir." Luther stared at his leather loafers. "Should have known better than to trust those two with such an important task."

"You would think common sense would prevail and you would not do something so stupid in broad daylight and even if you thought it was a good idea, you would not use your real names when carrying out the assault." A look of disgust crossed Silas' face.

"Well, me and the boys can handle it from the station," Dalton said, "We can make him doubt his story enough. I mean he was pretty roughed up, probably has a concussion."

"Any chance the press is going to be snooping around here?"

"No sir, we have kept a pretty tight lid on things." Dalton shifted his large rear in the chair, "To be honest, I'm not sure anyone cares about an ex-inmate getting roughed up a little."

"Good point," Silas said. "God, you're sweating and starting to stink."

Dalton wiped his forehead self-consciously.

"Get out of here." Silas motioned to the door with his sausage shaped fingers. "Get your boys up to Mill Creek. I want the Boone boys standing in front of me right now!"

Dalton wedged himself out of the chair as he stood. "Yes sir," he said through gritted teeth. He lumbered toward the door and left the room.

"Get some paper towels and wipe the sweat out of the seat," Silas said to Luther. "That's genuine cowhide. I don't want it to stain."

Luther nodded and left the room in search of the cleaning supplies.

"Imbeciles," Silas muttered, leaning back in his chair.

28

Harper sat in the driveway. Her Subaru clicked and popped as it cooled down from her commute home. It had been an exhausting day. The emotional response she had when taking care of Alex surprised her.

She had been a nurse long enough to know it was not smart to get close to your patients. Maybe it was because she had taken care of his mother as well.

Maybe it was because, oddly enough, she thought of herself and Lando. If something happened to her, he would be all alone in the world. She loved her sister but Vanessa wasn't mother material yet.

The pain of seeing your child in the state Alex Hollins had been in would be unbearable. He had not lived a perfect life, neither had she, but no one deserved that type of treatment.

Everyone was someone's child.

She stepped up the cracked concrete steps leading to the back door. A single light illuminated the kitchen through the door. She opened the creaky screen door and tried not to make too much noise in case Lando was asleep.

She stepped into the kitchen and went through the ritual of taking off her work shoes and tossing her keys onto a small wooden stand next to the door. Unconsciously, she let out a loud sigh.

Walking to the cabinets, she grabbed a glass and filled it with water at the sink.

Why was she fixated on Alex Hollins?

There was a tug in her chest.

She tried to play it off as just being tired.

The soft sound of padded pajama feet coming into the kitchen interrupted her train of thought.

"Mama!!!" a small voice exclaimed.

Landon charging right towards her. She swooped him up and gave him a giant squeeze, blowing some raspberries on his neck. A burst of giggles erupted.

"What are you still doing up?" she said, playfully poking his belly.

"Aunt Nessa said I could."

"I'm sure she did!" Harper looked up to see Vanessa walking into the room, a tattered copy of Goodnight Moon in her hand.

"I tried….sorta," Vanessa said with a slight smile.

"Mama, will you read Moon to me?" Landon was in full manipulation mode.

"OK sweety, let mom get out of her gross work clothes." Harper put him back on the floor. "Why don't you go lay with Aunt Nessa while I get changed and I'll be right in there."

He let out a victorious whoop and charged back toward Vanessa.

"Thanks, Sis." Vanessa smiled, "How was your shift?"

"Exhausting."

Vanessa grabbed Landon and walked back to his bedroom.

Tears welled up in her eyes. She did not know where these emotions were coming from. Through the experiences of the past couple of shifts, she had come to the realization that motherhood was a lifelong commitment and only grew harder and more complex the older your children got.

The fact she was doing it alone was overwhelming.

29

Dalton struggled to keep the old Crown Victoria on the dirt road as he made his way toward the Boone residence. The road had two ruts made from years of rain and vehicle traffic. The shocks in the car needed replacing and Dalton's weight did not help. He jostled about in the car, striking his head on the ceiling a few times.

He was fuming.

In what other county did a preacher get to order the sheriff around?

Dalton regretted the day he began taking the bribes. While the extra money had been nice, he was beginning to see it was not worth the toll it had taken on him emotionally. The constant stress of being found out. The total impotence of power when he was in front of Silas.

His mind began to wander as he made his way down the road. He needed an exit plan.

Looking up, there was a large Rottweiler standing in the middle of the road. Dalton slammed on the brakes, stirring up a cloud of dust surrounding his car.

His heart pounded in his chest.

Bruce was the Boone brother's beloved dog and security system. He might as well dig his own grave if he hit the dog.

The dog glared at the white car.

Dalton laid on the horn.

The dog stood defiantly. Its pointed snout and muscular limbs daring Dalton to move forward.

Dalton opened the door and stepped out of the car.

"Shoo!" he yelled.

The dog did not budge.

"Go on!" he yelled, growing increasingly frustrated. "Stupid mutt!"

Reaching down on his belt he unclipped his can of pepper spray. Rolling the cool cylinder between his fingers he contemplated his next move. He leaned on the horn a couple more times.

The dog remained unfazed.

"Well, I hate to do this."

He flipped the cap on the pepper spray, aimed it at the dog, and squeezed the trigger. A thin stream of fluid shot out, hitting the dog directly in the face, eliciting a loud yelp from the dog. It lunged forward and struck his head on the bumper of the police cruiser. Dazed, he backed up and ran off into the woods, whimpering and howling.

Dalton grinned and slid the pepper spray back onto his belt. Squeezing himself back into the driver's seat, he put the car in drive and proceeded down the poor excuse of a road. A mile later the familiar sight of the Boone trailer came into view. A stream of smoke came from the chimney. Dalton could never be sure if this was a wood stove or meth lab but had never asked.

He pulled up next to an old, beat-up Chevy truck that had seen better days. He recognized it as Eddie's piece of junk. As he stepped out of the cruiser, he was met with the familiar scents of stale beer and marijuana.

The place was quiet, although he could still hear the occasional whimper of the dog. He climbed up three wooden steps that were tested by his weight.

He knocked on the door.

No answer.

Glancing at his watch, one o'clock. They should be awake. He pounded harder on the door.

"Who is it?" a gruff voice called out from behind the door.

"Sheriff Blackwood. I need to talk with you."

"Go away," the voice replied.

"I'm sorry, I can't do that," Dalton said, his hand unconsciously resting on the handle of his service revolver. "Eddie, Zeke I know you are in there. Silas and I need to talk with you. No one is in trouble."

A muffled laugh and the sounds of heavy footsteps approached the door. A clink sounded as the deadbolt disengaged. The door cracked open and the heavy smell of cannabis hit Dalton. Zeke Boone peeked through the door frame. His eyes were bloodshot, pupils pinpoint.

"Sheriff…" Zeke's voice slurred. "To what do we owe the pleasure?"

Dalton caught a glimpse of black metal hanging at his side. His throat tightened.

"Zeke, no need for a gun," Dalton said. "Silas wanted me to come down and get you two. He had a few questions."

"Are we under arrest?"

"What?...No…I'm just here for Silas."

"Are we going to church jail?" Zeke said and a boisterous laugh erupted from behind.

"Church jail, good one Zeke," Eddie Boone whooped from inside the trailer.

"Sheriff, seeing as we are not under arrest, my brother and I are not in the best state to visit Pastor Weston. Why don't you give us some time to get freshened up and maybe we could meet with him tomorrow."

Dalton could feel rage develop deep in his throat as his neck muscles tightened. "We would both appreciate it if you come on down now. I am happy to drive you both. I think that would be safest."

Zeke opened the door a little wider, raising his hand wielding a forty-five-caliber pistol and aimed it right at Dalton's chest."

Dalton stepped back, his heart racing. "Zeke, I ain't here to cause trouble."

"I know sheriff, and seeing how you ain't here on official business, I consider this trespassing." He stepped closer to Dalton. "I kindly ask you to get your large posterior off my porch and back into that car."

Zeke took the gun and placed the barrel into Dalton's rotund abdomen, pressing hard. The soft flesh enveloped the gun. Dalton broke out in a sweat and began backing off the porch. The steps groaned under his weight.

Zeke stayed put on the porch.

Dalton backed up to the car.

"Zeke, you'll regret this. You know how much stuff I've allowed you and your brother to get away with." Dalton's face turned red. "If you weren't on Silas' payroll, you'd both be in jail by now."

"Sheriff, I'd suggest you stop talking and start figuring out the quickest way to get your large ass into that car."

Zeke raised the pistol above his head and fired a shot. A loud boom echoed through the trees as a flock of doves scattered into the sky. Dalton jumped and hurriedly compressed himself behind the steering wheel, cracking his head on the door frame in the process.

Zeke howled with laughter. "Maybe that will knock some sense into you."

Dalton barely shut the door before starting the car and throwing the police cruiser into reverse. He did a quick U-turn and floored it.

Zeke laughed, turned around, and went back into the trailer.

30

Alex rested his head against the passenger side window, the glass cooling his forehead. His neck was too sore to keep upright. He was ready to get back into bed. The oncoming headlights from other cars caused him to wince.

"You alright?" Emory asked.

"Yeah, thanks again for coming to get me."

"No problem, you're lucky you caught me before I went to bed. Once I turn my CPAP on, I'm dead to the world." Emory laughed and looked at the clock on the car's console. "Seven-thirty is past my bedtime."

Alex grinned, "You are a wild man."

"Any idea who may have done this to you?" Emory asked.

"I wish I knew. I've not been out of jail long enough to make any enemies, or friends for that matter."

"Did you talk to any police about why you were in the emergency room?"

"The sheriff stopped by Dalton something..."

"Blackwood, Dalton Blackwood and he is worthless." Emory sounded disgusted, "Silas Weston has him in his back pocket. Good luck on ever finding out who assaulted you. Our whole law enforcement team here is corrupt."

"Well, that's encouraging."

They sat in silence as the silent whine of the highway filled the car. Alex tried to stave off some nausea from the pain meds he'd had in the emergency room. To keep his mind off it he thought of Harper.

She'd been kind to him despite knowing his past. Alex was pretty sure he was the talk of the hospital, but she hadn't shown any judgment at all.

Such a polar opposite experience to the encounters with his father, the "man of God" Silas Weston had been harassing him pretty much since he got to town.

"Wake up."

There was a nudge in his ribs.

"We're here."

Alex opened his eyes, confused, head back to pounding.

"You were snoozing pretty good." Emory said

"Sorry," Alex said, rubbing his forehead. "Thanks again for the ride. Sorry to keep you out late."

"No problem. Happy to help you and your mom out."

Alex opened the door and stepped out. The cool night air felt good.

"Hey," Emory yelled out. "Call me if you want to go visit your mom tomorrow."

"Sure, thanks for the offer."

"But don't call until after 8:00, I'm going to be sleeping off my wild night."

Alex grinned. "Noted."

He shut the door and walked up the sidewalk. Emory's car slowly pulled away. Stepping inside his mouth went dry. The entire living room had been ransacked. Pictures were ripped off the wall, the furniture was turned over. The carpet had a large crimson stain on it which he assumed came from his head. The air still had a lingering scent of marijuana.

Too tired to even process this he went directly to his bed and sprawled out across the soft mattress. Sleep came quickly.

31

Silas hated his life.

He bounced around the interior of the large Lincoln Town Car as it made its way down the sorry excuse for a road that led to the Boone home.

Luther sat behind the wheel sweating as he tried to avoid the larger holes and defects in the road. Dalton Blackwood was in the back seat looking out the window with an ice pack on his head.

How had he ended up in Pinehurst of all places?

Silas had graduated seminary fired up and ready to start a megachurch. He was thinking of the Richmond area or some large metropolitan area in Virginia. He learned quickly his style of fire and brimstone preaching did not attract the crowds he anticipated. When his dad died, he welcomed the opportunity to move back to Pinehurst and take over his church. He was a big fish, small pond type of person anyway.

Initially, it was a struggle, but soon his congregation started doubling every Sunday. The parishioners ate up everything he said. With the growth came land, a new building, and power.

His head bounced and nearly struck the roof of the car.

"Luther!" he barked, "Slow down and watch where you're going!"

Luther's face turned beet red. "Sorry boss. This road ain't necessarily the best."

"I can see that!" Silas muttered.

The only hesitation about moving back to Pinehurst was Alex. Before he had left for seminary, he had started dating Nancy Hollins. A moment of indiscretion in the back seat of her father's car led to an unforeseen development in their relationship.

Silas had no desire to be weighed down by a wife and kid, so quickly separated himself from the relationship. Fortunately, Alex's drinking troubles took care of that problem and Silas was able to grow his church and influence without much concern, until now. He had not expected Alex to return to Pinehurst after being released from prison.

Soon the tan rusted double-wide trailer of the Boone boys came into view. The same beat-up truck sat in the gravel driveway. Silas could see one of the boys sitting on the front porch with a long object in his hand.

"Is that a …" Luther began to say as the man leveled the object and pointed it straight at them. Luther slammed on the brakes, raising a cloud of dust behind them.

Silas pressed the down button on the window and stuck a handout.

"It's me!" he yelled. "Silas!"

"I know who it is," the man yelled back. "I'm tired of you all harassing me and my brother."

"Look, we just want to talk," Silas said. "I may have another job for you."

"You still haven't paid us for the first one!"

"Zeke, that's what I'm here for." Silas said producing a white business sized envelope from inside his sportscoat, "I can pay you double for this job."

"Ha!" Zeke waved the rifle toward the car, "For some reason I'm having a hard time believing you.".

Silas looked at Luther and shrugged his shoulders.

"Can we at least talk?" he yelled.

"Get off my property!" Zeke shouted and shouldered the rifle.

The front window of the Lincoln exploded into a spray of safety glass.

"What the…" Dalton yelled from the back seat.

Silas brought his head to his knees screaming. Luther looked pale as he fumbled with the gearshift and tried to throw the car in reverse.

"Go! Go! Go!" Silas yelled his head as close to his knees as his large belly would allow.

"I'm trying!" Luther shot back, glancing from the rearview mirror back to the front porch.

Zeke loaded another round, still cackling.

"Look at them go!"

Luther's face went pale and he pressed the brake.

"Luther, why are you stopping?!?" Dalton shouted from the backseat.

"The dog."

Dalton tried to turn his large frame around to look out the back window but physics would not allow it.

"What do you mean?"

"A dog is behind the car."

A large Doberman had wandered directly behind the car, snarling.

"Just run over him, we gotta get out of here!" Silas shouted.

"I'm not hitting the dog," Luther argued, "or the next shot is going to shatter more than the front window."

Zeke made his way down the front steps, rifle hanging by his side.

"Preacher man, get out of the car!" Zeke yelled, pointing the rifle toward them.

"Dalton, can't you arrest these jokers?" Silas asked.

"Are you crazy?" Dalton said, "If I haven't arrested them yet, I ain't going to start now, alone in the boondocks."

Silas paused, sticking one hand out of the passenger window. "OK, Zeke. I'll get out, but put the gun down man, we ain't here to hurt you. I've brought you your check from the last job."

Zeke laughed, turned to the side, and spit a stream of black saliva from his mouth. "That's a good one preacher. How about you get out of the car first?"

Silas looked at the other passengers who kept their gazes uncomfortably straight ahead. "Alright, Dalton, you better have your pistol ready, you got a clear shot out of where the windshield used to be."

Silas opened the door and slowly exited the car, keeping both hands above his head. This is ridiculous, feels like I'm being arrested by a hillbilly. Once out of the car, Silas stood still with both hands in the air.

"Alright Zeke, I'm out," Silas said. "Now you put your rifle down."

Zeke grinned. "I don't remember making that promise, preacher." He walked towards Silas, keeping the rifle leveled at his chest. "Don't make any sudden movements, and 'show me the money' preacher." Zeke's speech was slurred. "I don't want to send you to heaven early, or is that where you end up?"

Zeke staggered towards him. Silas had a pretty good suspicion he was tweaked out on some illegal substance.

"Zeke, you're high," Silas said. "Don't do something you'll regret once you sober up."

"My life is a big regret, pastor," Zeke said. "Something you should know about as well."

Zeke made it to the hood of the Lincoln and rested up against it.

"Alright Zeke, why don't you hand me the rifle and we can go inside and talk about things."

"Good one preacher. Nice try."

Silas reached into the pocket of his suitcase and pulled out the envelope.

"See here you go," Silas held the envelope up, "I think you will be happy with what's inside."

Zeke took one step forward and fell face first on the ground, his rifle clattering off harmlessly to the side. Silas stepped back, the large bulk of the man just missing him. Zeke's head struck the open car door with a sick thud and he bounced back onto the ground with a groan.

"Jesus!" Luther yelled from inside the car. "What did you do boss?"

"Nothing," Silas said, kneeling next to him. "He is still breathing. Probably just high and it got the best of him."

Dalton rolled down the rear window. "No way we are getting him back to the trailer."

Silas looked at the large unconscious figure sprawled out on the ground. A small stream of blood ran down Zeke's forehead.

"Yup, Zeke here may need to sleep it off for a bit," Silas said, getting back into the car. "I think we may need to go check on his brother."

32

Alex woke with a start, sitting bolt upright in the bed. He was met
with a sledgehammer pounding deep into his skull.

"Ugh…"

The room spun as his stomach churned. Sunlight streaming
through the blinds hit his eyes like a million hypodermic needles. He
closed his eyes and laid back down placing the pillow over his head.

His mind cleared as he remembered he was back at his
mother's house. The bouts of nausea were getting more frequent and
the increased saliva in his mouth only pointed to one inevitability. He
had enough hangovers to know this feeling.

Lowering himself to the floor, he crawled toward the
bathroom across the hall. The shag carpet burning his knees as he
slid across it.

Any movement set his head off like a fire alarm. He made it
into the bathroom and the cool tile floor soothed his skin. The
almond colored toilet sat in front of him. He lifted the lid and leaned
over, vigorously retching into the commode. With each heave, his
head filled with pressure like it might explode.

The room went black.

• • •

Knock…knock…knock.
Knock...Knock...Knock

The steady knocking noise brought Alex back to the bathroom floor, where he lay arms outstretched around the base of the commode. The smell of fresh vomit filled the room. His mouth had a taste of acid and sulfur.

"Alex...Alex...you in there!" the voice said.

Emory.

"In here..." Alex tried to say, his words hanging in his raw throat.

Fortunately, the nausea had gone away, but the headache was still present in full force.

Knock...Knock...Knock.

The storm door open and the doorknob rattled.

"Alex. It's Emory!" the voice sounded concerned. "I'm worried about you. The hospital's been trying to get in touch with you. It's about your mom."

Alex used the commode as support and pushed himself off the floor.

"Coming," he tried to say.

The room spun as he stood, like he was on a raft in the middle of a whirlpool. He quickly leaned over and grabbed onto the sink. Bearing weight on his right leg was excruciating.

Knock...Knock...Knock...Knock

Turning on the cold water he splashed some on his face. The shock was refreshing and knocked some cobwebs loose in his mind. He paused and then made his way slowly down the hallway.

One...foot...in...front...of...the...other...

He steadied himself against the wall.

"Coming..." his voice was stronger now.

The headache was severe enough that his ears were ringing. He finally made it into the living room and to the front door.

Knock....Knock....Knock...

"I'm here," he said unlocking the door, turning the deadbolt away.

The sun flooded in across his face, causing him to bring his hand up to cover his face.

"Alex!" Emory said, "I was worried sick about you! My God, you look awful."

Emory put his arm around Alex's waist and guided him to the sofa.

"I feel awful," Alex managed to say, attempting a laugh.

"Can I get you some water or a coffee?"

"Both would be great," Alex said, "How about a bottle of ibuprofen?"

Alex laid his head back against the sofa. Soon the house filled with the familiar smell of coffee brewing.

Emory walked over and handed Alex a glass of ice water with a straw in it.

"Here." Emory held out a clenched fist. "Give me your hand."

Alex raised a hand to him, open palm. Emory dropped three red tablets in his hand.

"Here is some ibuprofen, probably should take it with food, but based on how bad you look, I don't think you'll be eating anytime soon."

Alex opened his mouth and threw the pills on the back of his tongue. He chased them down quickly with the ice water. It was the most glorious experience he had in the past 24 hours. The ice water cooled his entire chest as it traced down his esophagus.

He let out a moan. "That's good."

"Drink up," Emory said.

Alex quickly drained the glass and held it up for Emory indicating he wanted seconds. After three cups of water and half a cup of black coffee, Alex began to feel like himself. His headache had gone from about a fifteen down to a standard ten.

Emory sat in a recliner. "You look a little better. I mean, still not great, but you're going to live."

"What brought you out my way?"

"I was worried about you," Emory said. "The hospital's been trying to get in touch with you. It's about your mom."

Alex was instantly alert. "Why? Is there a problem?"

"She had a little setback." Emory shifted forward in the seat. "She started running a fever and having a little more trouble breathing. They were moving her back to ICU for observation."

Alex looked down at his cup, steam rising from the top.

"Don't worry, the doctor sounded like this was all precautionary."

"Well, it doesn't sound too good," Alex said. "I should get over there."

"Today?" Emory looked surprised.

"Yes."

"Are you sure?" Emory asked. "I mean, you just got out of the emergency room last night. I'm sure your mom understands. I am happy to let her know."

"No. I asked to see her last night, but the nurse felt like it wasn't the best idea." Alex paused. "I want to see her today. I am afraid something might happen."

"Well…ok. Just make me a promise."

Alex looked a little confused. "Sure."

"Make sure you shower before I take you over there, you are ripe!" Emory laughed.

Alex smiled. "Sure. I don't want any unnecessary casualties on the way over."

"Probably wouldn't hurt if you gave your teeth a good scrub either."

33

A cacophony of beeps, hisses, clicks and whirs filled the room. The patient in the bed was unrecognizable surrounded by tubes and lines snaking over and around her. A large plastic mask covered most of her face and a long plastic tube coiled off the mask and connected to a large tower at the bedside. A lone monitor traced undulating flow of her respiratory pattern, a slight hum with every breath.

The doctor had called it Bi-Pap and explained it was a step to try to keep her from needing a breathing tube. Alex had never heard of it.

He was in a wheelchair, pressed as close as he could to her bed. Finding some skin between the tape and tubing, stroking her cool hand. He wasn't sure she even knew he was there. The nurse said they were keeping her sedated so she wouldn't fight the breathing mask.

Tears formed in his eyes; the only signs of life were the steady stream of squiggly lines going across the monitor above her head paired with the subtle rise and fall of her chest.

He had put her through so much.

Growing up he had been through all the teenage vices. Smoking, drugs, porn, and the occasional pregnancy scare with various girlfriends. She had stayed up pacing the floors until he was safely back home. She had held his head after he became violently ill from drinking too much. She ignored the extra body in the bed when he snuck girls in overnight. He had grieved her more than any single person should have to suffer.

Pinehurst was a small town. After the manslaughter charge, she became the community pariah. Her friends soon dried up. She didn't feel welcome at church. When she stopped going to church, no one even checked in on her.

Emory had been the one consistent friend and Alex was grateful for him.

A tear ran down his cheek and he squeezed her hand. "I'm sorry Mom."

The door to the ICU bay slid open and the sound of soft footsteps came in. Alex turned around to see the nurse walking in with a couple of syringes in her hand. She was a young African American woman.

"You doing all right?" She asked, working with some IV tubing.

Alex wiped his eyes with the back of his hand., "Yeah, just hard seeing her like this."

"I'm sure," the nurse said wiping off one of the IV lines with some alcohol. "It is always hard seeing your loved ones like this."

She connected a syringe and slowly pushed some clear liquid through the catheter. "It's ok to feel sad or anxious." She looked at Alex again. "Your mom is in great hands with our intensive care team."

"That's good to know." Alex leaned on the bed. "I've also had a rough day or two." He pointed to his eye.

"I can see," she said. "I heard you were in the ER earlier."

"Yep, I've been here lately more than at home."

"Well, I tell you what," the nurse said, walking to the foot of the bed. "I gave her some more sedative and visiting hours are over soon. Why don't you go on home and get some rest?"

Alex sat quietly looking up at his mom.

The nurse said, "I promise, if she were awake, she would be telling you the same thing."

"Alright," Alex said. "A soft bed is sounding pretty good about now."

• • •

The Oldsmobile rumbled down the road, the heater blasting, trying to chase off the oncoming evening chill. Alex sat in silence.

Just as I am without one plea

But that thy blood was shed for thee

Alex recognized the familiar hymn coming from the speakers. Emory squinted into the evening sky and hummed along.

"Can't beat the classics," Emory said.

Alex grunted.

"Nowadays those big city churches are more like rock concerts," Emory said. "Lights, dancing, people jumping around. Nope, not for me. Just give me a piano and a classic hymn. That's all I need."

Alex remained silent, feeling the twinges of another thumper of a headache starting.

"How was your mom?"

"Well..." his voice quivered, "she didn't look good...all those years of smoking are catching up with her."

"I'm sorry Alex," Emory said. "Your mom is a special lady."

Alex wondered if that was an indirect jab at him. "I know, special for putting up with a son who is a convict."

"Alex...that's not what I meant." Emory sounded deflated. "I mean it. She is just all around special. She means a lot to me."

"Sorry Emory. I guess I'm a little extra salty tonight."

"Understood. Hey, do you mind if I stop by Walmart really quick? I need to grab some more coffee filters and a couple of other things."

There was nothing Alex wanted to do less, but Emory had been so good to him over the past couple of days he relented.

"Sure, not a problem. I need to get some antibiotic ointment and more ibuprofen anyway."

They sat in silence as the music finished. Soon the southern twang of Silas Weston filled the car.

Bless Gawd! This is Silas Weston senior executive pastor of New
Ministries. The Lord works in mysterious ways and there is change comi
town. Join us this Sunday for our morning worship service. Let us equip
the full armor of God. Our small town is under a full-scale demonic attac
However, even as I record this, I sense the tides changing. I sense Satan I
I sense the unrepentant yielding.
See you Sunday!

Alex winced. Ashamed of hearing his owns fathers voice.

Emory turned the radio off.

"I can't stand him."

Alex grinned. "I thought you liked everyone, Emory."

"Almost everyone!"

Pulling into the large parking lot of the local Walmart, it
looked unusually crowded for a Tuesday evening.

"Everyone loves Walmart," Emory said, trying to find a
parking space.

He snuck into a spot midway back.

"You feel like walking? Or do you want me to get you one
of those scooter things?" He laughed.

Alex grinned. "I think I'll be fine."

They made it into the store. The bright fluorescent lights
hurt Alex's head, causing him to squint to ease the pain.

"I'll go grab what I need if you want to get the ibuprofen,"
Emory said, "The medical section is over there to the left."

"Sure."

Alex followed the signs towards the health care section.
Moving gingerly, but much better than this morning. He found the
pain reliever aisle, pausing to take in all the options while trying to
find ibuprofen. The vast array of choices made him wonder if there
were that many people hurting all the time. He found a bottle of
ibuprofen and grabbed it.

He made his way to the wound care supplies to get antibiotic
ointment for his staples. If the pain aisle was impressive, the selection
of band-aids, dressings and ointments was equally impressive.

Between the selections of pain medications and dressing supplies, he wondered just how clumsy people were.

He found some triple antibiotic ointment. The tube said it prevented infection so he guessed it would work.

"I would avoid that one," a female voice said from behind him.

Startled, he turned around to find Harper. She was in a gray quarter zip fleece with a pair of black jogging pants and Nike sneakers. A little boy with blonde hair and blue eyes stood beside her. He wore a blue striped shirt and red plaid pants. A tattered stuffed dog hung from his left hand.

"Harper!" Alex's face burned, "Didn't expect to see you outside the hospital."

She smiled. "I know. I do occasionally get a day off. What better way to spend it than in Walmart?"

He laughed. "Well, I'm here too, but I have nurse's orders," he said, holding up the ointment.

"I am glad you're being a good patient, but the triple antibiotic can be irritating. I would get bacitracin. It usually is in a green tube."

She stepped past him her arm brushed against his chest, brief, probably accidental but stirred something in him he couldn't quite name. Pausing, she knelt and came back up with a green tube of ointment.

"Here you go." She handed it to him. "And it's a bargain at $2.98. We would have charged you $300 for the same tube in the hospital and only used it once."

"Thanks," he said. "Who is this guy?"

Harper looked down at the boy, "You want to tell him your name?"

"Lando!" the boy yelled, "and this is Pupster."

He raised the tattered stuffed animal high.

"Lando, what a cool name!" Alex said. "My name is Alex. Fist bump?"

Alex went to kneel, but a sharp pain shot through his right knee, reminding him he had just left the hospital.

Alex held up a balled fist and Lando instantly reciprocated, bumping his fist against Alex's.

"Can I get one from Pupster?"

Lando laughed and grabbed the tattered paw, tapping against Alex's closed fist.

Harper laughed as Alex slowly stood up.

"Still sore?"

"Slightly." He laughed, "I can't take a punch like I used to." They both laughed.

Her dimples and her brilliant white teeth as they flashed out from under her lips.

"Well, I promised a certain someone they could look at the Hot Wheels," she said.

"Hot Wheels!!!" Lando jumped for joy.

"You wouldn't guess that he already has like a hundred at home," Harper said, patting his head.

"I am a firm believer you can never have too many Hot Wheels," Alex said. "It was great seeing you. Thanks again for all you did for my mom and me. You are an awesome nurse!"

Harper blushed. "Just doing my job. How is your mom?"

Alex looked down at his feet. "They had to move her back to the ICU."

"Oh no, I'm so sorry!" Harper said, "What happened?"

"She started running a fever and was having trouble breathing. They have her sedated. They are trying to keep her off the breathing machine with a Bi…something."

"Pap."

"What?" Alex looked confused.

"Bi-Pap. It's called a Bi-Pap. It helps her breathe," Harper said, "Well, I work tomorrow. I'll try to sneak up and check on her. We have a great critical care team, so she is in good hands."

"Thanks," Alex said. "That would mean a lot if you could check on her. I don't necessarily have any transportation so I'm not sure if I can get up there tomorrow."

He self-consciously touched the row of staples across his forehead.

"Don't touch those." Harper reached out and grabbed his arm.

It was like an electric jolt. The pressure of her hand through his jacket. It had been over twenty-five years since a member of the opposite sex had intentionally touched him.

Reflexively, he stepped back.

"I'm sorry!" Harper said, pulling her hand back. "I guess it's the nurse in me."

"No apologies needed. I'm a little jumpy after the past 24 hours." He laughed.

"Mommie!" Lando pulled his mother's arm. "Hot Wheels!"

"Ok, baby! I haven't forgotten."

"I know Hot Wheels are a big deal! They were when I was a kid also," Alex said to Lando.

"Ok. Well, we're off to do some car shopping," Harper said. "I'll check on your mom and let you know. Do you have a number I can call you with an update?"

His face turned red with embarrassment. "I don't have a phone yet. I am still using the old school landline at my mom's house."

"No problem," Harper said. She dug through her purse and produced a pen and a scrap piece of paper. She jotted something down and handed it to him.

"This is my number. I get off at 7:00 pm tomorrow. If you want to call me and check in, that is fine."

Alex looked at the scrawled numbers on the wrinkled piece of off-white paper.

"Thanks! This means a lot....to both of us."

Harper looked down at Lando. "Say goodbye."

"Bye!" the boy waved and turned to walk away.

"We will talk tomorrow," Harper said.

"Looking forward to it!"

Lando skipped off down the aisle with Harper in close pursuit.

There was an ache in the pit of his stomach, the slow familiar sadness of being alone.

34

Silas scanned the men assembled around the large mahogany table. Most had been with him since he founded the church, a few members had changed, some quietly, some not as much. But the mission remained the same, grow the churches influence and eliminate anything that stood in the way. Silas called those obstacles 'spiritual barricades'. It was easier to convince people to skirt around the law, if they were though they were doing it in the name of God.

Today's discussion was about his Alex Hollins. Only a select few new the dark truth that he was Sila's son. He had hoped that prison would bury the secret permanently. However, thanks to the anemic, liberal justice system, his son who had murdered one of their own had been returned to society to kill again.

"Gentleman," Silas said, "we need to get this situation under control. Our hired 'help' made the idiotic decision to confront Alex in broad daylight. If that wasn't enough, went on to refer to each other by name, while committing the crime."

Silas glared at Zeke and Eddie Boone who were seated in some chairs lining the back wall of the room. Zeke had a large, bruised goose egg protruding from his forehead compliments of Luther's cars fender. Eddie sat beside Zeke half asleep and probably high.

"Zeke, I hope you are satisfied with your payment?"
Zeke let out a little grunt.

"We are likely going to need you and your brother's services again soon so I do hope you would be open to doing business with me again."

Zeke slowly raised his left hand, extending a middle finger to Silas.

The whole table erupted in laughter.

"I'll give you a pass on that one since you just suffered a head injury, compliments of Luther's Lincoln."

Zeke lowered his hand and rested his head against the wall.

Silas looked at Luther Evans who was leaning back in the leather chair.

"Luther, any thoughts?"

Luther leaned forward, placing his hands on the table. "Well, I think we have mitigated most of the damage. The police have interviewed the neighbors, and no one reported seeing anything. Those that did, let's just say have been paid for their silence."

"That's good news." Silas leaned back, "Dalton, what are your plans?"

"Well, right now Mr. Hollins is distracted by his mother still being in the hospital. I'll swing by house in a day or two. We will go through the motions of a photo line up and see if he can pick out who assaulted him. Of course, I will be selective about whose photos we include."

Silas grinned. It was expensive to keep the sheriff on payroll, but times like these made the investment pay off.

"Excellent, Dalton." Silas rubbed his large jowls. "We need to figure out the next steps to get this piece of shit out of our town. Does anyone have any bright ideas?"

Silence filled the room.

Then Dalton spoke up. "I could have one of the boys at the station trail him in one of our unmarked cars. That way we could at least get an idea of what he is up to and maybe would give us some information."

"You sure your boys won't get caught?"

"They're good," Dalton said. "Also, I don't think Alex has been back in town long enough to recognize if something is off."

Luther spoke up. "I don't believe he has a car; it may be a boring assignment. They may only be traipsing back and forth to the hospital."

"Well, something is better than nothing and right now we have nothing," Dalton replied.

"Alright," Silas said. "Have your boys tail him for a week or so and report back. In the meantime, I'll continue to mount some pressure as well. Let's just say I see some unique lawn decorations in his future."

Silas was determined to make Alex's life in Pinehurst so miserable he was either going to force him to leave or commit another crime that would put him back to prison. Either way, Silas would feel vindicated.

Dalton nodded. "On it boss."

"And Dalton, for God's sake be more subtle than Beavis and Butthead over there in the corner."

The table erupted in laughter as Zeke's face turned red.

35

"No way!" Vanessa Layne shouted. "You are not having that man over here!"

"Vanessa, he is harmless." Harper pleaded, "I feel so bad for him."

"Harper, he killed someone!"

"Accidently…"

"While he was drunk…"

"Twenty-five years ago…"

"Harper, I am not having this argument with you." Vanessa sounded exasperated. "You not only have you to look out for, but also Lando."

Harper looked at the moisture forming on the outside of her glass of Moscato, slowly raising it to her mouth, taking a sip of the sweet liquid.

"Harper, I love you. I just know your track record with men….well…it's not great."

Harper sat the glass down. "Says the perpetually single girl."

Vanessa jerked back as if Harper had physically hit her. Harper immediately regretted what she said. "I'm sorry. I'm frustrated because deep down I know you're probably right. It's just he is so pitiful. He is alone, his mom is critically ill, and he just got beaten up in his own home."

Vanessa remained quiet.

"Look, I know you are watching out for me and I appreciate that. You also are the one encouraging me to put myself back out there."

Vanessa took a slow swig from the bottle of beer in front of her.

"I am doing this to be friendly. It's not even romantic. I'm trying to help a fellow soul who happened on hard times. Like you've done for me, sis."

"I don't have a good feeling about this," Vanessa said. "And to clarify, I am not perpetually single, I have high standards. One of which is not dating convicts."

"I have standards also. But I believe in giving people a chance," Harper said. "Maybe I'm a little too optimistic."

"And maybe I'm a little too realistic," Vanessa said finishing off her beer. "Fine. Have him over for dinner, but I need to be here. I don't want him here in my house without me."

"I understand. It's your house," Harper said.

She wasn't entirely sure how to feel.

A part of her was happy, part of her was nervous.

Was she crazy, desperate, or both?

36

Alex woke up to the silence. The morning sun snuck through the closed blinds. It was the first morning he had not awoken with a blistering headache. His knee had improved to a dull ache with the occasional full body jolt to remind him it was still there. He sat on the side of the bed and looked around the room.

In one corner his meager possessions sat in a cardboard banker box issued from prison. He hadn't had time to fully unpack yet with the events of the past couple of days.

On the nightstand, a black plastic alarm clock with faux wood grain sat, its bright red LED display read 9:00. This was the latest he had slept in years. Beside the clock sat a crumpled piece of paper. He picked it up and smoothed it out, looking at the numbers. 434-401-8492. His pulse quickened, remembering his encounter with Harper. Seven tonight was a long way off.

Who was he kidding?

Why would a beautiful lady like her want anything to do with a convicted felon like himself?

He showered, taking advantage of the unlimited hot water and trying to avoid the staples in his head as they were still sensitive. He got dressed, made some coffee, and scrambled some eggs.

Maybe his first few days back at Pinehurst had been an anomaly. He would be ok with some boredom at this point.

By around eleven he had done everything and was sitting on the sofa in his mom's living room trying to figure out the remote when there was a knock on the door.

Peeking out the living room window, he expected to see Emory's familiar Oldsmobile in the driveway. Instead, it was a Pinehurst County sheriff's cruiser.

"Coming!" he yelled, hobbling towards the door.

He opened the heavy wooden door to see the large figure of Dalton Blackwood on his front porch.

"Morning, Mr. Hollins," Dalton said.

"Good morning, Sheriff. Is everything alright?" Alex asked.

"Everything's fine. I was following up on the investigation around your assault." He said, "You mind if I come inside for a bit?"

Alex unlatched the storm door and pushed it open the tension springs squealed in resistance. "Sure, come on in."

He stepped aside to let the large man in. The smell of cheap cologne and sweat invaded his nostrils.

Alex pointed towards the recliner. "Have a seat."

"Do you mind if we go to the table?" Dalton lifted a folder. "I have some photos I would like you to look at."

"Sure," Alex said, leading the way into the dining room. The table was rarely used so Alex cleared off some old papers and mail. "Apologies about the mess, I am getting settled in and Mom is in the hospital."

"I heard. I hope she is doing ok," Dalton said, "She is a sweet lady."

"I am waiting to get an update." Alex placed the mail in an empty chair. "Would you like a cup of coffee?"

"That sounds nice," Dalton said. "I take it black."

"Great. Make yourself at home and I'll be right back."

As Alex disappeared into the kitchen. The sheriff sat down in a chair; it let out squeak as it strained under his weight. A few moments later Alex returned with two steaming cups of coffee and sat down at the table.

Dalton had arranged a grid of nine polaroid mugshots on the table. Each photo was about three inches by three inches.

Dalton took a slow sip of the coffee. "We are trying to locate the men who assaulted you. We interviewed your neighbors and no one witnessed anything unusual that morning, which is a little bit of a setback."

Alex nodded his head.

"Anyway, I thought since you got a look at both of them, I wanted to see if you recognized any of them from this photo lineup."

Dalton waved his pudgy hand over the grid.

"Take some time and look at these photos. Let me know if any of them look familiar."

"I'm happy to help," Alex said, "but my memory of that day is vague, thanks to a wicked concussion."

"Oh, I understand. Just take your time. If someone looks familiar point and I'll pull that picture out."

Alex looked at the photos. A hybrid collection of ethnicities, facial hair, and tattoos. Any one of them looked like they could have done this. However, both of his attackers had large burly beards. One had a rudimentary tattoo of a tear coming from the corner of his eye.

He stared at the pictures until his eyes crossed. Since he had spent time with men who argued their innocence every day, he didn't want to be responsible for sending the wrong person to jail.

Rubbing his temples he gave up. "I'm sorry," he said. "None of these guys look familiar. Like I told you in the hospital, they were two large bearded white guys. One had a tattoo on his face and the other called him Eddie. I would imagine that might narrow things down in a small town like Pinehurst."

Dalton laughed. "You would think, but with the interstate running by here, we will occasionally get some bad actors passing through. You know, random acts of violence. Drug related, usually."

Alex nodded, taking a sip of coffee.

Dalton stood, trying to free himself from the chair. He gathered up the photos. "Well, I do appreciate your time. Thank you for the coffee. If you happen to think of anything else let me know."

He handed Alex a business card. "Cell number is the best way to reach me."

Alex stood and took the card. "Thanks. Maybe as time passes, I will remember more."

"Sometimes that happens," Dalton said. "In the meantime, this is an active investigation, so don't go asking a lot of questions. If anyone comes snooping around let me know."

"Sure thing." Alex began walking to the door.

"I can show myself out," Dalton said. "Thanks again for the hospitality and sorry your return to Pinehurst has been less than welcoming."

"Sheriff," Alex said.

Dalton turned around. "Yes sir?"

"What do you think they meant by saying I wasn't welcome here? I mean it doesn't sound very random to me, based on my history."

Dalton paused. "You know, the same thing has been bothering me also. I don't really have a clue." He turned and walked out of the house.

Alex was not convinced by his answer.

37

Harper had survived another shift in the understaffed, overcrowded emergency room. No one had died and that was a plus. She had been able to sneak upstairs during lunch and visit Ms. Hollins. Unfortunately, not much had changed, she was still lightly sedated on Bi-Pap. Harper grew concerned about her prognosis. With her advanced age and COPD, Harper was worried she might end up on a ventilator.

"It's after 8:00, you leaving soon?" Sarah Crawford, her night shift replacement asked.

"Soon, just finishing up my charting in our super efficient computer system." Harper laughed.

"Tell me about it, nothing makes a bad day better than clicking hundreds of boxes."

Harper laughed again and went back to typing. Her phone vibrated in her work bag. Looking down she did not recognize the number, but it was a Pinehurst area code.

"Hello?" she sounded cautious.

"Harper? It's me, Alex."

"Oh, hey!"

"Is this a good time?"

"Sure, I'm wrapping up," she said, stepping away from her computer. "I was able to get up and see your mom, earlier."

"Thank you," Alex said. "I have been worried about her all day. I spoke with the doctor this morning after he rounded and it sounded like she was about the same."

"Unfortunately, that's the case. She is still using the Bi-Pap, but they are trying to keep her less sedated."

"I guess that's a good thing?" Alex asked.

"Yes. The good news is they haven't had to put the breathing tube in yet. I think once they get this pneumonia to clear will help her the most."

"Was she responsive when you went in?"

"She did seem to recognize me and gave me a little nod. I talked to her, put some lotion on her arms and tried to fix her hair. Which was tricky with the mask on."

"Harper, I don't know how I can ever repay you." Alex tried to keep his voice strong. "I haven't had the warmest reception back in the area. My mom has always had to bear the burden of me being her son."

There was a moment of silence.

"Alex, we all make mistakes," Harper said. "My mom told me God doesn't keep score and neither should I. So, I make it a point to live my life like that. Being an ER nurse, I see all types of bad decisions every day. If I got too judgmental, I couldn't function." She laughed.

"Well, I appreciate that," Alex said, "Emory is bringing me to the hospital tomorrow to visit her."

"Maybe she will be a little more alert and you all can have a good visit."

"That would be nice."

Another awkward pause.

"Hey, listen…" Harper said. "Would you like to come to my sister's house this weekend for supper?"

"Excuse me?"

"Do you want to come to my sister's house this weekend and have supper?"

Alex laughed. "That's what I thought you said. You do understand I just got out of prison?"

"Yes. I also know you are alone in a small town, your mom is in the hospital, and if I had to guess, you probably have not had a decent meal?"

"Well, you are right on all counts, It's that I'm not necessarily a popular dinner guest in this area."

"Well, there aren't too many folks in this town whose opinions matter to me," Harper said.

"I'd love to come over," Alex said. "Is your sister cool with it?"

"Of course she is," Harper said sheepishly, "I could get your staples out and save you another trip to our lovely ED."

"That would mean a lot," Alex said. "There is the uncomfortable subject of transportation. I don't necessarily have a way to get there."

"No problem," Harper said. "Lando and I will pick you up. He will be excited to talk your ear off about Hot Wheels!"

"Great! Sounds like a plan!"

"Alright, let's aim for 5:00 on Saturday," Harper said.

"I'll see you then," Alex said.

"OK." Harper said, "Are you forgetting something?"

"What?" Alex sounded confused.

"I need to know where you live." She laughed.

"Oh, good point," Alex said, "220 Wildwood Dr. do you know where that is at?"

"I know the area very well," Harper said, "My sister's house is a few streets over on Cambridge, we are practically neighbors!"

"I'll see you then," Alex said.

38

The days that followed were as close to normal as Alex had experienced since he had been released from prison. Emory took him to see his mother a couple of times. Thankfully, she had been taken off the machine and moved to a standard oxygen facemask. The doctor said he still wanted to keep her in the ICU a bit longer, but it appeared like the pneumonia was clearing.

With Emory as his sole source of transportation, Alex's only view of Pinehurst was the hospital, Walmart, and Hardees. Alex did not complain. It beat being trapped in the four walls of a prison cell.

He got a prepaid cell phone during one of his trips to Walmart and was still trying to figure it out, although it did make him feel a bit more human. He was excited to share his new number with Harper. He was looking forward to Saturday, not only to see her but to get the staples out of his head. They were itching and beginning to get on his nerves.

So far in his travels to the hospital, he had not run into Harper, but that was alright. They had been speaking on the phone a fair amount and she was always friendly.

He needed a decent outfit for Saturday since his wardrobe choices were slim. He had worn enough orange in his life to never want to see that color again.

During one of their excursions to Walmart, he ventured into the clothing section and picked up a pair of jeans and a decent looking button down shirt.

"Getting ready for your date?" Emory asked, sipping on a soda he had gotten earlier at Hardee's.

"It's not a date. She invited me over for dinner and to take my staples out. If anything, it is a mercy social excursion. I think she feels sorry for me."

"Well, when I was young, the guys always asked the girls out," Emory said. "These liberated women confuse me. I'm glad I'm not back on the market."

Alex grinned. "Emory, you still got some mojo, you should put yourself back out there."

"No way, I'm too ornery. No woman in her right mind would put up with me!"

"I'm sure there are plenty out there who aren't in their right mind who would love to call you their own."

They both laughed.

"Hey actually, I need to grab one more thing and then we can go," Alex said. "Is that ok with you?"

"Sure," Emory said. "I got all the time in the world. This is the most excitement I've had on a Thursday in a long time!"

Alex made his way to the toy aisle. He found the selection of toy cars and a display of Hot Wheels sat on the end cap.

"Is this a new hobby?" Emory asked, sounding confused.

"No. Harper has a little four-year-old boy, a cute kid. He loves Hot Wheels." Alex looked through the rows of cars. "So, I figured I would come bearing gifts."

"Great idea," Emory said. "Hot Wheels were big when I was growing up, too. I guess some things never really go out of style."

Alex wasn't sure which car to get Lando, but he chose a souped-up bright red 1964 Ford Mustang with fire running down both sides of the car. He figured cars and fire would speak to a boy on multiple levels.

"Alright, I'm ready."

They checked out and headed out to the car. The sun had begun to set behind the mountains bleeding a purplish-orange glow through the clouds. For the first time in a while, Alex had a slight sense things would be ok.

As he and Emory pulled out of the parking lot, they didn't notice the gray Ford Taurus turning on its headlights and following them out.

39

Trevor Adams shifted in the stiff faux leather interior of the car. It smelled like stale tobacco and fast food. The department only had one unmarked car since Pinehurst was not necessarily the hotbed for undercover investigations. He tried to keep the windows from fogging up on the cold winter morning.

The bad thing about being the new kid on the block is you get stuck with the worst assignments. He had been trailing Alex Hollins for the past week and it was painfully boring. To be a dangerous ex-convict he lived an ordinary life.

Largely staying inside except about every other day a large gray Oldsmobile would come and take him to the hospital. After a couple of hours, the car would return and either take him back home or take him to Walmart or Hardees or some combination, but he always ended up back home.

It was easy money, but he would rather watch paint dry as they say. However, when the sheriff asks you to do something, you don't have much choice. He wasn't even sure what he was looking for. His only instructions were to keep an eye on him.

40

Saturday arrived quickly. The week had been uneventful. His mother was moved out of the ICU and into a regular room. Alex had adolescent level butterflies in his stomach as he got ready for his dinner "date" with Harper. He had gotten the hang of using his phone and had become somewhat proficient at this thing called texting, which was the primary way he and Harper had been communicating.

He scrolled through their latest exchange with a grin.

Good morning!

Morning!

You still on for this evening?

Yep, if you and Lando are.

We are. He hasn't stopped talking about it.

Looking forward to it, except for the getting my staples out part.

LOL, it won't hurt a bit.

LOL?

Laugh Out Loud. You really do need a primer on texting.

LOL, you're right (How did I do?)

That is acceptable.

What time are you going to pick me up?

How about 6:00?

That works, I feel like a loser having you pick me up.

Don't feel bad! I don't mind.
Ok, see you at 6:00.
👍

Alex had noticed a grey Ford Taurus parked on the street a couple of houses down. Initially, he hadn't thought much of it, however, one evening when he was leaving the hospital he'd seen it parked a couple cars behind Emory's.

He hated to be paranoid, but twenty-five years in prison tends to do that. Drinking his morning cup of coffee, he went over to the front window. Sure enough, there it was, parked in the same spot, he could make out the faint silhouette of someone sitting in the driver's seat.

Why would anyone be following him? Maybe it was a local reporter trying to get the big story on the homecoming of a local convict, or it was one of Silas' men keeping an eye on him.

Emory was coming over later to take him to the hospital, he would ask him if he noticed anything.

41

It's not a date. It's not a date. It's not a date.

Harper kept repeating this mantra to herself as she turned onto Wildwood Street.

Looking in the rearview mirror, Landon sat in his car seat looking out the window, bouncing his feet to the music of "Baby Shark" as it played over the car stereo.

Harper smiled. It was probably her 1,000th time hearing the song and the joy it brought Lando never stopped amazing her.

In 500 feet your destination will be on your left, her phone blurted out.

The street narrowed, with cars parked along the road. She was anxious she was going to scrape one. She got particularly close to a Ford Taurus and gave the man sitting in it a scare.

Your destination is on your left.

She cut her turn signal on. A large mailbox with name Hollins on it sat at the corner. Relieved, she turned onto the concrete driveway, placed the car in park, and grabbed her phone.

I'm here.

Shortly after the front door opened and Alex stepped out.

Wow, he cleans up nicely.

His hair was still damp from the shower and combed over to the side. He was wearing a nicely fitting pair of jeans and a blue and gray checked shirt with a worn leather jacket. He had a small bag in his hand.

He waved and made his way to the passenger door.

She unlocked the doors and he slid into the front seat.

"Hello," he said.

"Hello," she said. "You look nice."

"Thanks," he said, looking at her. "Same goes for you."

"Hey, what about me?" A tiny voice came from the back.

"What's that sound?" Alex feigned confusion.

Harper caught on. "I'm not sure. I didn't hear anything."

"Hey, I'm here! Look behind you," the voice giggled.

"There it was again," Alex said.

"You know, I think I heard it that time." Harper grinned.

Alex turned slowly in the seat and jumped.

"Wow! Where did you come from!"

"I've been here silly!" Landon laughed.

They all laughed as Harper backed out of the driveway. Harper loved the fact that Alex didn't seem to mind Landon.

"I hope you don't mind I brought a chaperone for the trip." Harper grinned.

"Not at all," Alex said. "I bought a little something to get on the chaperone's good side."

Alex held up a tiny gift bag and handed it back to Landon.

"Oh, Alex, you didn't need to get him anything!"

Alex probably didn't have a lot of money didn't need to spend it on Landon.

"It's not much. I don't mind at all."

"Hot Wheels!!" Landon screamed, pulling the package out of the bag and holding it above his head like he had won a trophy.

Harper smiled. "Alex that was so thoughtful. You definitely know his love language!"

They made small talk and soon were at her sister's house. They pulled into the driveway of the tiny Cape Cod. The front porch lights were on and lamps shown through the open windows giving it an open, warm feel on the cold winter night. Harper turned the car off.

"Here we are," she said.

"Very pretty home," Alex said.

"Well, it is all my sister. She has a natural touch for decorating. I am a natural disaster."

Alex smiled.

They stepped out of the car. Harper got Landon out of the car seat and they walked up the steps to the front door. They didn't notice the headlights turning off a couple of houses down.

• • •

It was around 6:00 pm and Trevor could barely keep his eyes open, when the lights of a car coming down the street filled the cabin of his car. At first, he thought it was the usual traffic, but the car slowed as it approached Alex's mother's house, then the left-hand turn signal came on and the car turned into the driveway of the house.

Trevor sat straighter leaning forward trying to make out the car. It wasn't the older gentleman who usually came. This was a newer model Honda CRV. He could make out the faint shape of a car seat in the backseat. Soon the front door of the house opened, Alex stepped out and walk to the passenger side of the car. The reverse lights came on and the car backed out of the driveway and pulled away. Trevor put his car in drive and started to follow the car.

42

The house smelled like freshly baked apple pie and the sounds of light jazz played softly in the background. Alex took a moment to take in the welcoming atmosphere. He had not been in a place this nice in a long time.

"Hello, I'm Harper's sister, Vanessa," a tall brunette with deep green eyes held her hand out to Alex.

"Hi, I'm Alex. Nice to meet you," Alex said, shaking her hand. "Beautiful place you have, Harper was complimenting your decorating skills. I have to agree with her."

"Well, this is what watching hours of YouTube and TikTok will get you."

Alex must have had a puzzled look on his face.

"Van, remember Alex is new to the social media scene," Harper said. "She means she found some inspiration online."

"I see." Alex nodded his head, "I knew the YouTube reference, the Tic Tac one threw me."

Van laughed.

"What?"

"Tik Tok," Harper gently corrected him. "Don't worry you will get it."

There was a tug at his back pocket, Alex turned around to find Landon staring up at him.

"My room, my room!" Landon said, jumping up and down.

"I think he wants to show you his room," Harper said. "Landon, why don't we let our guest get settled in, and then he can come up."

Landon looked disappointed.

"I don't mind," Alex said, extending his hand toward Landon.

A broad grin spread across Landon's face as he clutched Alex's outstretched hand and pulled him toward the steps.

"I'm sorry," Harper said, falling in behind them.

"Seriously, it's not a problem." Alex laughed. "I'm excited to see if he has your sister's decorating talents."

Harper laughed. "Let's say it is more of a toy store vibe than a modern farmhouse motif."

Lando led Alex up some steps and into his room. The bed had a Hot Wheels comforter on it with rows of stuffed animals lying across it. He ran to a toy chest and pulled out a bucket of toy cars and promptly dumped them on the floor.

"Landon, I just straightened up in here," Harper said.

"These are my cars!" Landon said proudly. He picked the cars up one by one to show Alex.

Landon plopped down on the floor and patted next to him. "Sit."

Alex looked back at Harper.

"You don't have to."

"I know. I don't mind. If you want to go help your sister in the kitchen that is fine."

Harper paused and Alex picked up a subtle hint of unease.

"If you are not comfortable, I completely understand."

Harper's face turned red. "No...it's...not..."

Alex grinned. "I get it...no hard feelings."

"Sit," Landon piped up again.

Alex sat cross-legged on the floor next to Landon and Harper sat on the corner of the bed. Soon Alex and Landon had created quite an impressive collection of cars doing various dare-devilish type things.

Harper watched the two of them playing together on the floor. Alex looked like a natural when it came to kids. Harper enjoyed seeing how much Landon loved playing with Alex. Sadness soon crept in, this is how it should be. A boy should have a father.

"You're welcome to join us down here," Alex said.

"No, I'm fine being an observer," she said.

"Mommy, come play with us!" Landon shouted, then went back to pushing a car across the carpet.

"How can you say no to that?" Alex said.

"Easy, I do it many times a day." Harper grinned.

"Supper's ready!" Vanessa's voice came from the base of the stairs.

"Saved by the supper bell!" Harper said as she stood up from the bed.

• • •

The rest of the evening went fine. Supper was great. Probably the best meal Alex had had since he left prison. Although he chose not to tell Vanessa this, since it could come across as an insult. The bar for 'better than jail' food was pretty low.

The highlight of the night, outside of getting the staples out of his head, was Landon asking Alex to read him a bedtime story. Landon requested Goodnight Moon which made Alex smile because it was a story his mom had read to him. He didn't even make it to the end of the story before Landon was out cold.

Alex snuck out of the room, trying not to waked Landon. Stepping into the hallway the sounds of a muffled conversation floated up the steps.

"Are you sure you're ok with this?" Vanessa sounded concerned.

"He is harmless," Harper said.

"I mean, you barely know this guy and he is upstairs with Landon alone."

"Van, you're being paranoid," Harper said. "I don't get any creeper vibes off him."

"Harper, you know your luck with men," Vanessa said. "Besides, he just got out of jail."

"Vanessa, I know. Trust me on this one."

Alex cleared his throat at the top of the steps.

"Well, he is out like a light," Alex said, making his way down the soft carpeted stairs.

"Wow, that was quick!" Harper said. "You are hired; I'm usually in there at least thirty minutes."

"Beginner's luck." Alex laughed.

Vanessa sat quietly on the chair sipping her coffee.

"Vanessa made a pot of decaf. It is a Sumatran blend from the local coffee shop downtown." Harper held up her mug. "It's really good."

"Thanks, but I probably should be going," Alex said. "I don't want to wear out my welcome. Plus, I just had a major procedure." He pointed to where the staples used to be.

Harper rolled her eyes.

"I'll get your coat," Vanessa said, standing up quickly.

Harper sat silently watching her sister leave the room.

"I'm sorry, it's a little past her bedtime."

"No, I understand," Alex said. "I'm sure it's a little uncomfortable having me in her house."

"What do you mean?"

"Harper, this is a small town. Everyone knows what I did," Alex said. "Some folks are more accepting than others."

"Alex, no. Vanessa has not said anything about that."

"Harper, it's fine really."

Vanessa returned holding both Harpers and Alex's coats.

"Here you go," she said.

"Thank you," Alex said, taking his. "I appreciate the hospitality. You have a beautiful home and the meal was delicious."

"You are welcome," Vanessa said, her lips tightening. "Well, I'm going to start cleaning up the kitchen. Hope you have a good night."

She turned and walked back into the kitchen.

• • •

Harper and Alex drove in silence until she pulled into his driveway.

"Thank you again for the night," Alex said. "I appreciate you getting my staples out. I have already racked up quite the medical bill. I'm not sure how I could repay you."

"You're welcome," Harper said. "I'm sorry my sister got weird near the end."

"No, I understand. Not many people have met a real life criminal before. I know she was uncomfortable."

"Well, I guess with me being an emergency room nurse I see all types." Harper grinned. "I have more compassion than a middle school teacher."

"That explains it." Alex laughed. "Well, thanks again."

Harper leaned across the seat and hugged him, her soft hair brushing against his cheek.

"We need to do it again." She smiled.

Alex sat too stunned to speak, his heart pounding in his chest.

"You're welcome....I mean...." he fumbled for the door handle.

Harper grinned.

He stepped out into the cold night air but didn't feel anything. Harper backed out of his driveway and headed down the street with a quick honk as she departed. Grinning, he opened the wooden front door and stepped inside.

43

The ring of his desk phone brought Silas out of the YouTube rabbit hole he had descended into around smoking brisket. He picked up the black plastic receiver.

"Hello."

"Pastor Weston, Mr. Blackwood and his guest are here to see you," his assistant's timid voice said.

"Thank you, Anna. You can send them back."

A few seconds later, there was a knock at his office door.

"Come in."

The door opened and the familiar figure of Dalton Blackwood came in wearing a tan sheriff department uniform. A lanky kid who didn't look any older than twenty followed him in. The kid also wore a similar uniform that looked about two sizes too large for his slender frame, barely clinging to his body. He had a pale complexion with fire red hair and a meager attempt at a mustache decorated his lip.

"Dalton, great to see you," Silas said, gesturing for them to sit in the two large leather chairs that faced his desk.

"Likewise, Silas," Dalton said as he and the kid settled into the leather chairs.

"Who do we have here?" Silas looked over at the kid.

"This is one of my new officers, Trevor Adams," Dalton said.

The kid attempted a smile. "Nice to meet you, sir."

"You don't look old enough to be driving," Silas joked.

Trevor's cheeks turned a bright red, competing with his hair.

"Of course, I am an old man, so everyone looks young to me nowadays." Silas laughed.

"I can vouch that he is legal!" Dalton grinned, "Anyway, he is the resource I put on tailing Mr. Hollins."

"Oh, I see." Silas grew interested. "I assume there have been some developments. That would explain why you are both here."

"Very perceptive." Dalton said, "Yes, Trevor here has discovered some information we believe will be helpful to your cause."

"Excellent!" Silas clasped his hands together, "Well, don't keep me in suspense, what has our little convict been up to?"

Dalton looked at Trevor.

"Well...I...I...set up...surveillance...outside...the...the...residence..." the kid stammered through his attempt to form a sentence.

Silas grew impatient. "Good Lord kid, spit it out!"

Dalton chimed in. "I'm sorry, he is nervous. I'll cut to the chase."

Trevor lowered his head.

"Trevor identified a couple of patterns regarding Mr. Hollins' activities," Dalton said. "He does not appear to be able to drive and spends most of his time in his mother's house. When he does leave the residence, he relies on someone to drive him. This typically has been a late model white Oldsmobile. We identified the owner as Emory Wright."

"Makes sense, he was with him at city hall," Silas said, "That was also the same car."

"Yep, that's him," Dalton continued. "It appears he either takes Alex to see his mother at the hospital or runs him on errands around town."

"How old is Emory now?" Silas asked.

"I would guess in his late sixties or early seventies."

"Well, he would make an easy target to intimidate."

"True. However, at the end of the week there was an interesting development," Dalton said. "On Saturday evening a different car arrived and appeared to have a female driver. Trevor followed them to a home in Ridgeview."

Silas looked surprised.

"Yes, it appears our man went on his first date," Dalton said.

"Wow, love is in the air in Pinehurst" Silas laughed "Any idea who she is?"

"The owner of the house is Vanessa Layne," Trevor spoke up.

Dalton looked surprised at this sudden interjection from Trevor.

"That's right," Dalton said. "She is a teacher at Pinehurst Middle."

"So, do we have some ways to make her life miserable?"

Dalton grinned and Trevor looked increasingly uncomfortable.

Silas listened as Dalton and Trevor relayed the findings of the stakeout. Silas grinned as he grew confident, he had a way to keep Alex Hollins out of Pinehurst forever.

"Dalton, get the Boone brothers down here. We have some work to do."

44

Zeke sat disgusted on the driver's side of his Ford truck. His brother sat next to him snoring loudly, strung out on something. Probably oxy, that was his drug of choice and easy to come by in Pinehurst.

He had always despised his little brother. Zeke always had dreams of bigger things. He wasn't great in school but knew the woods of Bucks County like the back of his hand and was a skilled hunter. Growing up his family never had to purchase meat unless they wanted to. He usually bagged his limit within the first week of hunting season. Not that he let that stop him. He had always wanted to start a hunt club and be a guide.

But nope, his little brother's drug problem drove his mother to an early grave, and he had been stuck taking care of him since she died about ten years ago. She left them the trailer and property, but it was mainly their jobs for Silas that helped provide any semblance of regular income for them.

Lately, Silas had been obsessed with the Hollins kid. Zeke had no idea what he had done to Silas, but he had managed to piss him off right good. You did not want to end up on Silas Weston's bad side, that was for sure.

Now he had instructed them to "warn" the old man who had been helping him out to stay away. Zeke didn't have much of a conscience, but he did get a twinge of guilt roughing up a seventy-year-old man.

Soon the old model cream-colored Oldsmobile pulled into the driveway. An older man stepped out and made his way slowly to the trunk, opened it, and pulled out some grocery bags.

"Wake up, he's here." Zeke elbowed his brother in the ribs, resulting in a large gasp and a snort as his brother jumped up.

"What...Who..." Eddie looked confused.

"That Emory fella, he just pulled in." Zeke opened the door. "Let's go!"

Eddie still dazed followed suit.

They approached the man as he was struggling with his keys and the groceries, trying to get into the side door.

"You need a hand mister?" Zeke yelled from the driveway.

Emory looked up confused, "No, I got it. Appreciate the offer though."

"Well, I'm already here now, might as well help." Zeke continued toward Emory.

A concerned look grew on Emory's face as he struggled with the key in the door. He finally got it and the doorknob turned, letting him into the house. Zeke stepped right up behind him, grabbed the bags off the porch, and pushed him inside.

"See, just took a little elbow grease." Zeke laughed and Eddie stepped in behind him pushing the wooden door shut.

Emory had backed up into the kitchen. "Who are you? Get out of my house or I'm calling the cops!"

He went for the pale yellow phone hanging on the wood paneling by the cabinets. Eddie stepped toward it and knocked the phone off the cradle, the dial tone fading away as the receiver hit the floor.

"Look, I don't have much but take whatever you want." Emory's hands shook as he reached for his wallet.

"Oh, we don't want your money, old man." Zeke laughed. "We need you to stop."

Emory looked confused. "Stop...stop what? I don't even know who you are!"

"You don't need to know. We need you to stop hanging around Alex Hollins," Zeke said, taking a step toward him.

"Alex? Why Alex? He is harmless…he doesn't know anyone here," Emory stammered.

"He is a murderer. He is a convict, and we need you to stop helping him. Trust me, it will be in your best interest," Zeke said, now an inch away from Emory, stale coffee breath blew in his face.

Emory cried, "Please, don't hurt me! I'll stay away; you won't see me near his house again."

"Sounds like a great idea," Zeke said, stepping back. "But remember, if we do hear of you hanging around him again, you won't get off quite so easy."

Emory clutched his chest, leaning back against the kitchen counter.

"You don't look so good, old man!" Eddie laughed.

"Now, if you'll excuse us, we will be leaving," Zeke said. "We can show ourselves out."

Emory had slid onto the kitchen floor, his face sweaty and pale.

Zeke and Eddie stepped out of the side door onto the carport.

"Poor old man." Zeke grinned.

"Surprised he didn't piss his pants!" Eddie laughed.

"He probably had diapers on," Zeke said.

They both laughed and made their way back to the truck. As they walked past the Oldsmobile, Eddie pulled a pocketknife out of his pocket, knelt, and jabbed it into the rear passenger tire. A slight hiss sounded as the air rushed out.

"Now that was just plain mean," Zeke said.

"I know, I couldn't resist."

In the distance, the sounds of sirens filled the air.

"Uh oh, we better scoot!" Zeke said hopping into the driver's seat. "They might be looking for us!"

Eddie laughed. "Not that it matters!"

45

The shrill tone of his cell phone woke him from a deep sleep. His mouth was still locked in a grin from the events of last night. He fumbled on the nightstand trying to find the phone.

"Hello?"

"Is this Alex Hollins?" a concerned female voice said.

"Yes."

"My name is Lauren and I'm the nurse taking care of your mom."

A surge of adrenaline quickly washed away the euphoria from last.

"Unfortunately, she has taken a turn for the worse and we are going to have to move her back to the ICU."

"What happened?" Alex said in shock. "She was doing fine when I checked in on her yesterday."

"It's her breathing. It got worse overnight," Lauren said. "I would recommend you get over here if possible. Dr. Carter is taking care of her and he can update you."

"Sure...I'll be over shortly..." the world turned surreal. "Lauren..."

"Yes?"

"Tell her I am on my way and I love her."

"I'll do that," Lauren said.

Alex disconnected the call. His mind was spinning. She had been doing so well. They were talking about getting her to a rehab facility this week, to get her strong enough to return home. The possibility of losing his mom descended on Alex smothering him, he sobbed.

He needed to call Emory.

Alex had learned how to program his favorites on the phone and hit Emory. The phone rang several times and went straight to voicemail.

"You've reached Emory. You know what to do and I'll get back to ya!"

Not having a car had largely been a nuisance, however in a situation like this, it was a big handicap.

Harper.

He could give her a call.

At this point, he only had two favorites saved on his phone so it made finding her easy.

He held the phone to his ear as it dialed her number.

After a few rings a tired voice answered, "Good Morning! To what do I owe the pleasure of this early morning wake-up call?"

Alex tried to speak but his voice hung in his throat.

"Alex?" Harper sounded concerned.

"It's mom...."

"Oh no. What happened?"

"The nurse called....she has gotten worse...they are moving her to the ICU."

"Oh, Alex. I am sorry," Harper said. "Do you need me to drive you to the hospital?"

"Please, I've tried Emory but got his voicemail."

"No problem. Give me about thirty minutes to get ready and I'll be right over."

"Thanks, this means so much."

"I don't mind one bit. See you soon."

46

Harper pulled up to Alex's home and gave the horn a quick beep. He had sounded upset when she spoke with him. She knew his mother's health was fragile. She had advanced COPD and any infection in her lungs, like pneumonia, could be big trouble for her. Harper was worried that if she went on a ventilator that would be the end.

The front door opened and Alex stepped out wearing the same outfit he had worn when he came to Vanessa's house. He opened the passenger door and slid in.

A pleasant smell of cologne filled the car.

"Hey there," she said. "I'm sorry about your mom."

She leaned over and hugged him.

"I'm scared," he said, his voice cracking. "Without her, I don't have anyone."

"Don't talk like that," Harper said, patting him on the leg and backing out of the driveway, "You got me and Lando now."

They drove most of the trip in silence, the dreary winter landscape of Pinehurst passing by. Pinehurst had long past its glory days. She worried about raising Lando here. She needed time to get back on her feet, then they could move on.

She did have a tug of attraction towards Alex. It had been at least a year since her divorce and she had not been in a serious relationship since. Alex was a nice, good-looking guy. He got along well with Landon. She was concerned about his past and how this impacted his chance for the future.

She had just gotten out of one relationship where she was the primary breadwinner. She guessed she could do anything for love, but she did have visions of being a stay-at-home mom with a 4-Runner, taking Landon back and forth to soccer practice while drinking her Starbucks.

"Look at the sunrise," she said, trying to break her cycle of self-pity.

The bright yellow sun crested over Bent Mountain, breaking through the clouds and sending prisms of color across the trees.

"It's beautiful," Alex said. "That is one thing I didn't see much of in prison. Not many opportunities to see the sunrise unless we were on work detail."

Harper grinned watching Alex drink in the sunrise like he was seeing it for the first time, it was a good distraction for what lay ahead.

• • •

They parked outside of Pinehurst Memorial.

"Do you want me to go in with you?" Harper asked.

"Sure." Alex didn't hesitate. "You're the nurse. You can help interpret whatever medical stuff they are trying to tell me."

Harper grinned. "Ok, let's go."

They made their way quickly across the parking lot. Despite the beautiful morning, a winter chill still hung in the air.

The automatic door hissed open and Harper led Alex across the lobby to the volunteer station. An elderly woman with frosty gray hair and horn-rimmed glasses wearing a pink vest with the word volunteer emblazoned boldly across her right breast pocket looked up at them.

"Good morning. How may I help you?" she asked.

"We are looking for Nancy Hollins," Harper said.

The volunteer hit some keys on the computer and raised her head. "She is in the Medical Intensive Care Unit bed number seven."

Alex looked concerned and Harper placed her hand on his shoulder. The volunteer hit another key and a thermal label printer hummed and produced two visitor stickers.

"Here you go." She handed the stickers to them. "Just put them on your shirts and you all are good to go. Take the elevator to the second floor, hang a left, and follow the signs."

"Thank you," Harper said.

Alex looked shocked as they made their way to the elevators. She could not imagine how he felt. Being away from your mother for twenty-five years and finally getting a chance at normal life only to have this happen.

She pressed the up button on the elevator and a few seconds later a soft ding announced the arrival of the elevator. The doors opened to an empty elevator and they both stepped inside.

Harper press the button for the second floor.

"You ok?" Harper asked, knowing the answer.

"Not really. I'm scared."

"I know," Harper said.

They remained silent for the brief trip to the second floor. The elevator chimed again as the doors opened to the second floor. A sign hung on the opposite wall with various hospital units listed. Harper had transferred enough patients to the Medical ICU from the ER she didn't need the signs. Leading Alex through the maze of hallways they soon were at the entrance of the medical ICU. They walked in and Tim Jenkins, one of her fellow nurse colleagues, started walking towards them.

"Harper! What are you doing here?" he said. "I'm not used to seeing you in normal clothes."

"I'm here with my friend, Alex. His mom just got transferred down here from the floor."

"Mrs. Hollins?" Tim said, sounding concerned.

"Yes, that's her," Alex blurted. "How is she?"

"She got up here about twenty minutes ago, I believe they are still working with her."

Harper could tell by Tim's demeanor that things were not going well.

"Why don't I walk you all around the corner to the family waiting room," Tim said. "Dr. Parker will be out to talk with you when we have her all tucked in."

"Is she ok?" Alex asked, his voice tense.

"Your mom is a sick lady right now, but Dr. Parker is one of our best," Tim said. "I'm not the nurse caring for your mom right now, so I don't know specifics, but I promise I will have Dr. Parker come out as soon as he is finished."

"Thank you, Tim," Harper said. "I know where the waiting room is, we will go over there and wait. I know you all are busy."

"It's been a day, Harper, you know how it goes. Hopefully, Dr. Parker won't be too much longer and can give you all an update."

• • •

Harper and Alex sat in the family waiting room. The hospital grade furniture was upholstered with a geometric pastel material made from plastic. It was like a gaudy slipcover. It was easy to clean and probably had to be approved by an agency with a lot of initials to be in the hospital. However, it was more comfortable than what they had in the ED waiting room.

An infomercial for a miraculous cream that made your wrinkles disappear played on the large flatscreen TV encased in a plexiglass block with a lock, hung in the corner of the room. Harper assumed there was probably a story behind that.

Sitting in silence, she had the urge to put her arm around Alex but wasn't necessarily feeling quite that bold. Soon, Dr. Parker came down the hallway. The tail of his white lab jacket floated behind him like a makeshift cape. His lime green hospital issued scrubs were wrinkled. He was one of the more seasoned intensivists in the hospital. The one everyone wanted working on them if they ever needed a critical care doctor, which was hopefully never.

He was probably in his mid-forties, with salt and pepper hair, with the perpetually tired face of someone who spanned the gap between life and death daily.

A quizzical look spread across his face, "You look familiar."

"I'm a nurse in the ED. We've done our fair share of codes together," she said.

"That's it. The jeans and t-shirt threw me." He grinned.

"This is Alex, Mrs. Hollins's son." Harper pointed toward Alex.

Dr. Parker extended his hand to Alex, "Nice to meet you, and sorry it is under these circumstances."

Dr. Parker grabbed a chair and slid it in front of Alex and Harper. He leaned forward with his elbows on his knees. "Listen, in my years of practice I've learned it is never wise to sugarcoat anything, so I am going to be honest with you. Your mother is a very sick lady."

Dr. Parker paused to allow a moment for that comment to land. Moisture formed in Alex's eyes; Harper instinctively grabbed his arm and pulled closer to him.

"Her lungs were in bad shape to begin with and this pneumonia has pushed them over the edge. We had to place a breathing tube to help her breathe. This will help her rest and not have to work so hard."

Alex sobbed, "Will she make it?"

"Alex, I'm not sure. The next twenty-four to forty-eight hours will be crucial. Your mom was not in the best health to start; this is going to be a big setback for her to recover from."

Alex stared at the floor, tears streaming down his face. Dr. Parker stood up and grabbed a tattered box of tissues from a nearby end table. Harper clutched his arm against her.

"Alex, unfortunately, your mother did not have a living will or document of the sort to help direct her care in a situation like this. We are committed to providing her the highest level of care, but with her age and frailty, I would estimate her chances of coming off the ventilator are very low."

"What does that mean?" Alex said.

"It means we may need to have a tough conversation when the time comes," he said. "I'm willing to give her forty-eight hours, but if there is no significant improvement, then we have some weighty decisions to make."

"She can't live on the breathing tube?" Alex asked.

"No, that is not an option," Dr. Parker said. "If that were the case, we would need to discuss a tracheostomy, feeding tubes, and long-term placement."

Alex looked confused.

"A nursing home," Harper clarified. "Alex, do you think that is what your mom would want?"

"No, Mom always told me she didn't want to be stuck on any machines. I guess this is what she meant." Alex stared at the floor.

"She is critical but stable right now." Dr. Parker tapped Alex on the knee. "Like I said, let's see how she does over the next couple of days. In the meantime, be getting your thoughts together about how to proceed if it looks like she is not making progress."

"Thanks, Dr. Parker," Harper said.

"You're very welcome. I am sorry about your mother Alex. I can assure you, though, she is much more comfortable now."

"Thanks, Doctor," Alex said. "I appreciate what you have done."

"That's what I'm here for." Dr. Parker stood. "Any questions?"

Alex paused and shook his head.

"I'll go back to the unit, if they have her tucked in, I'll have the unit clerk come take you to her room."

"Thanks," Harper said.

47

"Alex, dinner is ready!"

Alex's ears perked at the sound of his mom's voice carrying across the neighborhood. He was down the street on his bike, off on some imaginary adventure, but that voice brought him quickly back to reality.

Turning the handlebars, he pedaled in the direction of his home. "Coming!" he yelled.

He must have lost track of time. In the subdivision of Wildwood, he was the only kid his age, so he relied on his imagination to help pass the long summer days. His mom had to pick up two jobs to keep a roof over their head and food on the table because she was too proud to apply for food stamps or any other assistance. He'd had to grow up faster than most ten-year-old's.

The bike chain rattled as he turned into his driveway early, going over a curb. He hopped off, letting the bike fall to the ground with a clatter.

Running up the side steps, he charged into the house, "I'm home!"

"Well, go wash your hands." His mom had her back to him as she stood at the sink.

He went down the hallway to the bathroom. Grabbing the yellow bar of Dial soap, he scrubbed his hands and went back to the kitchen/dining room.

"Smells good!"

"Thanks, sweetie!" his mom said. "It's your favorite, Hamburger Helper."

His heart dropped a little, it wasn't his favorite, but it was cheap and easy for his mom to fix.

"Mmmmm…." he rubbed his belly and his mother's face light up.

She sat a casserole dish at the center of the table on an old dish towel.

"Do you want to pray?" she asked him.

"Sure!" he said, reaching across the table and grabbing his mom's hand, dry and cracked from her work as a nurse.

He closed his eyes, "Good food, good meat, good Lord let's eat."

Both he and his mom erupted in laughter.

"Alex!" She tried to sound mad. "Serious!"

"Yes, Ma'am," he said, closing his eyes. "Dear Heavenly Father, thank you for this food we are about to eat. Thank you for providing it. Thank you for my awesome mom who took the time to prepare it. I know she works really hard and is very tired. Amen!"

"Thank you dear," his mom said a tear ran down her cheek.

"What's wrong, Mom?"

"Nothing. It was just a special prayer," she said, reaching toward the casserole dish and scooping a steaming portion of the meat and noodle concoction onto his plate.

• • •

A familiar sense of dread returned as the nurse led Harper and him through the ICU to his mother's room.

They stopped outside the large glass door with a plastic number seven.

"I will warn you now she looks a lot different than when you saw her last," the nurse said.

Harper placed her hand on his back.

"She has a breathing tube in and we had to give her a lot of fluid, so she is swollen."

Tears moistened his eyes, "I can't....I can't do this."

Harper moved her hand around his waist and pulled him close. "Yes, you can, we are going to do it together."

The nurse had a solemn yet compassionate look on her face. "You ready?"

Alex nodded.

She slid the door open and the three of them walked into the room. They were met by a cluster of sounds from the quiet hiss of the ventilator to the occasional alarm on the vital signs monitor, to the whirr of the IV pumps. Alex looked at his mother in the bed and could not believe it. Her body shrouded in tubes, lines, and tape. A collection of bags hung on poles around the head of the bead. A bag collecting urine hung at the foot of the bed.

Harper nudged him closer to the bed.

"Hold her hand, let her know you're here," she said.

He could barely see anything his eyes were blurred with tears.

"Mom...."

He and Harper took a few steps to the side of the bed. Harper lifted the warming blanket to reveal a swollen, bruised hand. She took Alex's hand and placed it on his mom's.

"Mom...." Alex said as he squeezed the swollen hand. The hard calluses still present, "I love you..."

Harper placed her arm around him squeezing him tight.

"I'm sorry..." Alex said between tears. "This is all my fault..."

"No, no it's not" Harper whispered. "Your mom was a sick lady and I think she covered it well."

"If I had not been absent twenty-five years of her life, maybe she would not have been so sick..."

"Alex, you don't know that..."

Alex went to one knee and pulled his mom's swollen hand to his face. These were the same hands that bandaged his scraped knees, worked twelve hours in the hospital, made his Hamburger

Helper, and faithfully dialed the Rockingham Correctional Center every day without fail.

Alex knelt in silence, stroking his mother's hand.

A short time later the nurse came back in. "It is almost time for shift change; I will need you two to step out. You are more than welcome to go back to the waiting room."

"Thank you," Harper said.

Alex slowly stood, letting go of his mother's hand.

"Thank you for being so kind," he said to the nurse.

"I am sorry about what you are going through," the nurse said.

"I can get us back to the waiting room," Harper said, taking Alex's hand and leading him out of the unit.

His muscles were heavy as they walked back to the waiting room.

"I know this is hard," Harper said.

"This is harder than twenty-five years in prison," Alex said, his voice cracking.

"You know what, Alex," Harper said. "Let's get you back home so you can shower, get a good night's rest and come back tomorrow."

"What about Mom?" Alex said. "I don't want to leave her."

"Your mom is in great hands, particularly in the unit," Harper said. "She has one nurse assigned to her. They will call if anything changes."

"I feel bad."

"I know, but you can't let yourself go down or you won't be any good to anybody."

Alex remained silent.

"I'm working a twelve-hour shift tomorrow." Harper said, "I could pick you up on my way in and then we could leave together."

Alex's eyes brightened a bit, "That sounds like a good idea."

Harper smiled.

"My bed is way more comfortable than any of the chairs in the waiting room," he said.

"Sounds like a plan," Harper said, squeezing his side.

48

Emory had finally stopped shaking from his experience this morning, living in Pinehurst all seventy years of his life he had never encountered anything like this. Pinehurst had largely been a safe town. The worst crime he could remember was when some bored teenagers went on a vandalism spree.

His heart had finally stopped pounding out of his chest. It took two nitroglycerin pills under his tongue to finally get the chest pressure to ease off. He managed to get himself to his recliner, but his t-shirt was still damp with sweat.

Alex was heavy on his mind. He could not stay away from him; he had an obligation to Nancy Hollins to watch after her son. He needed to warn Alex.

His cell phone sat on the end table beside the recliner. He picked it up. There was missed a call from Alex. He pressed the icon and dialed the number. After a few rings, a familiar voice answered.

"Hello?"

"Alex, it's Emory. I saw I missed a call. Everything ok?"

"No, they had to move Mom back to the ICU and things aren't looking too good."

Emory's chest tightened, "Oh Alex, I am sorry."

"I just got back from the hospital."

"What's the update?"

Emory listened with a sense of sadness settling into his soul as Alex relayed the recent events with his mother.

"Alex, I am so sorry to hear that." Emory sighed. "Anything I can do for you now?"

"No, I am exhausted so I will probably be going to bed soon," Alex said.

"Alex there is something I need to tell you," Emory said. "I understand this is not the best time for you, but I feel like you need to know."

The line was silent and Emory continued.

"I had two unexpected visitors in my house this morning." Emory paused. "Probably the same two that paid you a visit."

"Emory, are you ok?" Alex's speech was pressured. "Did they hurt you?"

"I'm fine, but they scared me right good. They threatened me and said if I was seen around you again, there would be trouble."

Alex remained quiet.

"Did you recognize them?" Alex finally asked.

"Yes, they were the Boone brothers, resident redneck criminals of Pinehurst," Emory said.

"Did you call the cops?"

"Nope. Wouldn't do any good anyhow," Emory laughed, "The Boone crew is on the payroll for Silas, he would make sure the charges didn't stick. If I reported it, things may have gotten worse for both of us."

"Emory, I don't know what to say." Alex sounded defeated. "I know you were being kind and didn't have to help me. You were doing it for Mom and I appreciate that, but listen, I don't want you to risk your life helping me out. I am an adult. I can fend for myself."

"I know," Emory said, "I lived long enough that a couple of burnt-out rednecks don't scare me."

"If something happened to you, I could never forgive myself."

"Alright." Emory paused. "Alex, be careful though, these guys mean business."

49

Silas stepped to the pulpit. The floor creaked under his weight. Despite it being the middle of winter, moisture glistened across his forehead.

"Thank you, choir." He nodded to the rows of seats behind him as the members slowly filed out and found seats in the main sanctuary.

"Ain't it good to be in God's house!" he yelled, slapping an open hand on the wooden podium.

A series of amens and hallelujahs went up across the congregation.

"I tell you what our little town needs us right now." Silas' mood became subdued. "The forces of evil are gathering. There is a darkness forming. There is an oppression coming."

He let the words hang in the air, the congregation sat enraptured by his words. Silas was in his zone. He loved the power he could wield from behind the wooden podium.

"We need to put feet to our prayers!" He slapped the podium with each word. "God has called us to be agents of his deliverance and we need to act!"

"The wiles of the world have infiltrated our town slowly. First, it was stores staying open on Sunday, then it was women wearing pants, then we started playing the lottery, then alcohol, then pornography…"

The congregation was getting vocal, members were on their feet, shouting amens, waving handkerchiefs.

"We've become sheep, wearing masks, taking vaccines all over some fake pandemic," he thundered. "Look at me! I never wore a mask, never got vaccinated, and I am still standing! I ain't going to let some sinful government control my body!"

More screams and a few members of the congregation were now running laps around the sanctuary.

"And then...a cold-blooded drunkard who killed an innocent girl was let go by our defective criminal system!!" Silas smacked a fist into his open palm, "Then...then...he has the audacity to bring his repugnant, sinful soul back to Pinehurst!" Silas yelled, the veins in his neck bulging out. "Our town has turned to Sodom and God's judgment will be on all of us!"

Shouts went out across the congregation. An older lady had fallen back, convulsing on the floor with a crowd of people surrounding her, shouting.

"God destroyed Sodom with fire and brimstone. Do we want that to be the fate of our humble town?"

Tears and wails went up. Shouts of anger. Most of the congregation was on their feet at this point.

Silas had them where he needed them, where he wanted them.

"We need to take our town back!" Silas yelled. "We need to run Alex Hollins away before he destroys our town. Or worse yet, kills again!"

The congregation was in a frenzy.

Silas had been successful; his plan was in motion. Soon he would not have to worry about Alex Hollins, ever again.

50

Alex looked at the digital clock on the nightstand. Five a.m.

Between the weight of his mother's illness and what Emory had told him, sleep had been replaced with a mix of anxiety, self-pity, and anger. So far, life outside prison had been far worse than he had anticipated. He had paid his debt to society but was now reaping the cosmic reckoning for what he had done.

Since coming home, nothing has gone his way. His mom is in the hospital, not likely to survive, he has been assaulted in his own home, and one of his few friends had been harassed. Harper was the only thing that had gone right for him, but he could screw that up as well.

He worried about Emory and that he had placed him in danger. The fact they would harass a seventy-year-old demonstrated a level of hate Alex didn't know could exist.

It was clear that sleep had escaped him. He rolled out of bed, made his way to the kitchen, and put on a pot of coffee. He wasn't sure there was enough coffee in the world to help him make it through today. His next stop was the shower. The warm water was refreshing and he lingered for a while, trying to wash away the stress of the past 24 hours. Turning off the hot water, he let the cold water rain down on him for as long as he could stand. This did about as good a job as a cup of coffee in waking him up.

Stepping across the hallway into his room he checked his phone, there was a voicemail from Harper. He opened it up and hit the play symbol.

"Hey Alex, it's me. Just checking to see if you were up. I'm going to hop in the shower and will be there to get you around six-thirty. Text me when you get this. If I don't hear from you, I will assume you are still sleeping and will pound on your door until you wake up. Bye."

He grinned. The highlight of his release was Harper, and he was lucky. He wasn't sure what she saw in him, but he did not want to question it. He shot her a quick text.

Out of bed, but not fully awake. See you soon.

He grabbed a pair of jeans and threw on an old gray crew neck sweater. He made his way to the kitchen and poured himself a cup of coffee. He had learned to like his coffee black in prison, although he was never able to make it quite as strong as they did there. Must be some secret state blend or something.

The clock on the oven said 6:15. He took his cup of coffee and went into the living room, sitting in the recliner that faced out the large window on the front of the house. It was still dark outside except for the sterile halogen light coming from the streetlamp.

He sipped his coffee in silence, waiting for that magic elixir to do its thing. Looking out of the living room window the sun had started to peek over Bent Mountain, casting burnt orange rays into the sky.

This living room was full of nostalgia for Alex. He had spent plenty of Halloweens helping his mom hand out candy to the steady march of ghouls and goblins. This was the same living room where he had opened many Christmas gifts and always was so excited, despite his internal disappointment, knowing his mom could not afford much for him. Often, she went without any gifts for Christmas. Now she was spending the last days of her life in a hospital plugged up to every machine imaginable. Life wasn't fair.

Soon a wash of yellow filled the living room as a car pulled into the driveway. Taking a deep breath in, trying to psych himself up for today, it was not going to be a fun one.

51

The side door to the house opened and Alex stepped out. Harper desperately hoping the car would warm up soon. These single digit winter mornings in Pinehurst were brutal. Alex made his way to the car not wearing a jacket and his hair was still wet.

"He is going to get pneumonia," she whispered, then laughed because she sounded like her mother.

Alex opened the door and hopped in.

"Hello," he said.

"Where is your jacket, young man?" Harper asked in mock motherly tone. "And why is your hair soaking wet? You'll catch your death in this weather!"

Alex at first looked a little caught off guard like he wasn't sure if she was joking. Then Harper broke down laughing and he grinned.

"Seriously though, where is your jacket?" Harper asked, "It's cold out here!"

"I didn't even think about it, I left it inside," Alex said, "Hold on."

He ran back up the sidewalk, disappearing back into the house and returned wearing a brown leather jacket.

He made it back to the car and slid into the passenger seat, "You happy now!"

Harper grinned, "Much better!"

They both laughed as she backed out of the driveway. Soon Harper was heading down the narrow roads of the Wildwood subdivision.

"Hear anything about your mom last night?" Harper asked.

"Nope. I assume this is one situation where no news is good news."

"That's probably true."

"Oh, I brought you a sausage biscuit and a cup of coffee." She pointed to a travel mug in the cup holder and a sandwich wrapped in a paper towel. "It's from Harper's kitchen, so no comments on the quality of the food or drink."

"Thank you so much!" Alex said looking delighted. "I didn't even think about grabbing breakfast, and I'll never turn down coffee."

"Well, be careful. The coffee is black, I wasn't sure how you wanted it."

"Black is perfect," Alex said, lifting the mug as some steam rose from the top.

"Vanessa says I like my coffee like I like my men," Harper said a sly grin on her face.

"How is that?" Alex asked.

"Pale and weak," Harper started laughing.

"Easy!" Alex said, grabbing his chest, "I resemble that!"

They both laughed.

They rode in silence as Alex ate his sausage biscuit and Harper focused on the road. The early morning inertia had overcome their initial banter.

"Are you nervous about today?" Harper asked.

"Yes, I can't say I am looking forward to it," Alex said. "Dr. Parker painted a pretty bleak picture; I may have a hard decision to make."

"Well, text me if you need me," Harper said. "I'm two floors down. If I am not busy, I can have someone watch my patients for me while I slip upstairs."

"Thanks," he said. "That means a lot."

Soon they were pulling into the brightly lit employee parking lot of Pinehurst Memorial Hospital. A lone security officer made rounds in his car. Harper found a spot close to the main campus, which was a plus. She parked the car and grabbed her backpack that carried all her essentials for the day.

They walked towards the hospital. She usually would hang a left at the radiology entrance and go to the employee entrance, but she escorted Alex in today to help him find the unit. An older gentleman stood at a computer station in the lobby. Alex told him who he was here to see and soon he sported a visitor sticker.

"Just go to those elevators down there." Harper pointed down the corridor. "Go to the second floor and take a left. The unit will be right there. If you hang a right and follow the hallway, you will end up at the waiting room."

"Thanks, Harper. I appreciate you being so kind. The biscuit from Harper's kitchen was great and the coffee is excellent."

"That is great to hear. I will tell the chef and the barista!"

"Have a good shift," Alex said. "I guess I'll see you…"

"Probably around 7:30 if all goes well. If the shift goes down the drain, I'll text you."

"Gotcha."

"Let me know if you need me sooner."

"Will do."

Alex leaned in, wrapping arms around her and giving her a gentle embrace. The clean smell of shampoo still clung to his hair. His powerful arms around her gave her a sense of comfort and strength that she had not experienced, ever.

He turned and made his way to the elevators. She had a sadness in the pit of her stomach that she could not identify. Maybe it was the sense of impending loss facing Alex; however, she would make sure he didn't face it alone.

52

Alex spent most of the day in the waiting room. Initially, the furniture was comfortable, but after the fourth hour, it was like he was sitting on a cement slab. Dr. Parker didn't have much in the way of updates on his mom. His words were "critical but stable" whatever that meant.

Alex had been back a couple of times to see her. She remained sedated and still connected to more machines than Alex imagined was humanly possible. The nurses gave him knowing glances of pity whenever he walked back.

Sally was the volunteer manning the visitor's desk in the waiting room. She was pleasant and had kept him supplied with a steady stream of coffee until he had to cry mercy because his stomach was starting to digest itself.

She did entrust him with the remote, which helped some, but after the local news, the only thing on all the channels were cheesy soap operas. He had enough drama in his life already. After a while, he landed on an infomercial for some miracle weight loss drug but instead of watching, he sat staring at his phone. For the most part, he had the waiting room to himself.

"You need any more coffee?" Sally asked, breaking him from mind-numbing scrolling through his phone.

"No, I'm good, thanks for asking."

"It's hard," she said.

Alex was a little confused and his face must have betrayed him.

"When someone you love is sick," she said.

"The hardest thing I've been through, and I've been through a lot," he said.

"My James went through it," she said, stepping out from behind the desk and walking towards Alex. "Went in for a routine back surgery and came out much sicker than he went in."

Alex caught a pleasant floral scent as she sat down beside him.

"I'm sorry to hear that," Alex said. "It's worse when you don't expect it."

"Oh, it is. I watched him struggle for weeks and I soon learned there are things much worse than death."

This was a realization Alex had been acutely made aware of recently.

"I am seeing that," he said. "How long had you all been married?"

"Forty-five years," she said, her eyes glistening. "We were high school sweethearts."

"Life does not seem fair," Alex said.

"You know, I used to think the same thing, but then I realized that life doesn't owe it to us to be fair. I thought we were all part of some cosmic puppet show driving toward a happy ending," she paused, "I now believe that life is just a random chain of events, good things happen to bad people, and bad things happen to good people. No rhyme or reason I can make of it."

"I don't know whether that is encouraging or depressing."

"Didn't mean to depress you dear." She tapped him on the leg. "Just some perspective so you don't think the universe is picking on you."

"What happened to your husband?"

"Unfortunately, he passed away about three months after surgery," she said. "I had to make a hard decision, but in the end, it was the right decision. He passed much more peacefully than he was living."

"I'm sorry."

"No need to be. We had a good life, two children, six beautiful grandchildren. My life is good now."

"I'm glad to hear that."

She glanced at her watch. "Well, it is almost time for my shift to be over so I need to go do a few things. It was nice chatting with you. I won't be back until next week, maybe I'll see you then."

"I appreciate your kindness."

She grinned, patted his shoulder, and stood.

Glancing at his watch, Alex saw that it was almost four o'clock. He had about three more hours until Harper's shift was over. His stomach reminded him he hadn't eaten much today.

"Sally," he called out.

She looked up from some papers on the desk, "Yes dear?"

"Which way to the cafeteria?"

"Oh sure, take the elevator to the first floor, hang a left and follow the signs. The grill is open 24 hours."

"Thanks," he said.

• • •

He made his way to the first floor and the cafeteria was surprisingly easy to find. The familiar aroma of institutional food hit his nose and brought back some memories of prison. He hoped the food here was better.

A college aged kid in an ill-fitting chef's hat and apron stood behind a large flat grill. Alex reviewed the menu knowing how much money was in his wallet.

"I'll take a grilled cheese and an order of fries."

The kid acknowledged him with a grunt, turned his back, and began getting the bread ready.

Alex grabbed a beige plastic tray and got some napkins, ketchup, and a cup of water. He went back to the grill, retrieved his order, and made his way to the cash register to pay. Finding a seat was not a problem.

Famished, he began devouring the sandwich. The gooey cheese stuck to the roof of his mouth, but he didn't mind washing it down with some water.

He had inhaled the meal. Leaning back in his chair he had just closed his eyes when a firm grip on his shoulder startled him.

"Well, if it isn't Pinehurst's prodigal son, Alex Hollins."

Alex looked at the pudgy fingers on his shoulder. There was a gold ring on each digit. His heart sank as he raised his head the familiar rotund figure of Silas Weston looming over him.

His stomach tightened as, his meal wanted to make a second appearance.

53

Silas had gotten word from one of his parishioners that Alex Hollins had been hanging around the hospital all day. Silas understood his mother was not doing well but couldn't say it was unexpected after all Alex put her through.

He got dressed and made his way over to the hospital. He arrived at the critical care waiting room to find it vacant, with no sign of Alex. With his clergy badge on he made his way back to the unit under the guise of Nancy Hollins pastor. He asked if any of the nurses had seen her son.

"Not recently," a pretty blonde in scrubs said. "He has been in and out all day. I don't think he has gone home yet. Maybe check the cafeteria?"

Silas thanked her and made his way back to the elevator. The doors opened and he was met with the smell of the hospital cafeteria. He walked down the long corridor that eventually opened into the hospital's main dining area. It was fairly empty. A young couple sat at one table solemnly talking over coffee. He scanned the room until he caught the familiar figure of Alex Hollins, with his back to him. Grinning, Silas made his way towards him.

He approached and placed a hand on his right shoulder. "Well, if it isn't Pinehurst's prodigal son, Alex Hollins."

Alex's muscles tightened under his hand and he slowly turned, his pale face looking up at Silas.

"I know, you're surprised, right?" Silas grinned. "Mind if I take a seat?"

Silas walked around the table and tried to compress his large girth into the one size fits most cafeteria chair facing Alex.

Silas sat silently, trying to regain his breath after the struggle. Alex looked rough. His eyes were heavy and tired, and a couple days' worth of stubble decorated his face. A stale aroma rose from where he was sitting.

"Silas, I'm not looking for trouble," Alex said, his voice guarded.

Silas feigned being hurt. "Alex, neither am I. Can't a concerned pastor check in on a member of the community?"

"I've never known you to be concerned," Alex said. "If you were, you wouldn't have walked out of our lives."

Silas's cheeks grew warm, "You have a lot of nerve to speak to me like that. I'm still your father and a respected man of God."

Alex remained quiet, looking down at the crumbs on his plate.

"Not in my eyes, you will never be more than a sperm donor to mom."

Silas grew infuriated. Alex had no clue how difficult the decision was to leave him. He was young, getting ready to start seminary. He couldn't abandon all that for a kid. Besides, look at all the good he had done for the Kingdom since then.

How could he have accomplished all of that while trying to support a wife and child? It was a momentary indiscretion that he could not let overshadow his years of good work.

"Listen here!" Silas raised a finger, pointing it at Alex. "You have only heard one side of the story. Your mother seduced me, she saw my potential and wanted to hop on my coattails. She tried to trap me."

"Last I heard it takes two to tango."

"I was a weaker Christian then; Satan was pulling out all the stops to prevent me from going into ministry."

"So, it was worth it…"

"Worth what?" Silas was confused.

"Worth abandoning a child, living a lie, and in constant fear of getting found out."

Silas gritted his teeth so tightly his jaws began to ache. He slammed his hands on the table, rattling the silverware.

The young couple behind them turned and looked.

"Here you sit, a murderer, and you dare bring up my past. Have you ever set foot in a church?"

"Outside of the major holidays, no" Alex said, "It's not like I had a great father figure."

Silas leaned back, causing the chair to squeak in submission. He crossed his fingers across his large belly and a soft grin came across his face.

"Since when did you become the moral police for Pinehurst?" Alex said through a clenched jaw. "I did my time. I have to live with what I did. I will carry that guilt with me for the rest of my life. I don't need a holier than thou pastor telling me how awful I am."

Silas stayed silent. He smiled at a family walking past him. Leaning in he rested his large arms on the table. "Well, that is where we have a slight difference of opinion. As a pastor of one of the larger churches in Pinehurst, I have a responsibility to the community. I thought you wouldn't have the nerve to return to Pinehurst, too embarrassed to show your face."

Silas paused, "The fact that Heather's parents still live here and you have the nerve to walk around, a free man, it's like rubbing her death in their face." He was hissing now. "You got drunk, killed someone and after twenty-five years of three hots and a cot you can live a reasonably normal life."

Alex was shaking, "If I could trade places with her I would in a heartbeat. I paid my price through the justice system. I thought as a pastor your job was not vengeance but grace and of all the people extending a hand to help it would be you. Instead, the most kindness I have received has been from a retired bartender and a divorced

- 192 -

mom. Both of these people probably fall somewhere in your general definition of folks who are bringing Pinehurst down."

Silas sat quietly, letting the words settle, "Son, I'm the judge and the jury. We just ain't figured out who the executioner is. God's word says it plain as day in Leviticus, 'he that killeth any man shall surely be put to death."

"Doesn't sound like a God of forgiveness to me."

"Your opinion doesn't matter" Silas leaned back. "Our justice system is anemic, and you are a beneficiary of that. However, I will encourage you to move on from Pinehurst, because I can guarantee you will not have a moment's peace in this small town. I will make sure of that."

Alex's phone rand, "Sorry, I have to take this."

"Oh, by all means. I need to be moving on anyway." Silas struggled to free himself from the chair. "Remember what I said. I'm sure I could find some church members who would be happy to give you a ride out of town."

Silas grinned and walked away. He wasn't sure his conversation changed anything with Alex; he had fired a warning shot. The real battle was about to begin.

54

Alex grabbed his ringing phone and hit the answer icon, "Hello..."

"Hey Alex, what's wrong?" Harper asked, "You sound upset."

"Nothing I want to talk about right now,"

"Okay," Harper was confused. "Does it have to do with your mom?"

"No, I don't want to talk about it. How close are you to being done?" he said, his voice strained, "I need to leave this place."

"Alex, listen I don't know what happened, but remember, I am trying to help you out, so don't take it out on me."

Harper listened to the silence.

"Alex..."

"Sorry...I... didn't mean to take it out on you." In a calmer voice, he said, "It's been a long, bad day and then I ran into Silas Weston and it went downhill from there."

"The crazy pastor that gave you and Emory a hard time at city hall?"

"Same one."

"Wow, it says a lot when you have a pastor after you." Harper laughed.

Alex laughed as well and Harper could tell he was starting to relax.

"Well, I called to say I am finishing up my charting and should be out of here in about thirty minutes."

"That sounds great," Alex said, sounding more like himself. "You want to meet me in the waiting room?"

"Sure," Harper said.

"OK, I'll let the staff know I'm leaving. You can text me when you are headed my way."

"Works for me," Harper said. "And Alex…"

"Yep."

"Sorry about your day, sounds like it may have been worse than mine and that says a lot coming from an ER nurse." Harper laughed.

Alex grinned, "Good perspective."

55

The car ride home was mostly silent. Alex appreciated Harper's company but was not in the mood to talk. Harper must have picked up on his vibe so the silence was mutually acceptable.

But after a while, she broke the silence. "You want to talk about it?"

"Not really," Alex said. "I mean I do, but I don't want to burden you with my problems. You are an innocent bystander in my life."

"Well, for one, it wouldn't be a burden," Harper said. "Two, I hope you see me less as a bystander and more as an active participant at this point."

"I do. I didn't mean any offense," Alex said. "I just feel bad for you."

"Alex, if you remember, I volunteered for this, it's not like you had to twist my arm."

"Fair enough," Alex said.

He proceeded to tell her about his interaction with Silas, carefully skirting around the fact he was his father. He wasn't sure if he was close enough to Harper yet to divulge that piece of his life. When he had finished, Harper stared ahead in silence.

"I mean, that is unbelievable," she finally said. "Getting bullied is one thing, but getting bullied by a preacher is a whole other level."

Alex looked out the window the night sky passing in front of him, speckled with streetlights, passing headlights, and storefronts illuminating the dark hour of Pinehurst. He despised winter and the fact it got dark so early. He already struggled with depression and the long dark days didn't help.

"I am the first to say I am not the most religious person, but it's folks like Silas that made me that way," Harper said. "I remember our family going to visit a church one Sunday and before we even made it to the sanctuary, my parents were turned away because my sister and I were wearing pants. That was the last time my family tried to go to church."

Alex shook his head. He wasn't sure Jesus enforced a dress code during his ministry.

"Well, I'm sorry that happened," he said, "I appreciate you listening, I feel better just talking about it."

They turned onto Wildwood Drive and made their way down the narrow street to his home. As they approached his mother's house it seemed brighter than usual. The closer they got, a series of spotlights had been staked in the front yard illuminating a cluster of signs placed in the ground.

"What is that?" Harper asked.

"I have no idea..."

Harper slowed as they approached the home.

The air in the car grew thick as they read the signs in silence.

A murderer lives here

Deut. 27:25: Cursed is he that murders the innocent.

Not In Our Town!!!

A copy of his booking photo for jail was enlarged and plastered on some plywood.

There was also a picture of the accident scene with Heather Grayson's demolished car displayed prominently.

"Alex," Harper said, placing a hand on his shoulder.

The macabre scene was a lot to process. Alex bounced between anger and embarrassment. He had brought this on his mom. She was living her quiet life until he returned.

Harper's eyes moistened, "Alex, I'm sorry. I don't know what else to say."

"I deserve this," Alex said, his voice resolute. "I did something stupid and someone died. This is my burden to bear."

"Alex, that's not true. I know nothing will bring Heather back, but I have always been taught the God they preach about is full of love and forgiveness." Harper was pleading at this point. "You can't let some misguided people claiming to be messengers of God run you off."

"Well, if I remember correctly, the Bible is full of references about an eye for an eye and thou shalt not kill, but also a God who killed a bunch of babies whose parents hadn't arbitrarily painted blood around their doors," Alex said. "I'm not so sure He would be any less merciful to a non-church going drunk who killed an innocent lady."

Harper sat silently. The sound of the car's heat cranked to full blast filled the car's cabin. The windows had begun to fog.

"I'm scared," Alex said. "My mom is dying and I've been a target since getting out of jail."

They both sat in silence.

"We have both had long days." Harper placed a hand on his leg and leaned in towards him, "Vanesa has an extra bedroom. Why don't you come stay the night at her house? We can call the police now and file a report. I know for a fact you are not going to sleep well here. I'm a little worried about your safety."

Alex looked at Harper. Her auburn hair was pulled back into a ponytail and her kind blue eyes stared into his soul.

"Harper, that is kind, but I can't impose on Vanessa and Lando."

"Lando loves you!" Harper grinned. "He will be excited he is having a sleepover. Vanessa won't mind, I think she is warming up to you."

"Harper I can't. It would be awkward."

"No more awkward than sleeping here with these signs in your front yard."

The car doors locked.

"I'm holding you hostage until you say yes." A grin spread across her face.

"Will you free me long enough to go inside and get a change of clothes?"

"Sure. Go ahead and call the police while you are in there. You may want to pull the plug on the spotlight, just be careful not to muck up the crime scene, wear some gloves or something."

"You watch too much CSI."

"I know, it's a problem."

• • •

Alex ran inside and grabbed a change of clothes, still shaking from the rage of what had happened to his mother's house. He searched for the number to the Pinehurst Police Department on his phone. He found it quickly and dialed the number.

"Pinehurst Police Department," a tired female voice answered. "How may I help you?"

"Yes, I would like to report a crime."

"Really?" The voice perked up. "What is the nature of the crime?"

"Vandalism."

"Ok." The voice lost some enthusiasm. "Is this public or private property?"

"Private."

"OK, let me have your name and address."

Alex answered the questions and after being place on an indefinite hold, the person on the other end came back on. She explained their officer was busy and the earliest someone could be out was a couple of hours. Alex would not need to be there but would likely need to come down to the station tomorrow for a statement.

Alex thanked the tired voice, locked up the house, and headed down the driveway to Harpers car.

56

Silas grinned as Luther reported on the events of the night, optimistic they had Alex on his heels. Relieved knowing Alex's time in Pinehurst would be short-lived. The fact his mother was so ill was a bonus. As if God was sending his seal of approval.

Sin may prosper for a season.

Luther's sources also said Alex went home with the harlot, Harper Layne. Silas could not believe a soul could be so far gone.

Silas liked to believe everyone had access to God's grace and forgiveness, but he had his doubts about Alex Hollins.

How could you redeem a murderous, drunken fornicator?

"Luther, excellent work!" Silas smacked his pudgy hands together. "I don't foresee Pinehurst being subjected to the scourge of Mr. Hollins much longer. Then we can turn our attention to other important matters of the church."

"Thank you, boss." Luther grinned. "I feel like this one rattled him pretty good."

"Agreed, and once his mom dies, he won't have a reason to stay in Pinehurst."

"Yep, except for maybe that fornicating temptress who is leading him down a path of destruction."

"True, but I think that is even temporary," Silas said. "We will cross that sinful bridge if we get there."

Luther stood looking at his watch. "It's been a long day. I'm going to head out unless you need something else from me."

"No sir, as always you have done more than enough!" Silas leaned back in his leather office chair. "I appreciate it. I'm ready to put this chapter behind us."

57

Vanessa, while understanding, still had the typical motherly qualities of an older sister. Growing up, their mother hadn't exactly been present, so she had to step in and assume that role at times. This translated to the ongoing assumption that Vanessa knew best.

Harper pulled into the driveway of her sister's house and placed the car in park.

"Are you sure this is not going to be a problem?" Alex asked, "I can sleep in the car."

"Don't be crazy!" Harper said. "You are not sleeping in the car. Grab your stuff and let's go in."

Harper opened her door and stepped out of the car. She stepped around the front of the car and met Alex.

"Alright, let's go."

They made their way up the wooden steps of the front porch which squeaked with each step. Harper retrieved her keys from her scrub jacket and opened the front door.

They stepped into the foyer. A pleasant cinnamon smell filled the air. Warm yellow light spilled from the living room to the right where Vanessa was bundled up in a large blanket on the recliner watching some reality show on a large flatscreen television that hung over the mantle of the gas log fireplace.

"Hey sis, how are ......"

Vanessa's voice stopped as Alex followed Harper in.

"Hey Van, I can explain," Harper said quickly.

"Hi Vanessa," Alex said.

"Hello, Alex. This is a surprise."

"I know, and I am sorry I didn't call." Harper stepped into the living room. "It's just Alex has had a bad day and needs to stay here tonight."

Vanessa's face betrayed her shock.

"I'm sorry. I really should have called but didn't have a chance."

"Harper, really if it is an imposition, I can land somewhere else," Alex said.

Harper turned, "Where?"

"What's exactly wrong with his house?" Vanessa asked, a slight tension in her voice.

"Well, it was vandalized," Harper said. "Someone placed all these awful signs in his yards and lit the entire yard with spotlights. He called the police but didn't exactly feel safe sleeping there and honestly, I can't say I blame him."

Vanessa remained silent although her displeasure was palpable.

"It was my idea. I asked him to stay here. With all that is going on with his mom and then the thing with his house, I couldn't in good conscience let him be alone tonight."

"I'm a big boy. I can go back to the house," Alex said. "I doubt anything would happen."

"What if it did?" Harper asked. "I would never be able to forgive myself."

"Tonight only," Vanessa said through clenched teeth, "He leaves when you leave for work tomorrow."

"That's the plan anyway. He wanted to get back to the hospital to sit with his mom."

"Thanks, Vanessa," Alex said.

"You know where the extra sheets are," Vanessa said, standing abruptly and leaving the room.

Harper and Alex stood in silence for a few moments.

"Well, that went as well as could be expected," Harper said. "Let me grab some sheets and a pillow."

Alex didn't say anything. His cheeks were red with embarrassment.

It wasn't fair to spring this on her sister, but she was concerned about Alex. Between his mother and the harassment in the community, he must be getting near his breaking point.

Harper ran up the stairs to the linen closet. As she turned to go down the hallway, she met her sister head-on.

"Harper Layne," Vanessa jabbed a finger in the air inches from Harper's face, "how dare you bring this man into my house and put me in this situation! You don't know what kind of danger you have invited into my home. What if whoever vandalized his house followed you here?"

"I'm sorry...."

"What about Landon? Do you know what type of danger you have placed him in? This man is a criminal and you have the nerve to bring him here uninvited to spend the night? What if the neighbors saw you walking in? What if he does something to Landon?"

Harper remained quiet, physically shaking from the confrontation.

"Vanessa, I would hope you know me better than that. It's not like this is the first time you have met him," Harper said. "I was trying to help a fellow human being. If I was in his shoes, I would want the same done for me."

"You were in his shoes, which is why you are with me," Vanessa snapped. "I can't be a charity for everyone."

The words were a slap in the face. Her cheeks flushed as tears lit up in her eyes.

"Harper, I'm sorry, I didn't mean...."

"I hate you!" Harper hissed. "Once I am able, Lando and I will be glad to stop being your charity cases!"

The sound of the front door shutting broke the silence.

"Alex!" Harper yelled, running down the steps. "Alex!!"

She ran into the living room and Alex was gone as well as his stuff. Running to the front door she swung it open, "Alex!"

The front yard was empty. She ran back inside, grab her keys and ran back to her car.

"Harper, wait!" Vanessa yelled. "I'm sorry…."

Harper started the car and pulled out of the driveway.

58

Trevor was bored and to make it worse he was only a few days into this assignment. He wasn't sure why he was following Alex.

What he was sure of was that Alex was a pretty boring dude to have been in prison for twenty-five years. He glanced at his phone, the bright white numbers showing it was 9:30. He had to watch how he used his phone at night, the screens glow lit up the inside of his car easily revealing his face. This made the boredom worse, he couldn't even scroll through social media.

Trevor had started to wallow in self-pity when the sound of a door slamming broke his spiral. He lifted his head up in time to see Alex running out of the house with his backpack dangling on one shoulder. At the end of the driveway, he ran directly towards Trevor's car. A momentary panic set in as Trevor slid himself as deep into the seat. He held his breath as Alex ran past his car, without even casting a glance his way.

This is interesting.

Shortly after that, a girl came to the door yelling for Alex. She disappeared, returned with keys and ran to her car, backed out of the driveway, and headed east following Alex.

Finally, some excitement.

Trevor turned the ignition on but kept the headlights off, which was good because soon another lady came to the door crying and shouting.

Something went down. Trevor needed to leave, or he would lose Alex, but he needed the other lady to go back inside to avoid being spotted.

Finally, she pulled the door shut.

Trevor threw the car into drive and took off.

The surge of adrenaline woke him up and he no longer felt the tug of sleep. In the distance, he could make out the bright red taillights of the girl's car. He accelerated, trying to close the gap.

Where was Alex though?

He could not have made it that far on foot.

Soon the slow moving red taillights of the CR-V came into view. The car came to an abrupt stop.

"Shit," he muttered.

What was he going to do now? He only had a few seconds to decide. He couldn't stop right behind her; that would be too obvious. Slowing as much as he could without being conspicuous, he quickly approached the stopped car. Moving into the left lane, he accelerated and passed the car. Looking over as he passed, the driver turned and they briefly made eye contact. He quickly turned and punched the accelerator.

He needed to find Alex.

59

Alex was tired of being a burden. A burden to his mother, a burden to the state, and now a burden to Harper. He had not set out to live his life in a way that he was continually bringing drama and disappointment to everyone he met.

Being optimistic about Harper was misguided. When he overheard her and her sister arguing upstairs, he figured it was time to go before he caused damage to another family.

He had often thought that getting the death penalty would have been better. Currently, it was like he was serving two sentences. The first to check off a box for the justice system. The second was the continued judgment of society, which was a debt he could never repay. At least not in Pinehurst.

For some unknown reason his own father, Silas Weston, had it out for him. Wasn't Christianity built on forgiveness? He remembered from his time in Sunday School that Christ forgave the thief on the cross. Maybe that grace doesn't extend to a murderer.

He made his way down the dark street perforated by the yellow haze of streetlamps. Harper lived only a few streets over from his mother's house. Having grown up in the area, he knew a shortcut ran through the woods that separated the subdivisions. These woods had been the site of many childhood games of hide and go seek and tree forts, and the older he got, a favorite place to make out with a few willing girlfriends. There was a chance Harper would come looking for him and he did not want to face her right now, the best way to avoid her was through the woods.

If he remembered correctly, there was a path behind the old Mayberry place. A buzzing in his pocket startled him, but it was just his phone. He pulled it out, Harper's number illuminated the screen. He hit the decline button and thirty seconds later the phone buzzed again in his hand. He hit decline again.

She is persistent.

Maybe Pinehurst wasn't right for him. If his mom ended up passing away, he wouldn't have anything holding him here. However, if she survived, she would need a lot of care and he didn't want her ending up in some home.

He approached the old, abandoned house which looked like something straight out of a horror movie. The door had dry rotted and split in half, and all the windows were missing along the front of the home. Weedy overgrowth had climbed up the porch railings and mostly covered the steps.

A light snow had begun to fall as he made his way around the corner of the house to the familiar backyard that had served as the entry into the woods for all the neighborhood kids throughout the years.

He had lost the benefit of the streetlights, but through the silver moonlight, he could make out the faint outline of a worn path leading through the backyard and terminating at the edge of the forest. He made his way cautiously to the back of the yard where the path led into the woods.

The woods appeared dark and skeletal in the winter moon. Back in his childhood, he could have navigated these woods blindfolded, but thirty years later, it was a little different. He did remember seeing a flashlight function on his phone. Pulling the phone out of his pocket, the screen lit up, pushing back the darkness around him. He found the flashlight icon and pressed the button. A beam of light shot out from the rear of his phone.

Magic.

It didn't take much to impress someone who had been in jail for twenty-five years. His fixation with the flashlight was broken by the sound of a car making its way slowly down the street. Looking back, two headlights slowly made their way past the house. He turned, disappearing into the forest.

60

"You lost him!?!?" Silas shouted into the phone in frustration. He had slipped into his silk pajamas on and was ready to watch an episode of Stranger Things. A show he condemned from the pulpit as full of Satanic references, teenage fornication, and foul language that no one from New Zion should be watching. However, he harbored a secret obsession with the show after he became hooked while researching it for his flock.

"I mean, not on purpose." Dalton's voice shook. "Trevor said he bolted out of the Layne girl's house and took off down the street. The girl came out shortly after and followed him. Trevor kept up the best he could, while still trying to be subtle, but the girl stopped next to the old Mayberry place so Trevor had to keep moving to avoid being caught."

"Dalton, you assured me this Trevor kid was up to the task," Silas said. "Do I need to come down there?"

"No boss. We have it under control," Dalton said. "I got a unit waiting back at his mom's house and Trevor is still making his rounds. I'm sure he will show up. I mean with his mom being sick and all he ain't going to run far."

"Unless he went and did something stupid." Silas took a bite of an open Snickers bar he had on his nightstand. "Anybody check on the girl and the kid? Make sure they are ok?"

There was silence on the other end.

"No sir, but I can get Trevor to swing back by the place."

"Do that. Have him go knock on the door and make up some BS about a noise complaint or something."

"Yes sir, good idea."

"Keep me posted."

"Yes sir."

"And Dalton…."

"Yes sir."

"Don't screw this up."

• • •

Dalton hung up the phone, his ears ringing with anger. His wife always told him he needed to man up and not let Silas push him around. After all, he was the sheriff, he had the true authority, not some overweight, fire and brimstone pastor who treated Pinehurst like his own playground. Silas used other's weaknesses to exploit them, control them, and give him power.

Hands shaking, Dalton picked up his phone and dialed the station.

"Bucks County sheriff's office," a voice answered.

"This is Dalton, let me talk to Pete."

"Uh...sure…" the voice became anxious as Dalton was placed on hold.

"What's up chief?" Pete's chipper voice came through a few seconds later.

"The usual, Silas causing us some work."

"Can't that man just focus on preaching instead of getting into everyone's business?"

"I agree," Dalton said. "I think he fancies himself a low-rate mob boss. He probably has enough dirt on everyone in Pinehurst that no one wants to push back."

"What's he want now?"

"There was a disturbance over on Cambridge," Dalton said. "We think the Hollins man was involved. Trevor is out that way in his car."

"You need me to get some men out there?"

"Yes, Hollins is on foot, he couldn't get too far tonight."

"I'm on it."

"Probably not a bad idea to get some men to comb the woods over in that area in case he decided to go off the beaten path."

"Where all the teenagers hang out?"

"Yep, that's the place. I'll have Trevor circle back and check the residence to make sure everyone is ok."

"I'm on it. I'll get a couple of units over there."

"Thanks, Pete."

"No problem boss!"

61

Harper leaned over the steering wheel sobbing.

Is this what her life had come to now? Arguing with her sister over whether an ex-convict could stay the night?

Her life had become unhinged and chaotic since the divorce. Landon was the only thing grounding her. With her new job, she had felt like things were settling down and the potential new relationship with Alex meant things were maybe starting to go her way.

She should have known better.

She was not that lucky.

Of course, Pinehurst was not necessarily the mecca of single men, but how in the world did the one man she had begun to fall for happen to be a convicted criminal? She was not sure she could ever convince Vanessa to accept him, but did she need her to?

Looking down the street, she did not see any sign of Alex, of course it would be hard to see anyone with it being this dark. She was deep into her pity party when headlights appeared in the rearview mirror.

They grew brighter and began to slow as the car got closer to her. She grew uneasy. Looking in the rearview mirror, she could not make out what type of car it was. Part of her thought it might have been her sister coming to check on her, but she knew better. The car was right on her bumper. Her mouth went dry and her heart raced. The car slowed, swerved left and pulled beside her. She made brief eye contact with the driver who looked like a lost twenty-year-old kid trying to find his way back home. He glanced away and sped by.

Harper hit Alex's number one more time. After four rings the phone went to a voicemail that had not been set up yet. She wiped her eyes with the back of her hand. She was embarrassed to go back and face her sister. Even if she could track Alex down tonight, he would not want to talk to her.

Cutting her losses, she put the car in drive, did a three-point turn and headed back to Vanessa's house to face the music.

62

The porch lights were on and light flooded out of the windows at the front of the house. If Trevor had to guess, he would say every light on the first floor was on. He pulled his car into the driveway. Turning off the ignition, he stepped out in the cold night air and made his way to the door. Walking up the stairs to the front door he pressed the doorbell.

After waiting a few minutes there was no response. By the number of lights on, there had to be someone home.

He pressed the doorbell again.

"Coming!" A voice called from within the house

A few moments later there were footsteps and the click of the deadbolt disengaging as the door opened. A woman who looked in her thirties stood there. Her long black hair was pulled back into a ponytail and her deep green eyes were accentuated by a pale complexion. She had pulled a white cotton robe tightly around her.

"May I help you?"

"Yes, ma'am. My name is Trevor Lawhorne with the Bucks County Sheriff's Department." He fumbled holding up his badge, "I need to ask you a few questions."

"About what?"

"It is regarding the gentleman who was here earlier."

"Is Harper okay?" she asked.

"Harper? Who is that?"

"Harper Layne. She is my sister. She is the one who was with the man."

"Oh…yes ma'am, everyone is fine as far as I know," Trevor said. "We received a report from a concerned neighbor who heard a disturbance and stated they saw a man run out of your house."

The lady's shoulders dropped in relief. "This is embarrassing. I had no idea it was that much of a scene."

"No need for apologies ma'am. I'm happy to hear everyone is ok." Trevor cheeks were starting to go numb from the cold. "Is your sister here?"

"No, she left shortly after he did. She took her car trying to find him. I've tried calling her cell phone but she is not answering."

"Do you mind if I ask the name of the gentleman your sister brought home?"

After a cautious pause, the lady said, "Alex Hollins."

"Did he attempt to hurt you or your sister?"

"Oh no…not at all. He is a nice man. It's just my sister has questionable taste in men."

"Understood. And you have not been able to reach your sister?"

"No. I've tried her cell several times."

"That's too bad. I would like to talk to her if possible."

"I'm not even sure when she will be back."

"Do you have her number?" Trevor asked. "Maybe I could give her a call, usually when the sheriff's department shows up on caller ID it gets your attention."

"Good point." Vanessa laughed. "It's cold outside, why don't you come inside?"

"Are you sure ma'am? I hate to impose."

"No, it's not a problem at all. With the events of tonight, I have no plans of going to sleep anytime soon."

Trevor grinned and stepped into her home.

63

It had been at least thirty years since Alex had been through the Cambridge woods. However, even under the cover of night, he could tell things had not changed much. He made his way cautiously down the path that had been forged from years of foot traffic. The meager light from his phone illuminated the area directly in front of him so he at least did not trip and kill himself.

The light occasionally picked up discarded artifacts of youth. An empty beer bottle here, a discarded condom wrapper there. Cigarette butts littered the trail. Despite the progress of society, the vices of youth remained consistent over time.

Carefully following the path, he continued to make forward progress. If he remembered correctly this would drop him out near the street behind his mom's house. He made his way slowly down, his visual field handicapped by the limited light from his phone.

In the distance, there was some rustling and branches breaking off to the left of the trail. He stopped. The noise grew louder.

"Who's there?"

No response.

The rustling grew closer as the sounds of limbs snapping and branches breaking increased.

Alex heart raced.

Raising his phone, he aimed the light in the general direction of the noise, but he couldn't see much. A large buck burst through the underbrush and darted across the path.

Alex jumped back, startled by the sudden appearance of the animal. Soon the sounds of branches breaking grew further away.

Shaking, Alex dropped to his knees and took some deep breaths to slow his heart rate down. He resumed his journey down the dark trail. Soon he was walking past a familiar landmark, a large rock wall stood off to the side of the trail. Where there wasn't moss creeping up the stone surface, various spraypainted profane sayings and pictures filled in the blank space.

The Wall, as it was called, was a favorite make out spot for couples. High enough to be off the main trail, it wasn't visible to other people and provided a quiet, out of sight location for couples. It was also a popular location to do any number of things from smoking a joint to drinking some cheap beer.

He continued through the dark woods, trying to avoid twisting his ankle on the exposed roots lifting through the ground. In the distance, the darkness was interrupted by tiny slivers of light cutting through the woods. When the faint silhouette of homes started to appear a sense of relief overcame him.

It bothered him that he had put Harper in a such bad spot with her sister. She was a lot like him in that she did not have a lot of support outside of a few people and he hated he may have jeopardized that.

The trail ended at a concrete storm drain running between two homes. Alex left the woods and stepped into a clearing of dead grass littered with discarded beer cans. He recognized the familiar cul-de-sac on Dogwood Street, he was close to his mom's house. Walking toward the road, he didn't even pay attention to the Bucks County Sheriff's Department car that sat idling in front of one of the homes.

64

Harper turned the corner and approached her sister's house. There was a dark gray sedan in the driveway. She did not recognize it at first, but as she got closer, it was similar to the one that had passed her earlier.

Pulling into her sister's driveway, she turned the car off and stepped out into the chilly night air. Her curiosity grew around whose car it was. The front porch lights were on and the living room lights spilling out onto the porch. Climbing the steps, she opened the front door and stepped inside. Her sister sat in the living room talking with a young African American man seated on her couch. He wore jeans, a gray crew neck sweater and a tan canvas barn jacket.

"Harper, thank God you are ok!" Vanessa stood up and ran over to her sister and gave her a big hug.

The man stood and walked toward Harper. Her breath caught in her chest as she recognized the man as the driver of the car who passed her earlier.

"Vanessa, this is Trooper Johnson." Vanessa pointed to the young man. "He got a complaint about a disturbance and was just checking on us."

He stood about six feet tall. He had rich dark skin with deep brown eyes. His face was cleanly shaven and its features made him look like a high school kid without the acne of adolescence, his jaw tensed as he approached her.

"Evening, Ms. Layne." The trooper dipped his head toward her. "Sorry to bother you so late. I was following up on a noise complaint. It appears both you and your sister are okay."

Why would a cop be following her?

"You look familiar." she blurted out.

Trooper Johnson had a brief panicked look on his face. "Well, I have been in the area for a while. Proud graduate of Pinehurst High School."

"No, I mean I think you passed me earlier tonight," Harper said. "Shortly after I left here."

"Harper, don't be silly." Vanessa stepped up and put an arm around her shoulder. "You were so upset when you left, I don't know how you could remember anything."

"I believe your sister is right," he stammered. "I've been at the station all night; this was the first call I've been on."

"I'm pretty sure it was you. Same car and all." She gestured back to the driveway.

"Maybe I have a twin." He laughed and switched gears. "How long have you and Alex been friends?"

"Wait...How did you know it was Alex who was over here?" Harper said.

His eyes widened, "Um...well...your sister told me you had him over."

Harper cut her eyes to Vanessa.

"He asked." Vanessa became defensive.

"Well...it...looks like you two are safe and sound." He began to back towards the door. "I guess I'll see myself out. You ladies have a nice night."

He quickly turned and exited out the front door.

Vanessa turned to Harper, "That was weird."

"Vanessa, I swear he was following me when I went after Alex. He passed right by me and we made eye contact." Harper was shaking.

"I will say the whole situation is suspicious," Vanessa said. "You need a glass of wine."

"I might need two."

Harper walked into the living room and sat on the couch, pulling a plush navy blue throw around her while trying to process the events of the evening.

Why would the police be staking out her sister's place? Or were they following Alex?

Both options sent a shiver down her spine. Had Alex done something illegal while he was back in town? She began to have doubts about her relationship with him. Maybe her sister was right. Maybe she was desperate to get back into a relationship.

"Here you go."

She looked up and took the wine glass from her sister's outstretched hand. It contained a heavy pour of dark red liquid.

"Thank you." Harper shifted herself into a sitting position, took a sip of the liquid, and a pleasant warmth hit the back of her throat.

"I'm sorry," Harper said.

"Sorry for what?"

"I should have listened to my big sister and not gotten involved with Alex." Harper took another sip of the wine. "I'm just so stupid."

"Harper, sweetie, you're too hard on yourself," Vanessa said. "I'm not sure any of this had to do with Alex. Probably just Mr. Buckholtz next door snooping and calling the police."

"No Vanessa. I'm pretty sure that cop was following Alex and me. There is no other way to explain it."

"I agree it all seems a little odd," Vanessa said. "But why would Alex have the police following him?"

"That's what I don't know." Harper said tears welling up, "Has he gotten involved in something else since he has been out of prison and I've been blissfully ignorant, overlooking the signs?"

"Harper, you are smart. I doubt you have unconsciously been aiding and abetting a criminal." Vanessa tried to reassure her sister. "Didn't he get assaulted in his home shortly after he got home?

Maybe all this comes from that? Maybe they are looking out for him?"

"Thanks for trying to put a positive spin on it," Harper said. "I'm going to reach out to him tomorrow and we'll have a hard conversation."

"Good idea." Vanessa smiled. "In the meantime, you have a big glass of wine to finish!"

65

Dalton pulled the police cruiser into the cul-de-sac at the end of Dogwood Street. He put the car in park and turned off the lights. The shortcut through the woods emptied right behind the homes at the end of the street.

He was still fuming about how he had tolerated Silas Weston talking down to him all these years. At first, he had been taken by religious conviction and the underlying principle of showing respect to a man of God. However, the more he got to know Silas, the less he saw a man of God and the more a power-hungry demagogue who chose to exact his power from the pulpit.

Unfortunately, for whatever reason, Alex Hollins was now in his crosshairs. In a way, Dalton felt sorry for Alex. He couldn't imagine going through what Alex had been through. Alex had paid his price. Nothing was bringing Heather Grayson back and that was something Alex had to deal with for the rest of his life.

The windows in the cruiser started to fog up. Dalton cracked a couple of windows to let in some cold air to help clear them. His cell phone buzzed in the passenger seat. Dalton glanced down, it was Trevor.

"What's up?"

"Boss, I screwed up." Trevor's voice sounded like a mix of panic and remorse.

"What do you mean?" Dalton's neck muscles tightened.

"She made me, boss, she made me."

"Trevor, calm down. What are you talking about?"

Trevor went on to explain the situation and Dalton's stomach sank. Trevor was a rookie in the department and as such, had made a rookie mistake. Now Harper knew he was potentially trailing them; he would need to pull him off the patrol.

Dalton tried to control his emotions.

"Trevor, why did you even pass her?"

"She stopped boss, stopped right in the middle of the road. I was right behind her. I had no choice."

"Trevor, there is always a choice." Dalton grew impatient. "Even if you did a U-turn, at least she would not have seen your face!"

"I'm sorry boss," Trevor said. "What do you want me to do now?"

"Nothing. Just go home before you cause any more damage." Dalton was frustrated.

"Yes, sir."

"Trevor."

"Yes, sir?"

"Did she seem okay? It didn't look like she was hurt or anything?"

"No, she seemed fine, other than she looked like she had been crying."

"We will talk in the morning." Dalton disconnected the call, threw his phone on the passenger seat, and returned his attention to the woods.

He hated waiting.

It wasn't long before there was a flickering of light in the woods. It grew brighter until the shadowy figure of a man emerged from the woods holding what looked like a flashlight.

There he is.

The figure moved slowly, coming up the side of the house and stepping into the driveway. Dalton could tell from his slow pace that he was tired. The streetlights spilled onto the man's face confirming it was Alex Hollins.

Alex stopped.

Dalton rolled down his window. "Everything alright?"

"Fine, just heading home."

"A little late for a grown man to be trapezing through the woods."

"Agreed." Alex sounded nervous. "I was visiting a friend."

"Understood. You need a ride home?"

"No sir. I'm right up the street here."

"Alright. Well, why don't you go straight home. I don't want to hear any complaints of someone snooping around."

"Yes, sir."

Alex walked away at a brisk pace.

Dalton rolled up the window, flicked on his headlights, and drove away feeling a sudden sense of sympathy for Alex.

66

Alex was exhausted, still shaken by his encounter with the police officer earlier. Probably PTSD from his prior life. He opened the front door to his mom's house and collapsed on the cloth loveseat that had been a staple in her living room for as long as he could remember. It still had the faint smell of cigarette smoke.

Flashbacks of him watching the A-team with her, a cigarette dangling out of her mouth. He didn't realize it at the time, but those were the best days of his life. A time when he was surrounded by people, although imperfect, who loved him unconditionally. His biggest stress was what to wear to school and whether he should try to hold Sarah Andrews's hand. He wasn't sure how his life had gotten off track. He was on the precipice of losing the only two people in his life who cared for him.

His mother was hanging onto her life at the hospital and now Harper was probably done with him as well. He hadn't had anything to drink since going to jail, but he had a sudden strong desire for a cold beer or a shot of Jack Daniels. He glanced at his phone, there were ten missed calls from Harper as well as a series of text messages.

Alex call me.

Alex, I am so sorry…

Alex, are you ok?

He wasn't okay. His entire return to Pinehurst had been a disaster. He'd had more security, comfort, and family in jail. Now that had been ripped from under him and he was starting over, from scratch.

The front yard was full of signs he had to deal with. His mom was probably going to die, and he was being driven out of the only home he had ever known. He had never been so lonely in his life.

. • • •

The harsh tone of the phone ringing brought Alex out of a deep sleep. He had a horrible crick in his neck, compliments of falling asleep on the loveseat. He tried to rouse himself to consciousness to find his cell phone.

The large grandfather clock in the living room read 7:00. He had passed out without the assistance of any substance. He finally found his phone wedged between the cushions of the loveseat.

He answered the phone, trying his best to sound awake. "Hello."

"Alex, sorry to bother you so early, this is Dr. Parker. I just finished checking in on your mom and wanted to give you a quick update."

"Is everything okay?"

"She remains critical but stable. She has a strong heart and that is in her favor. Unfortunately, her lungs aren't healthy. Right now, we still have her on the breathing machine. We tried to give her a few trials coming off, but she has failed them."

"What does that mean?" Alex figured she couldn't stay on the breathing machine forever.

"Well, it means that in a couple of days, if we can't wean her, we may need to make a decision."

Alex's mouth went dry.

"Right now, she has the tube in her mouth through her windpipe and patients really can't have those long-term. So, the next step would be to consider a long-term solution which would be placing a tracheostomy."

Alex recalled those horrible anti-smoking ads with people talking into boxes making strange robotic voices or taking a puff of a cigarette from a hole at the base of their neck.

Dr. Parker continued. "That involves making an incision at the mid portion of her throat and placing a breathing tube."

"I'm not sure she would want that," Alex said trying to process the gruesome image.

"Unfortunately, she does not have a living will and you are her only next of kin, so we will need to have a discussion. I'm not saying she is there yet, but I am planting the seed. If she does not improve in the next couple of days, this is the direction we need to consider."

Alex's life had been a turbulent ocean with a steady succession of waves knocking him down each time he tried to stand.

"I don't know what to do." His voice cracked.

"I understand, and we don't have to decide now," Dr. Parker said. "Just start thinking about it."

Alex nodded, "Is she awake?"

"Yes. We have gone down on her sedation, so she is more alert."

"Great. I'll try to get over today to see her."

"I think she would like that," Dr. Parker said. "I'm on until seven this evening. If you have questions, the nurses can find me."

"Thank you, doc."

Alex hung up. Tears filled his eyes.

Maybe you never are truly forgiven for your sins. Maybe Silas was right, maybe he was a scourge to Pinehurst. Now he was impacting the ones he loved. He looked down at his phone and pressed the contacts icon. He had a meager two contacts listed:

Emory

Harper Layne

He pressed Emory's number and brought the phone to his ear.

67

Silas grew increasingly frustrated with Dalton's insubordination. He stared at the sweaty excuse of a man sitting across from him. The dark stereotypical mustache sitting across his lip made Silas cringe. It must be a requirement of the job to work in the Bucks County Sheriff's Department, although Silas always thought it made Dalton look like a God-forsaken porn star.

"So, you're saying you saw him, you spoke with him, but you didn't arrest him?" his voice shook. He didn't like to lose control. "I mean, what part of bring him in did you not understand, Dalton?"

Sweat begin to bead across Dalton's forehead.

"I understood what you wanted. However, I could not legally arrest him for walking alone in the dark." Dalton's voice wavered. "I still have a code to go by."

"That's a good one, Dalton!" Silas laughed. "How many times have you bent that code when it suited you or me?"

Silas specifically remembered the night he had drank a little too much and one of Dalton's boys had pulled him over. However, after a quick call to Dalton, the officer came back to Silas looking pale and apologetic. He offered to follow Silas home to make sure he got there safely.

"You witnessed a known murderer emerging from the woods and the end of a quiet residential neighborhood and you don't think that is suspicious enough to at least bring him down to the station for questioning?"

Dalton remained silent.

"Are you going to answer me?"

Dalton took a deep breath. "I had heard from Trevor and the girl was fine. Alex served his time in Buckingham. I did not have a reason to bring him in."

Silas threw his large beefy hands onto the desk with a thud. He leaned forward, face beet red and pointed a pudgy finger at Dalton.

"Listen here Blackwood, if it wasn't for me, you would not be sheriff!" Spit flew from his mouth. "The Bucks County Sheriff's Charity fund would not be sitting close to six figures. I'm sure the governor would love to come in and do an audit of that fund. And I don't know too many county sheriffs who are driving a new Ford F-150!" Silas grinned, "As a concerned citizen and donor, I want to know what is going on with my money."

"Well, if we are going to play this game," Dalton said, voice quivering, "then I'm sure your wife would love to know where you go every Thursday night for your staff meeting, and why they are always held at the Pines Motel. I believe we may have some video surveillance on file of you and Mary Rogers leaving these meetings together. Last I checked she wasn't on staff at New Zion."

Silas grinned and leaned back in his chair. It protested against his weight with a crescendo of creaky sounds. It was natural things would eventually come to this type of posturing. He'd had his reservations about Dalton all along. He was weak and didn't have the fortitude it took to participate in the necessary gray areas of business. Silas wanted to kick himself. If he had known then he would have never been such a fool and given Dalton a chance.

He had learned as a pastor he had great power and authority. His congregation was putty in his hands. He could have accomplished all he had without the need to dirty himself with local law enforcement. But he was here now. They both had enough dirt on each other to effectively destroy their lives in Pinehurst. It was probably better to play nice, start to wean himself from using Dalton and start looking for other avenues to accomplish what he needed.

"Look, Dalton," Silas said, "I'm tired and frustrated. I need Alex Hollins out of here. The longer he hangs around the harder it is for me to focus on my ministry."

"I understand, Silas."

"Listen, why don't we pause," Silas said. "Let's regroup in a couple of days and develop a plan."

"Sounds good."

"Alright." Silas stood and reached out his hand.

Dalton stood, slid his sheriff's hat under his left arm and reached out his right hand to shake Silas'.

"I'll see myself out," Dalton said.

"Ok, we'll talk in a couple of days."

Dalton walked out of his office, pulling the door shut behind him, picked up his phone and scrolled until Zeke Boone's number popped up. He pressed the number and after a few rings the tired, probably drugged out voice of Zeke answered.

"Hallo."

"Zeke, it's Silas. Are you and Eddie up for some work?"

68

Vanessa let Harper sleep in. It had been a tough night for both of them. Looking out her bedroom window the ground had been covered with a white blanket of snow overnight. The tree branches sagging under the weight of the white powder. Pausing to take in the beautiful scene, trying to forget the events of the past couple of days.

Landon got up early and had managed to find his way into her room, not his mom's. She brought him downstairs and set him up in front of the TV watching Paw Patrol, happily eating a cherry Pop-Tart and drinking some chocolate milk. Not exactly the Breakfast of Champions, but hey what are Aunts for?

It was a beautiful white Sunday morning. The day was supposed to get warmer later, so maybe she could take him out to play this morning in the snow before it melted.

She looked in awe at the cute little kid, who was staring intently at the television, with the wave of disheveled black hair surfing across his head. Lost in his own world, laughing at the antics of a cartoon dog. Vanessa often wished she could regain the innocence of childhood and not have a care in the world.

"You want to go play in the snow later, Lando?"

"Uh huh," his face stayed transfixed on the screen.

"Maybe we can make snow angels??"

"Uh-huh."

"Ok, Aunt V is going upstairs to change."

"Uh-huh."

Between her getting dressed and wrangling Lando into his winter clothes to go outside, it took about an hour. The sun was up and Harper remained asleep.

"Alright Lando, do you want to build a snowman?"

"Yes!" He tried to raise an arm but was so bundled up he could barely get it up.

He yelled and charged toward the door.

"Wait!" Vanessa said, scurrying after him.

Stepping onto the front porch, Vanessa was surprised at how chilly it was despite the sun shining and her triple layer of clothing. Landon bounded down the steps and charged full force into the snow with shouts of joy coming from behind the thick scarf covering the lower part of his face.

"Lando, wait up!" Vanessa yelled. Her breath steamed out in front of her as she gingerly made her way down the steps, knowing that even in her mid-thirties her bones would not bounce back quite as easily as Landon's four-year-old body.

She knelt scooping some of the snow off a step, forming it into a softly packed ball and tossed it at Landon. It hit him squarely on his backside.

"Hey!" he yelled. He tried to scoop up some snow, but his mittens made it impossible.

They had a blast playing in the snow. Vanessa showed him how to make snow angels, a skill Landon picked up quickly. He enjoyed falling backward into the soft powder and leaving his winged impressions. Vanessa was having a good time and the events of last night were quickly fading from her memory.

They transitioned to building a snowman. The snow was not quite sticky enough, but they gained some momentum as they rolled the base for the frosty figure.

At one point Vanessa glanced up to see Harper looking out the living room window at them. Vanessa tried to give her a gloved thumbs up sign. Harper nodded, holding up her coffee cup.

The front door cracked open and Harper yelled out, "Looking good Lando!"

"Mommy!" Lando charged toward the open door. "Come outside and play!" He slowly navigated up the steps in his snow boots and gave his mom a big, wet hug.

"Maybe later baby! Momma just woke up and I need to get some coffee in me."

"Ok. Aunt V and I are building a snowman!"

"I see sweetie!" Harper stepped back. "Ok I'm going to pull the door shut so we don't lose all of Aunt V's heat."

"Come back after you have had your drink."

"Love you, baby!"

"Love you, Mommy!"

Lando turned and charged back down the steps towards Vanessa.

After a while, they had constructed what could pass for a snowman. Landon was ecstatic.

Three misshapen balls of snow stacked on each other, Landon had gathered some old acorns for eyes and some dead twigs for arms. Vanessa took her scarf off and wrapped it around what was supposed to be the snowman's head. Landon squealed in delight.

"Take a picture!" he shouted.

She had left her phone inside. The thought of going back inside and getting partially de-winterized was not a fun one, but she didn't want to disappoint Lando.

"Ok," Vanessa said, "I'm going to walk to the door to call your mom and have her bring me my phone. You stay right here."

"Yes, ma'am!"

Vanessa made her way up the steps and opened the front door. A welcome blast of heat met her face. She yelled out, "Harper!"

There was no response, except for the sound of the shower running upstairs. Vanessa sighed, understanding the inevitability of having to extricate herself from her snow boots. She looked back at Landon who danced happily around the snowman.

"Landon!"

"Yes, Auntie!"

"I'm going to grab my phone. You stay right there. Do not leave the front yard!"

"Yes, ma'am."

"Do you want some hot chocolate?"

"Yum!"

Vanessa stepped into the foyer and began the process of getting her snow boots off.

Landon played with his new frosty companion, oblivious to the late model Chevy truck slowly making its way down the street.

69

Zeke hungover, head throbbing looked over in disgust at his mouth breathing brother asleep in the seat next to him, probably still high.

Zeke was typically not up this early. However, when Silas Weston called, you jumped. At least that's what the man expected. If Silas wasn't the only thing standing between him and his brother having a long stay at Buckingham prison, Zeke wasn't sure the money was worth the effort.

The snow was unexpected. Their road was a low priority on the county's snow removal list, which is why he was glad he had ole Cletus, the name he affectionately gave to his late model diesel truck. The Chevy had seen him through many snowstorms, floods, and other bad weather.

Dropping the truck into four-wheel drive he navigated the white space where the road used to be. The truck shook as they hit a few surprise divots and bumps in the road. Eddie's head bounced against the window and he let out a few grunts but kept sleeping. A steady stream of drool had formed in the corner of his mouth.

Cletus was a faithful truck, but it took a while for him to heat up. Zeke tried to blow into one hand while maintaining control of the truck. He took a quick swig from the bottle of Jack Daniels beside him, hoping it would warm him up.

Silas had been vague in his request. Sounded like he was getting frustrated with Dalton and wanted Zeke to help him turn up the heat on this Hollins dude. Zeke looked down at the crumpled piece of paper with 127 Cambridge Street scrawled on it. Silas had said this was where Alex's girlfriend, Harper Layne, was staying.

How in the world can a man spend twenty-five years in prison for killing someone and be out less than a month and land a prize like Harper? Zeke looked into the rearview mirror at his leathered complexion complete with a teardrop tattoo at his left eye.

What did Alex have that he didn't?

Zeke had spent one night in prison about ten years ago for a DUI and that is when he met Silas who was supposed to be doing a prison ministry. Zeke soon learned he was looking for cronies to do his dirty work. Anyway, they hit it off and Zeke agreed to help him out in exchange for bail. They had been "business partners" ever since.

Zeke made it off the narrow back road and turned onto the main drive. It was white with no tire tracks. It looked like they were the first ones out. Bucks County was not known for its robust civil infrastructure so no telling how long it would be before the roads were plowed. Snow like this could shut the town down for days.

The truck handled much better on the road allowing him to increase his speed. The cabin had begun to warm up or the Jack Daniels was kicking in. Heading into town he turned the radio dial trying to find something to listen to other than his brother's snoring.

"Gawd will bring his vengeance on the fornicators, the adulterers, and the homosexuals! Amen!"

Silas' familiar voice came out of the speakers. Zeke grinned. If his congregation only knew what good ole Silas had been up to.

"We are now under the scourge of the Democraps! We had a Godly man in office and he was persecuted from day one!"

Some chords from an organ filled the car with shouts.

"You know what? Our great Lord was persecuted to death and on the third day he rose!"

Silas sounded possessed, he really must be feeling it today.

"Well, I believe our nation is nearing the morning of our third day and soon our great nation will rise and our godly president will return!"

The organ erupted into a static reverie followed by whoops and hollers from the congregation. Zeke had about as much hypocrisy as he could stand and cut the radio off.

• • •

He navigated the small unplowed streets of the subdivision trying to locate Cambridge Street. He did not see how people lived with their houses on top of each other. Give him his trailer and sixty acres of land any day. He didn't have much tolerance for human interaction. Looking down at the corner there was a signpost that read Cambridge St.

He elbowed Eddie.

"Wake up!" he yelled. "We're almost there."

Eddie groaned and violently snorted as he tried to hang onto sleep. "Leave me alone!"

"Eddie, I ain't joking. Get up!"

Zeke looked at Eddie who had fallen back to sleep. Zeke curved his thumb and middle finger together and plucked Eddie square on the forehead. A dull thud echoed through the cabin of the truck.

Eddie came to, sitting bolt upright in the seat with his fist cocked back. "What the…."

"Go ahead," Zeke said. "It will be the last time you hit me."

Eddie grumbled but situated himself into a more appropriate sitting position.

Zeke turned left onto Cambridge Street. The road had a few more tire tracks on it, letting Zeke know that Cletus wasn't the first vehicle down the road.

He scanned the house numbers.

"Help me find 127."

"Zeke, you know I ain't good with numbers," Eddie whined.

"I ain't asking you to add. I'm asking you to look."

119

121
123
125

Zeke slowed the truck down. "Alright, should be the next one."

A small cape cod style home came into view. Snow covered the roof and the dormers. A large tree stood naked in the front yard; some snow angels were on the ground. He slowed further, double-checking the address.

Silas had said to "put a scare" in the girl as they had done with Emory. Zeke didn't like the thought of getting too tough with a lady and sometimes Eddie was a loose cannon. No telling what might happen if the lady started giving them a little lip.

Easing in front of the house there was a snowman in the yard, soon a child bundled in a winter jacket emerged from behind it. Zeke panicked. The child dance around, jumping up and down in the snow. Zeke pressed the accelerator down and drove past the house.

"Where are we going?" Eddie asked.

"Did you not see the kid?"

"Yes. What, are you afraid of a kid?"

"No, I'm not afraid of a kid. But a kid is not part of the plan."

Zeke drove in silence trying to clear his mind. After a few minutes, he had an idea. A way to kill two birds with one stone. Make a little extra money and send a message to Alex.

"I got an idea."

Eddie grunted. "If it gets me back home sooner, I'm game."

"We take the kid?"

Eddie looked shocked, "Are you crazy?"

"No. We take him, blame that Alex dude, hold the kid for ransom, split it with Silas, return the kid safe and sound, and we'll be a couple grand richer."

"I don't know Zeke," Eddie said. "Sounds risky."

"Eddie, the police chief is wrapped tight around Silas's pinky. Shoot, we can even split the ransom three ways."

"I guess." Eddie sounded less than convinced, "Still, a kid?"

"Eddie, we will take good care of him. We ain't going to hurt him," Zeke said. "We have a warm house. I got plenty of TV dinners, and we have a dog."

Zeke did a three-point turn at the end of the street and circled back. They reached 127 again and the kid was still out in the front yard, doing snow angels now.

He put the truck in park.

The kid continued running around in the snow, unaware they were even there. They needed to act quickly. The kid was alone, but he wasn't sure for how long.

"Ok, Eddie, go grab him."

"In broad daylight?" Eddie laughed. "Are you crazy? This was your plan. I ain't touching the kid."

"I need to be the getaway driver. I have to get us out of here."

"I ain't doing it."

"Jesus, Eddie. When have you ever had a conscience?" Zeke threw open his door and hopped onto the street.

Looking up and down the street he made sure no other vehicles were out this morning. He walked toward the yard. The little kid, oblivious to the world, lying in snow fanning his arms & legs out..

"Hey, buddy!" Zeke said.

A small head popped up and looked right at Zeke. Big blue eyes showed out from under the hood of a heavy winter jacket. A scarf lay discarded beside him in the snow. His cheeks were bright red and a steady stream of thick but clear drainage ran from both nostrils.

The boy stared at Zeke.

"Are you making snow angels?"

The boy nodded his head slowly.

"Cool. I have a little boy about your age at home. Would you mind showing him how to do that?"

The boy nodded again.

Zeke made his way closer to Landon.

"Wow, that's a big one!" Zeke pointed to the winged impression on the ground. "Did you make that one?"

The boy shook his head. "Auntie V did."

"Cool, where is she?"

"Inside," the boy said. "Making hot chocolate."

"You all have some cool stuff here."

Like a snake striking its prey, Zeke grabbed Landon and with one hand across his mouth, ran toward the truck. The boy kicking and trying to scream against Zeke's hand.

Eddie pushed open the driver's side door and Zeke fought trying to get the struggling child into the front seat. Eddie grabbed him around the waist and pulled him into the cab. The kid let out a blood-curdling scream as soon as Zeke's hand dropped from his mouth.

"Kid, we ain't going to hurt you!" Eddie tried unsuccessfully to calm the child.

Zeke hopped in, threw the truck into drive, and gunned it while he pulled his door shut. Landon continued screaming as Eddied tried to restrain him. The rear of the truck fishtailed in the snow and they were off.

Zeke accelerated out of the neighborhood while Eddie had the kid in a bear hug. They were both yelling at the top of their lungs. Zeke fumbled for his phone, found Silas's number, and hit dial.

He hoped church was over.

70

Alex bundled up and walked out in his front yard to start removing the signs. It had taken a little convincing, but Emory had agreed to come take him to the hospital to visit his mom. Alex could tell he was still gun shy from the earlier threats.

It wouldn't help much if he pulled up and saw the lawn decorations. Fortunately, the signs were not secured well and everything came up easily. He gathered the cardboard and plywood and walked it behind the house, tossing it into a pile.

With the events of the past couple of days he had not slept well, his mind raced with thoughts of his current situation. The easiest solution would be to leave Pinehurst, but he could not do that to his mom. He also still had a sliver of hope things would work out between him and Harper. Also, part of him did not want to give Silas the pleasure of winning.

Walking back around the house, Emory had arrived and was waiting in the driveway. Alex waved and made his way toward the car. Emory popped the locks and Alex slid into the passenger side. The smell of cheap cologne and mothballs hit him. The heat was running at full blast welcoming Alex with a wave of warmth.

"Morning Alex," Emory said. "Got a surprise snow."

"I know, thank you so much for picking me up," Alex said pulling the door shut. "This means a lot."

"Not a problem." Emory backed out of the driveway. "At my age I welcome a little excitement!"

"Well, I appreciate that, but I don't want you ending up in the hospital."

"I know, but the thought of having some pretty young nurse taking care of me makes it worthwhile."

Alex laughed.

"How's your mom?"

"Not too good." Alex's voice choked a little. "Spoke with the doctor and it sounds like I'm going to have a hard decision to make."

Emory stayed silent.

"They want to consider a trach and I just don't think that is how she wants to live."

"Oh, I agree. Your mom valued her independence, having something that potentially will tether her to home or a bed would devastate her."

"I know," Alex said. "The doctor said she had a strong heart and was more alert. I can't imagine asking them to do anything less if she can look at me, even smile."

"I can't imagine," Emory said. "I'll be praying for sure."

"I hope you're praying to a different god than Silas."

Emory didn't respond right away. His eyes stayed on the road.

"How does a man like that, calling himself a pastor, get away with it?" Alex's voice shook. "My mom is fighting to stay alive and he is out there selling hate like it is gospel?"

"I don't have an answer." Emory said quietly.

"I'm not perfect, I've screwed up plenty. But my mom?" Alex shook his head. "She doesn't deserve this."

Emory sighed, "Life's not fair. My mom used to say we shouldn't expect it to make sense at least not from down here."

Alex stared out the window.

"Whatever Silas is preaching," Emory continued, "That's not Christ, its cruelty in a three-piece suit."

Alex nodded, "I agree, but I don't understand why a 'loving God' would let someone like Silas thrive."

"Maybe we're not supposed to get it."

"Well, I'm taking a break from God for a while."

"Okay," Emory said, "Just know he won't take a break from you."

They drove in silence.

The sounds of police sirens soon filled the air. Emory checked his rearview mirror, nervous as two Bucks County police cruisers flew by them, lights and sirens blazing.

"Hmm. Wonder what's going on?" Emory said.

They arrived at the hospital and Emory drove around to the terrace entrance.

"Here you go, sir," Emory said.

"Thank you, Emory. I appreciate your kindness."

"Tell your mom I'm praying for her and, for what it's worth, I'm praying for you also."

Alex stepped out into the cold winter morning. Emory drove off leaving a trail of white exhaust. Alex made his way toward the automatic sliding door leading into the hospital. A sense of dread washed over him.

• • •

He was in the familiar setting of the intensive care unit. The usual beeps and hisses filled the room. His mother lay in the bed looking a little more human with several of the contraptions now gone. Still, a clear tube protruded from her mouth, secured to her face with surgical tape and connected by a long opaque accordion-like tubing to a large machine by her bedside.

"Hi Mom.", he stepped beside the bed, rubbing her cool hand.

Her eyes flitted open, a moment of recognition occurred and she grinned. Her hand tightened around his. She tried to say something against the machine and this resulted in her coughing, setting off alarms from the ventilator.

"It's ok Mom," Alex reassured her. "Don't try to talk."

She nodded her head.

"I'll be here for a while; you go on back to sleep."

She was already there. Her respirations had settled down to the rhythmic cadence delivered by the ventilator. The bruised skin on her hand opened up a childhood memory.

Not wanting to be late for supper, he charged across the lawn and bounded through the front door, colliding with the male figure standing in the living room.

"Watch out buddy," the man said angrily and pushed him out of the way, almost sending him sailing back down the front porch steps.

Roy Hodges had been another of his mother's attempts at dating. So far, her track record was far from stellar and Alex knew she could do way better than Roy.

"Sorry, Roy."

The fabric around his collar tightened as Roy grabbed him, "That is sir, to you. Understand?"

Roy walked down the front porch steps, got into the large green Cadillac El Dorado, and sped off.

Alex continued into the house. He smelled lasagna and his mouth started to water.

"Mom!" he yelled.

The house was strangely quiet. He went down the hallway.

"Mom?"

The bathroom door was closed.

A slight whimper came from inside. He tapped gently on the hollow plywood door.

"Mom...you, okay?"

"Yes dear, I'm fine." She said followed by a slight snort.

"I'll be out in a second and we can eat. Why don't you go set the table?"

She wasn't ok and Roy was likely involved in whatever made her that way. He made his way back to the kitchen.

The generic wooden table was bare. He assumed he would only need two place settings.

He placed the plates, silverware, and napkins out. He got ready to serve some lasagna as the bathroom door opened.

"I'm coming dear," his mom said.

She rounded the corner into the kitchen, "Oh, the table looks nice.

Turning he was too stunned to speak. Her left eye was black and swollen shut.

"Mom, what happened to your eye!"

"Just a dumb accident."

He could tell she was lying.

"I left a cabinet door open, got distracted, and turned away. When I turned back around…well." She pointed to her left eye. "Me and the corner of the cabinet got really close."

He may have been eight, but mechanics of the story were not possible.

"Mom, did Roy do this?"

A sharp blow landed across his cheek.

"How dare you!" she said, "Roy would never hurt me."

Alex slid to the floor holding his cheek, the pain throbbed in fiery waves across his face. He was embarrassed to be crying, but the tears were not from pain, but from anger.

"Oh sweetie!!" his mother lunged to the floor and grabbed him close against her breast. "I am sorry! I don't know what came over me!"

He sat in silence.

"I lost my temper," she said, wiping her tears with the back of her hand. "Baby, oh my baby!! I am so sorry!! Please forgive you mom!!"

Alex had started to calm down but still didn't feel like talking. He nodded.

"No matter what, we have to stick together." She pulled him closer, "We stay thick…."

"Thick as thieves…." Alex finally said melting into his mother's chest.

Thick as thieves.

Alex stroked his mother's hand. She looked peaceful despite all the technology keeping her alive. He didn't know how he could agree to shut all this down and let her die.

Thick as thieves.

71

Vanessa stood in the kitchen, hands on her hips, waiting for the kettle to boil. A watched pot never boils. But she wasn't complaining. She was warming up. Her cheeks were no longer numb and she was starting to feel her fingers.

The shower was running upstairs and she was glad Harper got to sleep in today, poor girl deserved it. Vanessa was enjoying her time with Landon. When the water in the kettle came to a rolling boil, she retrieved two mugs from the cabinets and set them on the counter. She went to the refrigerator to get the whipped cream, because what was hot chocolate without whipped cream?

The throaty growl of a truck going down the street distracted her briefly. It must be the snowplow clearing the snow, this took her as a surprise because her street was the last on the list.

Pouring the steaming hot water into the mugs she added the chocolate powder, giving each mug a good stir and topping them with whipped cream. Stepping back, she looked at her creation. Not quite Martha Stewart level, but still impressive.

Making her way to the door with the two cups of hot liquid, using her hip, she pushed the storm door open. "Lando, hot coco is ready."

No response.

"Lando," she yelled, leaning further out the door. "Come get your hot chocolate!"

Still nothing.

Vanessa grew aggravated. "Landon, it's cold. You need to come here now and get your drink."

Silence. The cool air of the snowy morning blew in through the open door.

An overwhelming sense of dread settled over Vanessa. Despite the cold air outside she was sweating. Stepping outside her wool socks grew damp from the snow coating her front porch. She looked over the railing.

The snowman still standing.

The freshly made imprint of snow angels dotted the front yard and little footprints circled the snowman. Scanning the front yard there was Landon's bright red scarf lying discarded in the snow.

"Landon!" she screamed. The mugs shattered as they stuck the porch, there hot contents steaming as they hit the cold concrete.

72

Harper sat huddled in a wooden chair in the corner of the room a tattered quilt pulled around her. The scene unfolding around her was surreal. Two police officers were questioning Vanessa, while another officer methodically walked back and forth through the front yard with a police dog. Harper's eyes burned and her chest ached from crying.

Landon was missing.

Landon was missing.

Even those words didn't seem real. She'd chosen a hot shower and her morning coffee over his wide-eyed invitation to play in the snow. Now that moment was gone, maybe forever. That may have been her last chance to ever play with him again. She pulled her knees tight against her chest and tears streamed down her face.

• • •

"No officer, as I said before, I did not see anyone unusual." Vanessa was clearly rattled, though she was trying to maintain her composure, despite having to answer the same questions.

"I left him outside while I came in to get my phone to take some pictures. I decided to make us some hot chocolate. I looked out the window before I went to the kitchen and he was still playing. After I made the hot chocolate, I went outside and didn't see him. I panicked, looked all around the front and back yard, and when I still did not see him, I ran back inside and called 911."

"Thank you, ma'am," the officer said, looking serious but sympathetic, "Do we know anything about the child's father?"

"He is locked up in Roanoke for drug and child abuse charges, no chances of him getting out any time soon."

"Your sister has no enemies you are aware of?"

"No, she has been living with me less than a year, she just works and comes home and takes care of Landon. She doesn't even have any friends…" Vanessa paused.

"Something wrong?" the officer asked.

"Well…" Vanessa paused again, trying to choose her words, "She had started seeing this guy, Alex. He was over at the house last night and we had, a disagreement."

"Ok. What is this gentleman's last name?"

"Hollins, Alex Hollins," Vanessa said. "Actually, one of your officers was here last night, said the neighbors called the police complaining of a noise disturbance."

The officer jotted some things down on his notepad. He leaned his chin to a radio on his shoulder. "Dispatch, this is Edwards."

"Copy," a distorted voice came through the radio.

"Can we get a 1080 on Alex Hollins?"

"Roger," the voice replied.

"Do you know if Mr. Hollins ever threatened or hurt your sister?"

"No, not that I am aware of." Vanessa stopped. Her mouth went dry. "Wait, you don't think he had anything to do with this, do you?"

"I can't say, but in situations like this we need to look at all potential suspects."

Vanessa's stomach dropped, "But he loved Landon. They got along so well."

"Doesn't matter. I've seen some crazy things," the officer said. "We will have our team look into it."

The room start to spin; Vanessa leaned back against the sofa with the sudden feeling she was going to be sick.

73

Dalton used to look forward to Sundays. He got to sleep in and he typically enjoyed the services at New Zion Road. However, today he lay in bed staring at the ceiling. He had already hit snooze on the alarm twice. The shower running in the bathroom and knew his wife was getting ready.

He had grown increasingly disenfranchised with Silas, having more guilt around his role in enabling this monster. When Silas first started New Zion, he had good intentions. The early years of the church were the best. However, as the congregation grew and the money began to pour in, Silas changed. He became more controlling, more power hungry.

The biggest change came when the Senatorial debates came to Roanoke and he was asked to open them in prayer. Silas was in front of the largest audience of his life and it was televised. After that, he became increasingly interested in politics, money, and power and less interested in being a spiritual leader for his flock.

The water stopped in the bathroom. His wife came out with her hair dripping wet and a towel wrapped around her.

"Honey, you better be getting up. We are going to be late."

"I know," he said. "Just moving slow."

She grinned and stepped back into the bathroom, shortly followed by the loud blowing of her hair dryer.

His phone chirped to life on the nightstand. Rolling over her picked it up, "Blackwood here."

"Chief, we got a situation." The voice sounded shaky. "We have a potential kidnapping over on Cambridge Street. Four-year-old male."

Dalton sat straight up, now fully awake. "You sure?"

A true kidnapping had never occurred in Pinehurst. There had been plenty of false alarms and the kids were usually found later. Either they were lost in the woods or it was an attempted runaway.

"I'm pretty sure boss," the officer said. "We got the crew down here. It is at 127 Cambridge."

"Ok," Dalton said." Let me get dressed and I'll be right down."

"Ok," the officer said. "And boss, we do have a potential suspect. What do you know about Alex Hollins?"

Dalton's mouth went dry.

• • •

Dalton tried not to speed in the snowy conditions, even with chains he had to be careful. He picked up his phone and dialed Silas.

"Well Dalton, what a pleasant surprise on this Lord's Day," Silas answered. "I assume you're on the way to the Lord's house?'

"Silas, what have you done?" Dalton tried to control his anger.

"What do you mean?" Silas sounded confused.

"I mean, what have you done?" Dalton was frustrated. "Have you gone rogue on me?"

"Well Dalton, first of all, I don't have a clue what you are trying to say, and second I don't need your permission for everything I do," Silas barked. "Would you please do me the favor of enlightening me?"

"I am on my way to the Layne residence which is now the site of a possible kidnapping." Dalton paused. "I am being told that Alex Hollins is a potential suspect."

There was silence and Silas chuckled. "I knew it."

"Knew what?"

"Numbers 32:23. 'Be careful your sin will find you out.'"
Silas recited the verse with ease. "This is a much better outcome than
I could have hoped for. I knew Alex was no good and a danger to
our community. Now, a little four-year-old boy is in danger because
of this man."

Dalton listened. Had Silas glossed over the fact a child was
missing? He seemed happier that Alex might have been involved.

"Silas, I said he was a potential suspect," Dalton said. "Did
you have anything to do with this?"

Silas gasped, "Dalton, I am offended you would even
assume I was involved. I know I am not perfect, but I would never
stoop so low as to endanger the life of a child. It is insulting that you
would even go there."

"Well, if this is a kidnapping it could turn into a federal case
and this place will be a media circus. A lot of folks other than me will
be poking around, so if you know anything, now is the time to say
something."

Silence.

Dalton had struck a nerve.

"Dalton, you have my word as a man of faith that I had
nothing to do with this." Silas sounded somber. "And I hope and
pray they find the child alive and that Alex Hollins goes back to jail
for the rest of his life."

74

Silas hung up with Dalton an unsettling feeling brewing in his stomach, sweat beaded on his forehead.

He walked to the atrium where the ministry team gathered before the service began. Luther was sitting in a chair reading scripture to the team.

"Luther, may I speak with you for a moment," Silas said. "In private."

"Sure," Luther said. He handed his Bible to an elderly gentleman sitting next to him.

Silas walked him back to his office and shut the large wooden door.

"Something urgent has come up and I need you to take me out to the Boone brethren's home."

Luther's face grew pale. "But...but Silas, what about the service, it starts in less than fifteen minutes."

"That is the least of my worries," Silas said, "Have one of the deacons cover for me. Tell the congregation we got called to the hospital for a sick member."

"What about the sermon?" Luther grew more confused.

"They can improvise," Silas said, "They can have testimony time for all I care; I just need to get out of here soon."

"Well....I...." Luther stammered

"Listen, figure it out. We have to go," Silas started to leave his office, "I'll meet you at your car."

"Is everything okay?"

"No."

Silas turned and stormed out of his office. His heart pounding. He kept replaying his conversation with Zeke Boone.

"Shake her up a little,"

He was fearful Zeke had interpreted that a too liberally.

Making his way into the parking lot, nearly slipping on a patch of ice, his leather loaders were no match for the weather. He made it to his way to Luther's Towncar.

Grabbing his phone he dialed Zeke's number. It rang several times, then Zeke's familiar voice came on. "It's me, you know what to do."

"Zeke, it's Silas. Call me as soon as you get this message!"

Silas tried to control the anger in his voice, but in his gut, he knew the Boone brothers were involved in the disappearance of Layne boy. They were unstable and this was the worst-case scenario. Silas didn't need the state police or FBI snooping around Pinehurst.

The familiar tune of Dueling Banjos resonated from his phone, Zeke's number flashed cross the display.

"Zeke," he clenched his jaws together. "Please tell me you didn't have anything to do with that missing child."

"Well, good morning to you as well pastor," Zeke laughed.

"Zeke, I am losing my patience with you."

There was a gruff laugh. "Boss, you know I can't lie to a preacher."

"Zeke! What the hell were you thinking!" Silas screamed. "I told you to shake her up a little bit, not take her child! Do you know what this does to both of us?"

Zeke laughed again. Silas assumed he was high, which made the situation worse. He and Eddie were probably strung out with a young child roaming around their trailer. No telling what the kid could get into.

"Boss, you don't give me near enough credit," Zeke said. "Me and Eddie have thought this out. We snatched the kid, that shakes her up real good. Then we ask for a ransom, you come riding in like some damn her and set up the swap. You return the kid unharmed, we grab the cash, split it even. You look like a hero and Pinehurst goes back to normal.

Silas remained silent.

"Zeke, you are a bigger idiot than I could ever imagine!" Silas yelled. "Do you realize that with a possible kidnapping, the sheriff is now going to involve the state police?"

Silence except for the heavy sound of Zeke's breathing into the phone.

"We are going to have state troopers, reporters and rubberneckers all over here in less than eight hours."

More silence.

"I hope you know you are not the first person who has tried this," Silas continued. "It doesn't work. I have no influence over the state police. If Dalton drags his feet, Harper Layne is going to have all of Pinehurst in an uproar demanding justice for her missing son."

"Uh....I....guess...we didn't think...."

"That's right, you didn't think. Period." Silas's voice began to crack, "I cannot protect you on this one. I hope you enjoy prison because when it comes to your story versus mine, I know who they going to believe!"

"We will take him back." Zeke sounded scared.

"What, are you just going to knock on her door and say here is your child?" Silas laughed. "That place will be a madhouse. Guess who suspect number one will be the minute you show up with the kid?"

"Maybe we could drop him off a few streets back and tell him to go home?"

"Zeke, your ideas are getting worse by the minute."

"Sounds like we screwed up."

"Yes, you did," Silas said. "Don't do anything. I'll be up

shortly and maybe we can figure out how to fix this colossal mess you created."

75

Alex woke up in the stiff chair besides his mother's bed; his neck
bent uncomfortably against the glass divider. Easing his neck upright
sent pain knifing through his spine. Looking over at his mom, resting
quietly, the ventilator causing a steady rhythmic rise and fall of her
chest. The gritty taste in his mouth let him know he had been asleep
longer than he intended.

Standing slowly, he walked to the head of his mother's bed.
Despite all the medical contraptions keeping her alive, she looked
peaceful. This was probably the most peace she'd had in years. He
slowly stroked her white hair, tarnished by a slight yellowish hue,
compliments of all the years she had smoked. His phone vibrated in
his pocket.

It was Harper.

He wasn't sure if he wanted to talk with her, but he couldn't
ignore her forever.

"Hey there."

He was met with an immediate blood-curdling scream,
"Where is he?!"

"You son of a bitch! I trusted you!"

"Harper...Harper...calm down...what's wrong?"

"Don't tell me to calm down! Where is Landon!"

Alex grew concerned, "Harper, is Landon, okay?"

"He is gone! You took him!"

"Harper, I don't know what you are talking about! I don't have Landon, I promise."

"Why should I believe you? I knew I shouldn't have trusted you from the first day I met you!"

Her words hit him like a hammer deep in his stomach. A wave of nausea passed over him.

"Harper, I am at the hospital with my mom, I swear I don't know anything about Landon."

The phone went dead.

"Harper! Harper!"

He dialed her number again and it went straight to voicemail.

Alex panicked.

What had happened to Landon?

Looking around the room he found the remote for the cheap flat-screen TV suspended against the wall. Turning it on he quickly found the local news station.

A young African American reporter with a microphone in her hand stood in front of Vanessa's house. She wore a station branded blue winter jacket and a pink toboggan covered her hair. A red breaking news banner scrolled continuously beneath her with the words AMBER ALERT, Four-Year-Old Male, Landon Layne, last seen 127 Cambridge Street. The scene behind her looked straight out of a crime show. Two police cars were in the driveway with their lights flashing. A couple of police officers with dogs walked methodically through the deep snow.

"Kara, all we know as of now is that four-year-old Landon Layne was playing in the snow with his aunt. She stepped inside to get her phone and when she came out, he was gone. All that was left was a scarf he was wearing."

The screen switched to a recent picture of Landon and Harper standing in front of a Christmas tree. Landon clutching pupster close to his chest his characteristic grin spread across his face.

Alex's legs became weak and he fell back into the chair with his eyes fixed on the television.

"Police made a rapid response to the house, but so far there have been no signs of the child. I spoke briefly with Pinehurst Sheriff Dalton Blackwood earlier."

The screen transitioned to Dalton's familiar face. "Emily, all I can say now is we have every resource on this case and we have reached out to the Virginia State Police for their assistance."

"So, you are classifying this as a kidnapping?"

"Well, we are still very early in the situation, thanks to Miss Layne alerting us promptly. And with the rapid response of my men, not a lot of time has passed since the child was last seen."

"So, he may just be lost?"

"Well, that is one scenario. We are concerned about the child's safety in this weather. Time is of the essence."

"Does anything lead you to believe it could be a kidnapping?"

"I'm sorry, I can't comment on that at this point." Dalton turned to the camera. "However, we do have a person of interest we would like to question regarding the disappearance of the child."

The dated mugshot of Alex Hollins appeared on the screen.

"Alex Hollins was last seen with the child's mother before the child disappeared. We are asking anyone who may know his whereabouts to contact our office. We would also strongly advise you do not approach him as we do not know if he is armed."

"Thank you, sheriff. Back to you Kara."

Alex ran to the small sink in the room and emptied his stomach contents. Wiping his mouth with the back of one hand, he grabbed the remote and turned the TV off.

Across the hall at the nurse's station, a small crowd of had gathered around a security guard. Someone was pointing towards his mother's room.

Alex panicked.

He looked back at his mom.

Thick as thieves.

He couldn't go back to jail, there was no way he could prove he was innocent.

Leaning over his mom he gently kissed her forehead.

"I love you, Mom. I'll be back, I promise."

The crowd had grown at the nurse's station. Alex stepped out of his mother's room, aware of the number of eyes on him. He made his way toward the exit.

"Wait, Mr. Hollins," a deep voice call from behind him.

Alex ran.

Charging down the drab beige hallway the cream-colored tiles reflecting the yellow, fluorescent light off them, creating the illusion of launching down a runway.

"Stop!" a voice called out behind him.

He had seen the size of the security guard and knew he was in no danger of being caught. He remembered seeing a sign for an emergency exit down the hallway from the elevator.

The overhead paging system buzzed on. "Code Silver, Code Silver, Code Silver!"

Alex didn't know what that meant but had an idea it was directed at him. He approached the door, pulled it open, and lunged into the stairwell. Charging down the steps, each footfall echoing of the cinderblock walls. Taking two or three steps at a time, he made it down several flights before the door open above him.

"Stop!!" The static of a walkie talkie echoed, "He is headed down the east stairs."

Alex didn't know why he was running. He was innocent, but there was a missing child and the court of public opinion in this town was strong.

The last flight of stairs ended with a door to the left. Big black letters read, Emergency Exit: Alarm will sound.

Alex pushed the door handle and a piercing alarm sounded burrowing deep into his brain. The door led him out into a large, covered area where a single ambulance was parked, its engine still running. Another security guard spotted him and ran towards him, struggling to pull some pepper spray from his utility belt.

"Stop right there!"

Alex, recognizing he didn't have any time to hang around, ran straight across the asphalt into a grassy area with a large helipad off to the left. In the distance, sirens wailed. A large section of forest backed up against the parking lot. If he could make it into the woods, he was pretty sure he could shake the rent-a-cops from the hospital.

He ran towards the parking lot as the shouting continued behind him. Some Bucks County sheriff cars had pulled into the hospital with lights blazing.

Word's out.

The parking lot was fairly empty for a Sunday morning. He zig-zagged among the few cars and soon was at the back side of the parking lot. He slid down a small snow covered hill that led into the woods.

He ran until his lungs were on fire, steam pouring off him like he had stepped out of a sauna. Looking over his shoulder he didn't see anyone pursuing him.

Collapsing into the cold snow he tried catching his breath. Every muscle ached like they were full of acid. His heart pounded so hard his eyes pulsed with each beat.

76

Harper hurled her phone into the darkness. It struck the wall with a sharp crack before skidding across the floor. Her eyes stung, raw from hours of tears. The recent emotional storm had exhausted her, shock, rage, despair all giving way to the heaviest feeling: shame.

How could I be so stupid?

Alex was a criminal. He could manipulate. The fact he might have Landon sent a chill down her spine. Her baby, alone with a monster. A monster she had tried to convince him wasn't real every night before bed.

Maybe Vanessa was right. I have a defective screening mechanism for men. Now it hasn't just impacted me, but potentially Landon.

She should not have called Alex. If the cops found out they would probably be upset. She had clued him in and this would only encourage him to run further, with her baby.

Sitting up in bed she started crying. Landon's tattered stuffed puppy dog lay next to her. She brought it to her nose and took a deep breath in. The familiar scent of her son flooded her nostrils, bringing back memories of bedtimes, bath times, and him giggling as he ran around the house.

A gentle knock on the door broke Harper out of her spiral. A crack of light spilled into the room as the door eased open.

"Harper," Vanessa's familiar voice called out, "I brought you some chamomile tea."

"Go away!" Harper screamed, "I hate you!! This is all your fault!!"

Vanessa paused in the doorway.

"You were always jealous that I had a kid and you didn't," Harper continued, "I trusted you with Landon, why didn't you bring him in with you!!"

Vanessa eased into the room; her figure silhouetted by the hall light. She made her way to the bed and sat on the corner.

"Harper, I am so sorry," Vanesa's voice cracked, "You have every right to be upset with me. I am still kicking myself for what happened. But you have to believe me that I would never have intentionally put Landon at harm."

Harper curled herself into a ball, sobbing.

Vanessa rubbed her sisters back, "I'm so sorry!"

They sat in silence for a while.

"You ready for your tea?" Vanessa asked.

Harper nodded and sat up as Vanessa handed her the steaming cup of tea.

"Be careful, it's hot."

Harper carefully wrapped both hands around the cup and took it. "Thanks."

Harper blew on the cup. "Any update?"

"No. I gave the police some of his clothes so the dogs could get his scent." Vanessa scooted closer to Harper. "They are combing the neighborhood now. They did notice some large footprints in the snow leading into the yard."

"Any word on Alex?"

"No. The news is running a breaking news piece with his picture," Vanessa said. "Has he reached out to you?"

"No, I have not heard from him." Harper lied, more out of embarrassment than anything.

"Listen, the police think it would be helpful if you went on the news and made a public appeal asking whoever took Landon to bring him back."

"I can't," Harper cried.

Vanessa leaned in and wrapped her arms around Harper.

"Sis, I know it's hard. I can't even imagine. It's hard enough for me. Landon was like a son to me." Vanessa squeezed Harper. "We need to be strong for Landon. That means we have to do hard things."

"I…can't…" Harper choked out the words.

Harper never imagined she would be in this situation. One of those parents whose face were broadcast all over the nation, making a tearful plea for the return of their child. This was surreal.

How was this happening to her?

How had her life fallen apart over the past couple of years?

"Yes, you can," Vanessa said. "Harper Layne, you can do hard things for Landon."

Harper leaned her face into her sister's dark black hair, and the familiar floral scent of her shampoo met her.

"Why do I even need to do this, when we know it was Alex?"

"Alex is a strong suspect, but you don't know for sure it was him," Vanessa said. "Also, maybe he will see it and respond."

Harper sat in silence. She took a slow sip of the tea; the sweet warm liquid soothed her soul.

"Ok…I'll do it…on one condition."

"Sure, anything…"

"I want you beside me."

"Oh, Harper…." Vanessa leaned in and pulled Harper tight up against her. "I would not let you do this alone."

77

Alex's entire body ached. His shoes were soaked and his wet pants suctioned to his legs like a second skin. His bare hands were numb, but he kept trudging through the barren, snow covered forest.

He did not know where he was going, just trying to put enough distance between him and the hospital. He had spent a lot of time in these woods surrounding Pinehurst as a kid so at least he was in somewhat familiar territory.

Fractals of the light blue sky peaked between the bare trees overhead; the occasional flicker of warmth struck his face. Lifeless trees shot up from the ground like arthritic fingers as the skeletal underbrush grabbed at his legs with every step. Even with no leaves, the trees still managed to keep out most of the warming rays of the sun. He grabbed a handful of snow and pushed it into his mouth trying to quench his thirst.

How had it come to this?

Hot tears streamed down his face, warming his icy cheeks.

After spending twenty-five years in jail, the thought of potentially going back was devastating. He had gotten used to the freedom. Coming and going as he pleased. Eating when he wanted. He was innocent, but who would believe him?

Emory.

Emory knew he wouldn't take a kid. He pulled his phone out of his pocket. The battery indicated he had about twenty percent charge left and he had a decent signal.

He scrolled to Emory's number and pressed dial.

The phone rang.

Alex grew nervous after the fourth ring when Emory answered.

"Alex, where are you?" Emory sounded uneasy, "Have you seen the news? Please tell me you are not involved."

"Emory, I swear I had nothing to do with it. I don't know who, but it wasn't me."

"Alex, the whole situation looks bad. Particularly with your history."

"I know, Emory, but I would never take a child. I loved Landon." Alex's voice cracked. "I made bad choices in the past and I have paid the price for those. I will never be able to outrun that shadow. But Emory, I have no desire to create more shadows."

The phone was silent.

"I believe you Alex," Emory said, "What can I do?"

Relief washed over Alex. Knowing one person believed him gave him the energy to keep going.

"Have the police or anyone come by your house looking for me?"

"No, I haven't seen anyone. Although you are getting popular. Some of the national outlets have picked up the story. Your face is all over the news. By the way, your mugshot is not very flattering."

Alex laughed. "Well, it wasn't exactly my best day."

"I'll give you that."

"Emory, I know this is asking a lot, but can I crash at your place until I figure out what to do?"

Emory hesitated. "....I mean…sure…but wouldn't it be best to go to the police and tell your story?"

"Emory, you know how that will end. Silas has the department in his back pocket. No one is going to believe me," Alex said. "I wouldn't be surprised if Silas is involved and trying to frame me for this whole thing."

"That is a mighty big assumption," Emory said. "Is it one you're willing to risk your freedom for?"

"I am," Alex said. "And honestly, I don't know any other options. It is on me to prove my innocence. I am not sure this is a situation even your God can get me out of."

"Alex…." Emory sounded hurt.

Alex didn't say anything.

"Alex?"

"Just a lot to process," Alex said.

"Alex, you can come over, just please be careful," Emory said. "I'm too old to end up in jail for aiding and abetting a criminal."

"Thanks, Emory."

78

Vanessa looked out the window into her front yard. It looked like a scene from a movie. Reporters and cameramen crowded in a semicircle around the front steps. Media vans from all the local news stations lined the street. Police had created a border with orange wooden sawhorses along the front yard to keep the spectators at bay. Harper could not understand why people would want to witness someone else's darkest moment. A small crowd had already gathered behind the barrier, some of the people were holding up their phones, probably live streaming or something. Everyone hoping for their viral fifteen minutes of fame.

Vanessa stepped beside her sister, hooking her arm and pulling her close. "You ready sis?"

Harper nodded.

Vanessa looked at Dalton. He pressed open the front door and the three of them stepped into the brisk winter morning and walked down the steps.

They stood in front of the gathered crowd as silence filtered its way to the back. A makeshift podium with numerous microphones reaching up like tentacles stood on the sidewalk.

"Good morning," Dalton said, stepping up to the podium. "My name is Dalton Blackwood and I am the Sheriff here in Pinehurst. At approximately 9:30 am we received a call concerning a missing child. Four-year-old Landon Layne was last seen by his Aunt Vanessa Layne, playing in the front yard of this residence."

Dalton paused and pointed to his left where the snowman stood with Landon's footprints in the snow still circling it.

"My office responded and we now have placed several K-9 units on the search. We have officers going door to door questioning neighbors." Dalton paused. "We are asking anyone who may have information about the child's whereabouts to please contact our office at 1-540-962-1920," Dalton continued, "As you have seen on the news, we do have one person of interest by the name of Alex Hollins. We ask that if anyone has any information on his whereabouts to please contact our office. We are asking you do not approach him as he is presumed to be armed and dangerous."

Some murmurs went across the crowd.

"I have asked Landon's mother, Harper, to give a brief statement." Dalton looked at Harper.

Harper froze. Vanessa gave her a gentle tug as Harper stepped to the nest of microphones.

"I...am...begging whoever took my baby please.... please...bring him back." Her voice cracked and Vanessa pulled her in tighter.

"Landon is an innocent child. If this was meant to hurt me...please don't make him pay for it. I'm begging you, keep my baby safe."

Tears streamed down Harper's face.

"Alex...if you have Landon...he loved you. Why would you do this?" Her voice broke again, "Don't punish him because of me. I'm sorry..."

The audience remained silent. Harper wiped her eyes with the back of her gloved hands.

"And Lando.... mommy loves you. Stay brave for me and Auntie Van!"

Harper began sobbing and folded into Vanessa's arms. Dalton's firm hand pressed on her back, gently directing them to the side.

Dalton stepped up to the microphones. "We plan on having another update around 5:00 pm or sooner should there be further developments. There will be no questions at this time."

79

Zeke was furious he had let Silas talk to him that way. He and Eddie had done what they were asked. Sure, he had improvised a little, but it created a win-win situation for everyone.

Walking out of his bedroom in the back of the trailer down a narrow hallway that smelled like mold, the sounds of a kid crying came from the living room. Stepping into the kitchen area, his jaw tightened. The kid had not stopped crying since they took him. Stepping into the living room, Eddie was trying to adjust the antenna on top of their old model tube television.

"Zeke, I can't make him shut up and it's driving me crazy!" Eddie had a look of panic in his eyes. "I'm trying to find him something on TV." Eddie pulled on the antenna again trying to make an image appear on the snowy screen.

Landon sat on the sofa wailing, "I want my mama!"

Zeke opened the refrigerator and found an unopened can of Pepsi. He was pretty sure kids could have Pepsi. He grabbed the drink and walked to the couch, sitting down beside Landon who jumped away from him.

Reflexively, Zeke reached out and grabbed the boy's leg.

"Ouch! You're hurting me!" Landon screamed.

Zeke took his large hand and placed it firmly over the kid's mouth. "Listen, this crying is not helping you, not helping me, it's not helping anyone."

Landon looked petrified, tears rolling out of his eyes onto Zeke's hand.

"We are trying to help you. If you want to see your mom again the best thing you can do is be quiet." Zeke slowly slid his hand off Landon's mouth. "OK?"

Landon sniffled, nodded, wiping the tears from his eyes. His blonde hair was damp with sweat.

"Now I got you a nice cold Pepsi here." Zeke pulled the tab back and a hiss escaped as he opened the can. "You go ahead and sip on this. Eddie is trying to find something fun for you to watch on TV."

Landon grabbed the cold can and took a sip.

"Taste good?" Zeke asked.

Landon nodded his head.

"Cat got your tongue? Where are your manners?"

"Yes...sir..." Landon's voice quivered.

"You like dogs?"

Landon's eye brightened for a moment and he nodded.

"We have a dog," Zeke said. "Maybe if you are good, we will let you see him. OK?"

Landon nodded again.

"Yes!" Eddie exclaimed as a black and white cartoon came on the screen.

Landon's eyes drifted to the animated rabbit on the screen currently being chased by a goofy looking dog. He sat transfixed, drinking his soda. For the first time since they brought the boy home, Zeke and Eddie enjoyed some silence.

80

Sitting in the front seat, Silas tried to keep it together as Luther navigated the large Lincoln Town Car down the snowy back road that led to the Boone boys' home. He had escalated past the point of being furious and sat in silence.

"Silas, you still haven't told me what's going on," Luther said, keeping his eyes on the road. The sun had started warm the road turning the ice into a messy slush.

Silas remained quiet.

"I mean, I've known you for a long time Silas and you know I would do anything for you. It's just I don't want to get myself in a bad spot. Nothing good ever comes out of going down this road."

Silas regretted ever getting the Boones involved in doing his dirty work. Their family tree did not have many branches and intelligence was not a strong suit. He had always worried something would go south. He also knew having Dalton in his back pocket could right most wrongs. He never expected a kidnapping though.

"Luther, do you trust me?" Silas broke his silence.

"Sure boss!" Luther said. "Just curious more than anything."

"Then shut up and keep driving."

Silas had to figure a way out of this one.

Pinning it on Alex made the most sense, he needed to do it in a way that would keep Dalton out of the loop.

Soon they rounded the corner and the Boone's rusted tan mobile home came into view. A stream of smoke rose from the chimney. A truck conspicuously free of snow sat in the front yard. A small, fenced pen behind the house held a tattered doghouse and Silas saw two eyes peering out from inside.

I guess Cujo doesn't like the snow.

"Stay here," Silas said to Luther.

Luther looked straight ahead, his face red and jaw tensed.

Silas wedged his large abdomen out of the front seat and made his way to the stoop on the side of the trailer. He was still in his church clothes and his leather dress shoes made navigating in the melting snow problematic.

His breathing was heavy as he managed to make his way up the three steps that led to the front door. He pounded hard on the door with the side of a pudgy hand.

"Zeke, open up, it's Silas!"

Up tempo, big band music blared from inside the trailer and soon the giggle of a child. The door opened, startling Silas.

"Howdy Pastor!" Zeke said, stepping out from behind the door.

Silas pushed his way in, barely squeezing between the door and Zeke.

"Come on in," Zeke laughed as he closed the door.

Silas looked in the living room where Landon Layne was laying on the couch a soda in his hand, watching television. Eddie Boone sat next to him equally transfixed by the cartoon characters running across the screen.

Silas could not believe they had actually done it.

"Unbelievable," Silas muttered.

"I know!" Zeke said, like a proud parent.

"No, I mean, this was an unbelievably stupid decision on your part."

Silas pushed a forefinger into Zeke's chest, sending him a few steps back. "And you are going to have to fix it."

Zeke grabbed Silas's hand, a look of anger on his face. "No, I was following your orders, so we are going to have to fix it."

Silas's face turned red. While mentally he had the upper hand, physically he was no match for Zeke and Eddie. A wide grin grew across Silas' face. "Zeke, I'm sorry. I got a little stressed and let my emotions get the best of me. Absolutely we will figure it out."

81

The old Clapper trail wrapped its way around Misty Ridge at the south edge of Pinehurst. It was a popular spot for day hikers to climb and get a beautiful view of the Blue Ridge Valley. It also served as a geographic dividing line for Pinehurst. As a child, Alex had learned he could transport himself all over the town without ever having to take a main road.

Emory lived in Maplewood Heights, which was to the east of Wildwood. His home backed up to the edge of the forest. Alex could make it there without being seen.

Under the partial cover of the barren trees, the snow was slow to melt and Alex's pants were saturated to the point it felt like he was walking with leg weights on. He had lost the feeling in his feet a long time ago. The cold air pummeled him in his chest like a baseball bat. His reserves were running low, but he was getting close to Emory's.

Why?

That question hit Alex from nowhere.

Why was he running? What did he have to live for? No job, his mom was dying and the only person who cared for him other than her now thought he had kidnapped her son.

Prison was looking like a better alternative.

Stopping, he rested against a giant oak tree. Cold air steamed out of his mouth. Leaning over he placed his hands on his knees, trying to catch his breath.

The decision was his.

Was the little semblance of normalcy he had started to develop worth fighting for?

Was getting back beside his mom in the hospital worth fighting for?

Was Harper worth fighting for?

Was clearing his name worth fighting for?

Clarity came to him in the middle of the frozen forest. An inaudible, but subtle 'yes' echoed back to him in his mind.

He pressed on.

After a while, some homes popped into view. Alex thought this was Maplewood, but wasn't sure what home was Emory's. Kneeling he crept forward, taking advantage of the cover of a few evergreens and some dead brush. He pulled out his phone and dialed Emory's number

"Hello," Emory answered

"Hey, I am in the woods behind your where you live," Alex said, "I don't know which house is yours."

"It's the one that doesn't have a fence," Emory said, "There is a tan shed in the rear corner."

Alex scanned the homes and spotted the shed, "I see it."

"I'll flick the back porch light on," Emory said.

A light blinked on beside the rear door. He could make out the faint yellow glow of light coming from a window. There was a deck that led to the door. The neighbors on both sides were spaced pretty far apart, but still, no guarantee he wouldn't be seen. Alex slowly made his way closer to Emory's backyard.

"I'm behind your house," Alex whispered. "Is your back door unlocked?"

"It is, but I'll double check," Emory said. "Be careful. I don't want the neighbors to see you."

Alex hung up. His phones battery was down to fifteen percent. Pausing, he took several deep breaths in. He debated whether he should run or walk. Either option wasn't great, anyone who saw a random man emerging out of the woods into a house would be suspicious.

Alex elected to run.

After an internal count to three, he darted through the snowy underbrush into Emory's backyard, up the three steps onto the deck. Emory pulled the back door open and Alex ran in collapsing onto the hardwood floor panting.

Emory grinned. "Well, that was exciting. Not quite James Bond level, but still, the coolest thing I've done in a while."

Alex grinned as he tried freeing himself from his waterlogged shoes suctioned to his feet.

"Well, what now?" Emory asked.

Alex looked up at Emory. He had no idea.

82

The room had descended into chaos.

"I need another Epi!" the doctor yelled from the head of the bed.

A nurse frantically performed chest compression on the frail body under his hands, the sickening crunch of bones breaking with each one.

The respiratory therapist had disconnected the patient from the ventilator and was manually bagging the patient, delivering precise, automatic breaths like she was keeping rhythm for the chaos.

Alarms chirped rapidly and randomly adding to the sense of anarchy. A small audience had gathered outside the ICU bay looking in, this included a couple of officers from the Bucks County Sheriff's office. The cardiac monitor above the left side of the bed was a scrambled mess of waveforms and readings.

"Hold compressions!" the doctor barked.

All eyes went to the monitor. The scrambled waveforms soon were replaced by a single straight line.

"Any pulse?"

"No pulse."

"Resume compressions."

The chaos resumed.

"Any luck getting the son?" the doctor asked the charge nurse.

"No, we've been trying," the nurse replied. "No next of kin either."

A chaplain stood in the corner trying to steer clear of the fight for a physical life so she could prepare for the transition to a spiritual one.

The red code cart looked like it had been ransacked by looters. Empty cardboard drug containers littered the floor around it. Yellow safety caps from syringes were flung sporadically throughout the room, plastic wrappers made it look like a morbid Christmas morning.

"How long have we been going?" the doctor asked the nurse who had been recording.

"Forty-five minutes," the nurse said.

A short objective reply with plenty of meaning.

"Anyone else have any other ideas?"

The room was silent as each member of the team focused on their lifesaving responsibility.

"Unless there are objections, I am going to call it."

Once again silence.

"Ok, let's call it."

Instantly, everyone stopped in unison and took a respectful step back from the patient. The straight line ran across the monitor with a loud steady alarm tone. The doctor stepped forward and placed two fingers on the patient's neck took his stethoscope and listened to the chest.

"Time of death?" the recorder asked.

The doctor looked up at the large digital clock in the room, "1445."

"Thanks, everyone," he said, looking around the room. "Good work."

He looked up at the charge nurse. "We need to get a hold of the son."

She nodded.

And with that, Nancy Hollins ended a life full of sorrow, disappointment, and heartache.

83

Emory lent Alex an old pair of sweatpants and a T-shirt. They were a little on the roomy side but much better than the cold wet mess he was wearing.

Alex had stretched out on the couch in Emory's basement. It was straight out of the 70s with its mustard yellow and orange patterned velour upholstery. A wood stove burning in the corner made the basement oppressively warm. The scent of the burning wood took Alex back to his childhood and the chores of having to split wood and load the stove. Despite the heat, Alex was still slow to warm up.

Soon footsteps were coming down the stairs.

"Your clothes were soaked," Emory said, stepping through the door into the finished side of the basement. "I'm surprised you haven't started to work on frostbite."

Alex grinned." I am starting to get some feeling back in my toes, thankfully!"

"I threw your clothes in the dryer. They might take an hour or so to dry."

"Thanks, Emory," Alex said. "I know this is putting you in an awkward position and I appreciate you helping me out."

"Don't mention it," Emory said, sitting down in a recliner. "So, what's your plan?"

Alex stayed silent for a moment, staring up at the white popcorn ceiling.

"I don't know," he finally said. "As you can see, I don't have Landon. I have no idea where he is. I can't help but think Silas is behind all this."

"I know Silas is not the most honest person, but I can't imagine he would stoop so low as to kidnap a child."

"Hate can make you do irrational things," Alex said. "Trust me, prison cells are full of examples."

"True," Emory said, "But I just can't see it."

"Unless he put someone else up to it?" Alex said. "What about those Boone brothers?"

"I guess it's possible," Emory said. "I mean, they are not the smartest tools in the shed. It would be a stretch, but not impossible to consider that they are behind this."

Alex spent the rest of the morning recovering and thinking about his next steps. Emory prepared them a lunch of tomato soup and grilled ham and cheese. He grabbed a couple of TV trays, sat them up in the basement and turned on the television. They were met with an image of Alex's mugshot.

"Hollins was seen Saturday night on Cambridge Ave. leaving the house of Vanessa Layne," a smooth female voice narrated. "Today, security officers at Pinehurst Memorial were involved in a foot pursuit with Mr. Hollins and he was last seen entering the National Forest behind the hospital. Police still have no leads and want to remind the public that Hollins should be considered armed and dangerous."

Emory turned off the TV.

"Well, I lost my appetite," Alex said.

"I'm sorry," Emory said. "You have to eat, though."

"I know."

Seeing that mugshot pulled a scab off a twenty-five-year wound he had been trying to heal. It hurt thinking people in this community still thought he was some kind of monster. Pushing the wooden TV tray away he sat back on the sofa.

He must have dozed off. When he awoke the TV trays were gone and it had started to get dark outside. Emory was passed out in a recliner. Alex stood and stretched. He walked to the end table where his phone had been charging.

He unplugged it and turned it back on. A series of missed call notifications flooded the screen. There were also several voicemails. He didn't recognize the numbers but figured they were likely the police trying to track him down, but there were no more calls from Harper.

He went to his messages and hit play on the most recent message.

"Alex, this is Dr. Horton. I need you to call me as soon as you get this message about your mother. It is important that you call me. You can call 200-2278 which is the intensive care unit. The staff can get me."

Alex's mouth went dry, and his hand shook as he tried to dial the number to the unit.

After a few rings a hurried, distracted voice picked up the phone, "Intensive Care Unit."

"Uh…yes…this is Alex Hollins…I was returning a call for Dr. Horton."

The line went silent, followed by a brisk, "Hold please."

The canned hold music went on for an eternity. Alex's stomach churned.

The music abruptly ended and a male voice picked up, "Mr. Hollins?"

"Yes."

"I'm Dr. Horton, one of the critical care doctors here. About an hour ago your mother went into cardiac arrest. We tried to resuscitate her but were not able to. Unfortunately, despite our best efforts, she passed away. I'm sorry."

The world closed in around him.

His vision was now a tunnel.

His respiration grew rapid.

"Mr. Hollins.?"

Alex tried to speak but couldn't. His throat constricted as the tears came. Sobbing, he dropped the phone and slid to the floor, covering his face with his hands.

Emory, now awake, ran to him.

"Alex?" Emory said, retrieving the phone. "Hello?"

"Who is this?" Dr. Horton asked.

"This is a friend," Emory said wise enough to not say his name. "Is everything okay?"

"I was letting Mr. Hollins know his mother passed away. I am sorry."

"Oh." Emory was shocked. "That is awful. I am sorry to hear that."

"We can keep her body in the unit for a couple of hours. He certainly is welcome to come to view her body here. We also need him to sign some paperwork."

"Understand."

"I also know this is not an optimal time for him." Dr. Horton paused. "There is a police officer here who would like to speak with him when he arrives."

Emory looked at Alex, now curled up in a fetal position on the floor sobbing.

"I don't think he is in any frame of mind to talk to anyone," Emory said. "Am I able to talk to the officer?"

"Hold on."

The muffled sound of people talking and then a brusque voice spoke, "This is Officer Carter, Bucks County Sheriff. Are you aware that Alex Hollins is wanted for questioning related to the disappearance of Landon Layne?"

"Yes, I saw it on the news."

"You are aware of his past criminal record." It was not a question.

"Yes, I knew about that."

"If you know his whereabouts, you can be charged with aiding and abetting a criminal. I suggest you tell me your location."

"Officer, with all due respect, I am seventy-two years old and this is the most excitement I have had in my life," Emory raised his finger, "This man has just lost his mother. He has been on the run for twenty-four hours. I am not about to tell you where he is so you   can   go   and   lock   him   up."

The line was silent.

"Are you prepared to go to jail then?"

"I am prepared to do what is right."

The office huffed on the phone.

"I will talk to him. I am sure he would like to see his mother before she goes to the funeral home."

"Well, if that is the case, let him know he will be leaving the hospital in handcuffs," the officer shot back in frustration.

"What happened to innocent until proven guilty?"

"Sir, we have a missing child, time is of the essence, this is not the time for a debate."

Emory hung up.

He knelt next to Alex and placed a gentle hand on his shoulder.

"I'm sorry, Alex."

• • •

Alex was racked with grief and guilt. He had let so many people down in his lifetime. Now he wasn't even able to be with his mother during her final breaths, because his past continued to haunt him.

He had to see her.

He could not let her lay there alone, in that hospital bed. However, this meant going back to jail, possibly for the rest of his life, but he was tired.

Tired of running from people.

Tired of running from his past.

Tired of isolation.

"I need to go," Alex said.

Emory looked down at him. "I understand, but you know what this means."

Alex's voice cracked. "I know."

Alex stood and the room spun. The whole situation didn't feel real.

"I'll go check your clothes," Emory said.

Alex nodded. His heart ached. Tears rolled down his face.

His mom was not perfect. She hadn't had an easy life, but she didn't deserve to die alone. She had spent most of her adult life alone. No husband, no son, no grandchildren.

She had been faithful to visit Alex every week while he was in prison. He owed the same respect to her, knowing what this likely meant for him.

"Here you go," Emory said, coming down the stairs holding a pile of laundry.

He handed it to Alex. The smell of fresh laundry was comforting along with the warmth of clothes straight out of the dryer.

"I'll step out and let you get dressed, we can leave whenever you are ready."

"Emory, you don't have to take me," Alex said. "I don't want to pull you into my mess."

"Nonsense! We are partners in crime," Emory said. "The two musketeers! All for one and one for all."

Alex grinned.

"Maybe we can even be cellmates," Emory said. "You can show me the ropes."

"Let's hope it doesn't come to that."

84

Silas stared at Zeke. The Boone boys had been nothing but a headache since he had begun working with them. Unfortunately, they knew too much at this point, although he was not sure how reliable they'd be as witnesses if it ever came to that. His word versus theirs, would be an easy battle to win.

Silas turned and looked at the boy sitting on the couch, whimpering, but transfixed by cartoons on tv.

His jaw tightened. He still could not fathom the stupidity of this move.

"What's your plan?" Silas asked no one in particular.

"Well, Eddie still has his burner cell phone from a prior job," Zeke said, "We would call the cops and say we had the kid, we wanted a ransom, and we would only work through you."

Silas stayed silent.

"Then we would ask for five hundred thousand dollars," Zeke continued, "We demand that you come by yourself. We leave the kid. You drop off the money and take the kid."

Silas groaned.

"And what's stopping me from taking the kid and the money?" Silas asked, "If you all are not there, I could just keep the money."

Zeke had a dumb look on his face.

"Well, I guess I hadn't thought about that part," Zeke looked perplexed, "If you go by yourself then Eddie or I could meet you and make the exchange. You could tell them we had a mask on or something?"

"Zeke, first of all, they are not going to let me go alone. Second, why don't you just wear a mask to begin with?"

"That's a good point," Zeke said.

"I know it's a good point," Silas said, "because I still have functioning brain cells that have not been destroyed by whatever drug of the week you and your inbred brother decide to put in your body!!"

Silas turned back around toward Zeke and pointed a lone finger right at his face. "This is the most ill-conceived, idiotic plan I have ever heard. You must have the mental capacity of a one-year-old to decide something like this. You have placed all of us in jeopardy."

Silas's voice continued to rise, "You don't have the sense of a damn rock and can hardly decide what to wear each day, much less concoct an elaborate criminal scheme!"

Silas stepped back from Zeke, his hands on his hips, "I regret ever getting involved with low-brow, mouth breathing hicks like yo…"

The crack of the gunshot shattered the silence like a sledgehammer through glass.

Silas jerked forward, his body seizing as a bullet slammed into his back, just below the shoulder blade. It punched clean through, ripping out through his left chest in a spray of blood and torn fabric.

For a moment, he stood there frozen, blinking, like his mind hadn't caught up to what had just happened. Then came the sound: a wet, sucking gasp as air fought to fill the lung that was no longer whole.

He staggered. One step. Two.

His legs gave out.

He hit the floor hard, face twisted in shock and pain, gasping like a man drowning in open air. Blood pooled beneath him, bubbling with each breath, slicking his shirt and smearing across the cracked linoleum.

His hand clawed weakly at the floor, trying to push himself up. Trying to speak. But all that came out was a thick, gurgled moan.

Alive. Barely.

His body racked with more pain than he had ever known as the world around him began to fade away.

• • •   ·

Zeke screamed, his face dripping with blood.

Eddie stood in the living room holding his bolt action Remmington rifle to his shoulder. A small tendril of smoke rose from the tip of the gun.

Landon sat on the couch grabbing his ears and screaming, "My ears!! My Ears!!" He buried his face into the sofa cushions as a puddle of liquid formed around his legs.

"Eddie, what the fuck?" Zeke said, spitting blood from his mouth.

"I couldn't stand it no more," Eddie said. "I couldn't let him stand there and disrespect you like that. I'm tired of him bullying us around."

"Eddie, you could have killed me!" Zeke said, a look of panic on his face.

He was surprised at how fast this situation was going south. From a kidnapping to possible murder this was not how he had expected this to play out. Maybe Silas was right, maybe he wasn't too bright.

"What was I supposed to do? Let him sit there and trash talk you? It never was gonna get any better. He was always going to talk down to us. We never got no respect from him."

Zeke stood in shock. He walked to the kitchen sink, half full of dirty dishes. Turning on the water he began rinsing off the warm, sticky organic matter from his face.

"Right Zeke?" Eddie's speech was pressured, "Ain't no holier than thou poor excuse for a preacher gonna insult us when all we trying to do is help him out, right Zeke? Right?"

Zeke grabbed some paper towels and dabbed his face. Smears of red highlighted the paper. He looked down at the body of Silas, a large pool of crimson now surrounded him. A harsh gurgling sound bubbling out from his mouth.

Zeke couldn't tell if he was dead or severely wounded. In any case they now had a bigger mess on their hands.

Landon continued screaming on the sofa with his eyes closed and hands over his ears.

"Zeke, you alright? I mean, you got me nervous not talking and everything. We're good, right? You would have done the same thing for me right?"

Zeke had committed a lot of crimes in his day. Most of them were small to medium stuff, theft, drugs, and occasional assault. Silas had made sure he got off every time, now who was going to bail them out.

The acidic taste of bile rose in the back of his throat and he spun around and vomited into the sink. He continued heaving until his chest and stomach were both on fire. The only redeeming factor was that he was sober and had a clear head because things just got complicated.

85

Luther sat in the Lincoln drumming his fingers nervously on the steering wheel. Silas had been in there a while. Internally, he struggled with whether he should go check on him. His decision to stay put was made partly by the fact he had not seen that beast of a dog. He was still in his church clothes and in no shape to tangle with the canine.

His debate was interrupted by a loud bang echoing from inside the trailer. It sounded like when he was a kid and dropped fireworks into an empty soda can.

A gunshot.

Fully alert now, his eyes fixed on the trailer.

"Silas…." he whispered.

Without thinking he threw the car in reverse and floored it. The rear of the car fishtailed on the wet snow, throwing snow and mud everywhere. Cutting the wheel sharply to the right he straightened the car out, shifted it into drive, and gunned it. The car found every rock and hole hidden by the snow. Luther jerked and bounced as he stayed focused on the road ahead. In no time though, he burst onto the main road the car skidding hard to the left as the tires contacted wet asphalt.

Luther fumbled with his phone as he tried dialing 911. He kept messing up but eventually got his pudgy fingers to cooperate.

"911, what is your emergency?" a young female voice said.

"I need to report a potential shooting." Luther caught himself screaming.

"Ok, sir, please try to calm down," the lady said. "Where did you witness the shooting?"

"Well, I didn't witness it. I just heard what sounded like a gunshot," Luther stammered. "Off State Road 22. I don't know the address, but there is a trailer at the end of the road. It is the Boone place."

"OK. We will get some units out there," she said. "Are you injured?"

"No, but I am driving away as fast as I can."

"OK, when you get to a safe spot, pull over to the side of the road and turn your hazard lights on. What kind of car are you in?"

"I'm in a silver Lincoln Town Car," Luther said, easing off the gas. "I'll pull over to the shoulder."

"Ok," she said. "A unit has already been dispatched."

"Thank you."

"You're welcome." The voice said, "Stay in your vehicle until the units arrive."

"Ok," Luther could hardly catch his breath.

In the distance a lone siren wailed, rapid response times were one of the benefits of living in a small town. Despite the cold weather outside he was drenched in sweat. His chest had an elephant sitting squarely between his breasts. He rubbed it, trying to ease the pain.

The siren grew closer.

He closed his eyes and took a deep breath in, leaning his head back.

86

"Are you sure you want to do this?" Emory asked.

"I need to do this," Alex said. "At this point, I don't have a lot to lose."

Alex had resolved himself that running was no longer an option. His mom was there for him at his worst, he needed to be there for her.

"Ok," Emory said, pushing open the front door. Cool air filled the room as it snuck in from outside. "Let's go."

They drove in silence. Grief had displaced the anger Alex had been feeling. He would never get over the fact he had let his mom down. He should have been with her instead of running.

What were her last moments like?

Did she struggle without him there to hold her hand?

Was she in pain?

The only images he had of a cardiac arrest were from the reruns of ER that played in the prison lounge. It was always a chaotic event and there was CPR.

The image of someone compressing his mother's bare chest brought a sick feeling to his soul. She had earned a better death, and if there was a God, he would have afforded her one.

Alex looked at Emory. Behind the thick glasses, his eyes were focused on the road. What was left of his snow-white hair was slicked back on his head. Emory had demonstrated more selfless acts of kindness than anyone Alex had encountered since being back in Pinehurst.

Alex had experienced persecution from people who were supposed to help him. But Emory, who had no skin in this game, had stepped in because of a friendship with his mom.

"Thank you," Alex said.

"What was that?" Emory said, glancing at Alex.

"I was thanking you for all of your help," Alex said. "You had no reason to help me. Now, there is a chance you could go to jail. I am not sure why you are doing it, but I appreciate it."

"Don't mention it," Emory said. "I know you are cynical of all this religious stuff, but I feel like I need to show a little bit of the love of Christ in what I do."

"Even if that means helping an ex-convict?"

"Yep! Especially if it means helping an ex-convict. I can't be selective about who I help." Emory grinned. "I mean, if you read the Bible, Christ was an equal opportunity lover of all people. Rich, poor, royalty, criminal, he didn't care."

Alex sat silently.

"If he saw what was happening today, he would be saddened at the hate shown by those who claim to love him."

"Like Silas," Alex said.

"Exactly. The church has become a big business now. Far away from how he had envisioned it. It is now a mixture of money, greed, manipulation, and celebrity status. Alienating the very people it was designed to help, like yourself."

Alex stared out the window, watching the white landscape pass him by.

"The church should have been the one opening their doors to you, bringing you in, helping you," Emory said. "The whole thing frustrates me."

Soon the familiar site of Pinehurst Memorial Hospital came into view. The parking lot looked crowded for a Sunday; filled with police cruisers and media vans.

"Well, looks like the words out," Alex said.

"Yep," Emory said.

Alex remembered the side door he had escaped from earlier. "Go over that way towards the emergency room."

"Why?"

"I know a less conspicuous way to get in."

Emory turned the car to the left, bypassing the circus at the main entrance. He drove slowly around to the ED entrance.

"Turn here." Alex pointed to a road that ran beside the helipad which was now covered in a blanket of white snow.

"OK, you sure you know what you are doing?"

There were a couple of Bucks County officers standing at the main doors to the ED, but they were busy drinking coffee and flirting with a young nurse.

"Drop me off right here," Alex said.

He saw the access door just off to the left, far enough away from the main entrance that no one would notice him.

"You sure?"

"Yep."

Emory stopped the car, "What do you need me to do?"

"You've done enough," Alex said. "Go home, enjoy your life."

"Alex, I can't just leave you."

"Emory, you can. Promise me two things."

"Sure."

"Come visit me in jail," Alex said.

Emory didn't say anything.

"And Emory," Alex voice tightened, "Keep praying for me."

"I...can...do...that..." Emory said, his voice clenched with emotion.

Alex stepped out of the car and walked briskly towards the door. He made it to the side of the building without being noticed. Turning the cold silver handle, the door opened and stepped into the warm corridor and started to climb the stairs.

Alex quickly made it to the third floor. Painted in black on the blue metal door at the top of the stairs were the words '3rd Floor' and 'Intensive Care Unit.'

Alex slowly opened the door and looked in. No one was around. The door led to a makeshift waiting room for families in a small corridor in the back of the unit. His mom's room was around the corner.

The nurse's station was in the center of the unit. It was a bustle of activity with hospital security, police officers, nurses, and techs all milling around. He stayed tight behind a corner where he could not be seen.

There was no way he could make it to his mother's room without being seen. Gathering his courage, he stepped out from behind the corner and started walking towards his mother's room. He made it to the large sliding glass door where the curtain had been pulled closed. He slid the glass door open and stepped inside.

"Hey! Stop!" a loud voice yelled.

The room was dark except for a fluorescent reading light that was on above the head of the bed. His mother lay there under the covers, hands crossed gently across her still chest, her eyes eternally closed. He recognized something on her face. Peace. For the first time in her troubled life, she had peace.

Alex ran to the bed and threw himself on her, weeping.

He didn't get to tell her goodbye.

"Mom, I'm sorry!" he sobbed. "I should have been here!"

The glass door slid open behind him with a thud. Soon a crowd of people descended into the room. A strong hand grabbed him by the shoulders and begin to pull him back. He squeezed his mom's lifeless body tighter.

"Stop it," a female voice said.

"I can't, ma'am. He is a suspect in a crime."

"At least let him have a few minutes with his mother!"

The hands dropped off his shoulder. He drowned out the argument going on behind him. His mom's body was cold, but he could catch the faint powdery scent she always wore, threaded through the sharp, sterile hospital smell.

He stared down. "Thick as thieves."

Soon, large hands were pulling him away again, forcing his arms behind his back. The familiar cold metal of handcuffs and the slight pinch to his wrist as they locked. Old memories flooded back into his mind.

"Alex Hollins," a deep voice said, "You are under arrest for the kidnapping of Landon Layne. You have the right to remain silent, anything you say can and will be used against you in a court of law...."

87

Dalton Blackwood sped down State Road 27, lights blazing and sirens howling. Not thinking about the condition of the roads, relying heavily on his cruiser's snow chains.

When the call came across the radio that there were shots fired at the Boone house, he knew he had to be the first one on the scene. He had a strong suspicion that Silas had gotten the Boone brothers wrapped up in the Layne boys disappearance. Over the past twenty-four hours Silas had become more unhinged with his obsession with Alex Hollins.

Daltons disgust for Silas had only grown, unfortunately he had enough dirt on him to bury Dalton with life. Of course, he had turned a blind eye many times while Silas had done things. It was the shared guilt that kept them begrudgingly close.

He slowed as he approached the old service road to the left. His car handled unusually well in the aftermath of the snow. Turning onto the road there were fresh tire tracks in the snow, letting Dalton know he wasn't the first down the road. He wished he could go faster, but the poor condition of the road only meant he was likely to destroy the cruiser's suspension in the process. Eventually the familiar tan trailer came into view.

In front of the trailer sat Silas's large black Cadillac Escalade. Dalton's chest tightened as he put the car in park. Hopping out he unholstered his pistol, making his way slowly up the steps. The terrified screams of child echoed from inside.

He pounded on the door.

"Zeke, Eddie! Open up! It's Sheriff Blackwood," he yelled through the thin metal door.

Initially, there was silence, soon followed by footsteps thumping through the trailer. The door swung halfway open and Zeke appeared.

"Well, howdy, Sheriff. What brings you out here?"

"We got a report of some gunshots in this area. I need to come in and take a quick look around."

"Oh," Zeke laughed. "That was just Eddie being stupid. His shotgun fell out of the gun rack and went off. Put a nice hole in the wall though."

"Why is Sila's car out front?"

Zeke's nervous eyes darted back and forth, "Oh…you see I was having some trouble with my truck and Silas, being the kind man he is, told me I could borrow it until I got good old Cletus operation again."

"Well, if that is the case, you won't mind me coming in to take a look around," Dalton said, lowering his gun to his side.

Zeke offered up a nervous laugh. "Well, this really isn't the best time. You know, all the commotion has gotten Eddie a little on edge and you know he isn't up for company when he gets like that."

Winking at Dalton, Zeke made a drinking motion with his thumb and pinky. In the distance sirens wailed.

"Zeke, I have more units on the way. Either you let me in now or it's going to turn into quite a scene."

"Dalton, I hate to pull this card, but if you want to come in, you're going to need a warrant," Zeke said. "I know we are friends and all, but it sounds like you may have an agenda."

"Well, that's unfortunate Zeke. I don't have an agenda, just hoping to clear this up quickly and I can move on with my day," Dalton said as the sirens grew closer. "I'm sure you heard we also have a kidnapping case that is a high priority, so this is pulling me away from that."

Zeke clicked his tongue. "Such a shame. Pinehurst used to be such a quiet town. Honestly, it all changed once that Hollins man returned."

Dalton nodded, "You may be right. Well, I guess I'll go talk with Judge Peters and see about getting a search warrant. I'll be back."

"See ya soon." Zeke grinned a black toothless grin as he began to shut the door.

Dalton could hear the sirens and wheels crunching on the dirt road. Just as Zeke had the door shut, Dalton raised his leg and with a swift kick knocked the door open. Zeke went sailing back and Dalton drew his gun, charging into the trailer and slipping on a wet substance on the floor.

Blood.

His eyes tracked the blood to the lifeless form of a man lying face first on the floor. Dalton suppressed the urge to vomit. A child sat on a couch in the living room screaming through a pillow.

"You no good piece of..." Zeke had recovered from his fall and charged toward Dalton.

Dalton quickly aimed and fired a shot hitting Zeke in his right thigh, which sent him howling to the floor in pain.

Landon continued screaming, trying to wedge himself behind the sofa.

"What the hell?" Eddies gruff voice called out

Dalton turned quickly to his right as Eddie appeared in the doorway of his bedroom with a rifle at his shoulder.

"Drop it!" Dalton yelled. "Drop the gun!"

"You shot my brother!" Eddie said, nodding his head past Dalton where Zeke lay writhing in pain on the floor.

"I said drop the gun!"

Eddie laughed, "Make me!"

"Eddie, I'm not playing!"

Eddie grinned, leveling the rifle directly at Dalton, "Neither am I!"

"Eddie, I have more cars on the way, this is not going to end well for you."

"You shot my brother!"

Eddie nodded over to Zeke's huddle mass writhing in pain on the floor.

"Eddie, I am not asking again, drop the gun."

"I am not telling you no again," Eddie's finger tightened around the trigger

Dalton fired a quick shot, striking Eddie in the chest, sending him backwards into the bedroom, the rifle clattered to the floor. Landon wailed and had managed to climb behind the sofa, now screaming at the top of his lungs.

Dalton lowered his pistol and ran toward the sofa. He knelt and, as he got closer, he detected the faint scent of piss.

"Come here big man, nobody is going to hurt you now," Dalton extended out his hand.

The sounds of footsteps running up the stairs came from outside and soon the trailer was swarming with officers.

"You ok Dalton?" one of the young officers asked.

"I'm fine," Dalton said, "Let's get a medical unit out here. In the meantime, someone put some cuffs on that one." He pointed to Zeke who on the floor, moaning and holding his leg.

"Jesus, what happened here?" another officer asked.

88

Alex sat in the hard gray metal chair, rubbing his wrist where the handcuffs had been. An empty chair sat across from him separated by a cold gray metal table. The interrogation room had not changed much in twenty-five years. A fresh coat of a drab two-tone gray covered the walls. A large two-way mirror filled the back wall, not fooling anyone. A lone black pendant lamp hung suspended above the center of the room, its flickering incandescent bulb casting an eerie glow in the room.

Alex looked down at his hands, knowing this was probably the last time in a while he would not see them shackled. In a way, he was relieved.

Relieved to stop running.

Relieved to know his mom was not suffering.

Relieved to be going back to the place he knew better than home.

It hurt more because he was innocent. At this point he did not have the money to hire a high-powered defense attorney so would be stuck with the public defender. He would still fight, but that would be like trying to press a boulder up a hill in wet grass. He had resolved himself to going back to jail, and at this point, he was okay with that.

After what felt like an intentionally long time, the door to the room opened and a middle-aged man with salt and pepper hair came walking in carrying two Styrofoam cups. His oxford blue dress shirt strained around his large abdomen as he walked toward the table and placed a cup of coffee in front of Alex.

"Mr. Hollins," he said, walking to the empty chair. It let out a creak as he eased himself into it. "My name is Detective Wilson"

Alex didn't say anything, just sipped the bitterly strong coffee.

"I suppose you know why you are here?" the detective continued.

"I have an idea," Alex said.

"Well, we can make this quick if you tell me where the Layne kid is."

"I don't know."

The detective remained silent; his eyes fixed on Alex as he took a loud slurp of his coffee.

"Mr. Hollins, I would like to believe that, but we have witnesses placing you at the residence the night before the child went missing, and with your history, things aren't looking good for you."

Alex was having a bad case of Deja vu from twenty-five years earlier when he had sat in a similar room being questioned by a similar looking detective, drinking similarly awful tasting coffee. The only difference was he was guilty then.

"I know things don't look good, but I swear I am innocent," Alex said. "I love Landon, and if I knew where he was, I would tell you right away."

"Then tell me."

Alex paused," I don't know."

The detective leaned back in the chair as it let out a series of creaks & pops. He clasped his hands together and rested them on his round abdomen.

"Look, Alex, It's Sunday. There is nothing less I would rather be doing than sitting here talking with you. The longer you hold back the truth, the worse it looks for you and the less patient I get," he said. "I'm sure you learned from time in prison that the more you cooperate the easier it is for both of us."

Alex stared down at his hands. Tears burning the corners of his eyes but fought hard to hold them back.

"What if I told you I had a pretty good idea of who was involved?" Alex said.

Detective Wilson leaned forward and placed his elbows on the table, his pudgy fingers pointing toward Alex.

"Well, I would be lying if I said I wasn't curious."

"Have you talked to Silas Weston?" Alex said.

"The pastor?" the detective laughed. "That man is a pillar of our community. Alex, you realize you are making this more difficult on yourself."

Alex's cheeks flushed

"I want an attorney," he said.

"Ok, so we are going to play that card now?" Detective Wilson sounded agitated. "Alex, for god's sake, why are you making it so hard on yourself? Do you want to spend the rest of your life in prison?"

There was a brief knock on the door and it swung open. A young officer looking pale, stuck his head in. "Jon, we need you for a second."

"Alright." The detective stood. "We were about to take a break anyway. Alex, why don't you think about what we have discussed and I'll be back in shortly."

The detective made his way to the door and stepped out, pulling the door shut with a dull thud. Alex stared around the empty room. Hopeless was the only word that could describe how he felt.

He was already guilty before proven innocent and a fight would be futile. He had lost his mom and any chance of a relationship with Harper. He didn't have a reason to stay here. At least he had a family in prison and for the most part, they treated him much better.

Alex had managed to finish his cup of coffee. He bent forward, resting his head on the cold metal table. After a while, Alex couldn't tell whether it had been minutes or hours, the door to the interrogation room opened and Detective Wilson stepped into the room.

"You're free to go," he said.

Alex looked up, confused. "Excuse me?"

"I said you're free to go."

"I don't understand."

"You don't need to. Right now you can leave. I would take advantage of that and get out of here."

Alex slowly stood, like he was waiting for the punchline of a bad joke. He walked towards the door.

"Can I use a phone to call a ride?" he asked.

"Sure, stop at the front desk." The detective motioned down the hall.

Alex considered saying thank you but started walking instead.

The station was unusually busy for a Sunday. Full of staff and officers milling around with somber looks on their faces.

A young receptionist sat at the main desk.

Alex smiled at her. "Detective Wilson said I could make a call."

"Sure," she smiled and lifted the phone onto the counter. "Press 9 to get an outside line."

Alex thanked her and dialed Emory's number.

89

Harper lay in her room, lights out, blinds closed, and the blankets pulled over her head. She hadn't moved in hours. She was numb. Her life had gone from promising to being destroyed in a matter of hours. A pervasive terror gripped her as she thought about Landon and what potentially could be happening to him at this moment.

Poor, little Lando.

He hadn't asked to be brought into the world to face an abusive, alcoholic father. He hadn't asked to be raised by an aunt. He was an innocent boy who happened to draw a short straw in the lottery of life. She had tried her best to give him the childhood he deserved.

She never let him see her upset or crying. She only wanted him to have positive memories of her and she hoped those were at least providing some comfort for him now. Feeling a self-pity spiral starting, she curled into a ball.

She must have dozed off because the sound of a commotion downstairs woke her up. Excited voices, shouts, and soon there was the thunder of footfalls on the steps and the door to her room burst open.

"Sis! They found him! They found him!"

Vanessa ran to Harper, yanking the blanket off her head. "He is safe!" She pulled Harper into her chest and they both held each other and cried. The nightmare was over.

• • •

Harper and Vanessa bounced around in the back of the patrol car as it sped down the snowy road. The young officer sat quietly in the front seat, focused intently on the road ahead. Vanessa had her arm around Harper pulling her as close as the seat belt would allow. "It's going to be alright, Sis," she whispered.

Harper smiled weakly, she wanted to believe that, but until she had Landon in her arms and counted all ten fingers and toes, she wasn't going to let herself get too excited. Harper had brought Pupster along, looking at the tattered stuffed animal her heart ached. Hoping soon their little family unit would be together again.

The officer turned off the main road onto a small side road. Fresh tire tracks were visible in the snow. Large trees with bare branches weighted down by the recent snow hung over the road. The officer drove cautiously down the road, still hitting the occasional hole or large rock covered by snow shaking the entire car.

Harper looked out the window at the barren forest passing by. Her heart sank at the possibility of her Landon being alone out there. After several minutes the road began to clear and a lone trailer sat in the distance.

The isolation of the road was soon replaced with a bustle of activity. Yellow police tape surrounded the property. There were several Bucks County Sheriffs and Virginia State Police vehicles parked randomly in front of the trailer along with a couple of vans from the local news stations. There was a lot of activity as people milled around taking pictures and talking to each other. The officer pulled off the road onto a makeshift parking spot.

"Here we are," he said, shifting in the seat and looking back at them. "Hold tight. I'm going to let them know you are here."

When he stepped out of the car a burst of cold air blew in. Harper stared ahead as he walked away, ducked under the yellow tape, and disappeared into the activity surrounding the trailer.

"Do you think he is ok?" Harper asked.

Vanessa grinned. "He is your son! He is tough!"

"I'm trying to tell myself that," Harper said.

She looked at the decrepit trailer. Rust stains ran down the drab tan siding and bedsheets covered the windows. She couldn't imagine what happened in there, what happened to her Lando.

She shook.

Vanessa rubbed her back. "You are going to make it sis."

Soon the officer reappeared, walking toward the car with another officer. He approached the rear door and pulled it open.

"Morning Ms. Layne," the new officer said. "I'm Officer Thomas, you ready to go see your son?"

Harper sagged as the officer guided her out of the car, his hand firm on her back. Soon they were surrounded by the camera crews. Vanessa's hand on the small of her back directed her forward. Harper kept her head down to avoid looking at the cameras.

"Ms. Layne, any comment?"

"Have you seen Alex Hollins?"

Occasionally the officer barked, "Stay back, give her some space."

When they got to the yellow tape, the officer held it up allowing them to duck under it. As if the tape possessed some magical force the reporters stopped not advancing any further.

The ground was muddy from where the snow had begun to melt. Harper's eyes were blurry from her tears, but she still managed to follow the officer. In the distance a black Chevy Tahoe faced them, its rear gate open. Several people were standing behind the vehicle.

"Almost there," the officer said.

Harpers throat clutched and her heart rate jumped. She reached back and found Vanessa's hand, squeezing it tight.

A young female State Trooper with dark brown eyes and black hair hidden tightly under her peaked service cap stepped out from behind the vehicle. She had a brilliant white smile, which put Harper at ease.

"Ms. Layne, I'm Trooper Walls, but you can call me Grace. Please follow me, I have someone who wants to see you."

Harper followed her around to the rear of the Tahoe. Sitting under an oversized green blanket and drinking a cup of hot chocolate was Landon.

"Oh, baby!" Harper yelled running towards him.

"Mama!" Landon screamed, dropping his hot chocolate, leaping off the back of the SUV to run to her.

Harper went down on her knees in the wet snow, not even noticing the cold as Landon leapt into her arms. She gave him the biggest bear hug she possibly could.

"Oh, baby! I love you. I'm so sorry!"

Landon squeezed her tightly. "Mama, I missed you!"

"I missed you too baby!"

Soon another body knelt beside her.

"Auntie Van!" Landon yelled.

"Aunt Van is so sorry she left you alone," Vanessa sobbed.

"I have someone else who missed you," Harper said bringing Pupster around.

"Pupster!!" Landon cried grabbing the stuffed dog and wrapping his arms back around his mom & Vanessa.

The three of them hugged, oblivious to the chaos surrounding them.

• • •

That night after finally getting Landon to bed, Harper stood at the doorway to his room, watching the subtle rise and fall of his chest. His room was illuminated by a single Paw Patrol night light casting a dim yellow glow to the room. Tears ran down her cheeks.

How had she come so close to losing him?

He was her everything, a tidal wave of despair washed over her, the fact she may never see him devastated her. This was her second chance to do better.

90

The early morning sun spilled through the partially open curtains finding its way to Alex's closed eyes. He rolled over and tried for a few more minutes of sleep, which would likely be impossible since it had eluded him all night.

Sleep and rest were two different things, both of which were in short order for him lately. Emory had dropped him off late yesterday evening and Alex had spent most of the night trying to process the events of the past forty-eight hours.

Emory had updated him on the news that they had located Landon. The sense of relief was overwhelming. Emory didn't have many more details to share.

Alex decided to get out of bed. The house was chilly, so he made his way to the thermostat in the hallway and turned it up. There was a click and soon the sound of warm air blowing out of the vents filled the house.

He put a pot of coffee on and went into the living room, turning the TV on to one of the local early morning news shows. A young blonde-haired woman with a fake smile and tired eyes no amount of make-up could disguise was talking about some upcoming local events.

"Now with your local news, here is Erik."

The camera shifted to a young man seated beside Jessica, looking more alert than his co-anchor.

"Thanks, Jessica," Erik Miles said, turning to face the camera.

An image appeared beside him: Landon's school photo with the caption: Local Boy Found Safe. Alex leaned forward; every nerve now tuned to the screen.

"The missing child case that thrust Pinehurst into the national spotlight has ended. In a joint effort between local and state law enforcement, Landon Layne was found safe yesterday afternoon."

A mugshot of Zeke Boone replaced the photo. Erik continued, "Zeke Boone is currently in custody and is being questioned in connection with the abduction. His brother Eddie Boone was found dead at the scene. Police have also confirmed that local pastor, Silas Weston was seriously injured, in what authorities are saying was a related incident. He is currently at Pinehurst Memorial Hospital in critical condition"

The screen split: a polished headshot of Silas Weston on the left, a grainy mugshot of Eddie Boone on the right.

Alex sat in a stunned silence.

He might never know exactly who took Landon or how everything unfolded, but he had always been certain Silas had been involved.

Alex didn't feel sadness when he learned his father was clinging to life, just relief. Silas had made his life miserable since he returned from prison. Now with Silas close to death it brought Alex a strange sense of comfort. Maybe there was a God after all.

The sharp beep of the coffee pot broke the silence. On screen, the news had shifted to a city council scandal, the anchor's voice now background noise. Alex clicked the TV off and moved to the kitchen, pouring a cup of coffee, the warmth grounding him.

What would the fallout be like in Pinehurst? Emory had always hinted that Silas had his hands in everything politics, churches, schools. It wouldn't unravel quietly.

• • •

The morning dragged. Alex nursed two cups of coffee and finally got his first real shower in days. The hot water was a godsend. Watching the dark grime swirl around the drain, a visual reminder of how dirty he had gotten.

Wrapping a towel around his waist he stared at the fogged mirror. There was still a lot to do. He needed to call Emory and head to the funeral home. His mother deserved a proper burial, but he had no idea how he'd manage to pay for it. His chest tightened. Grief had a way of creeping up when things got quiet.

Freshly dressed, he was about to call Emory when the doorbell rang. His heart jolted. Unannounced visitors never meant good news lately. For a brief second, he imagined flashing lights, handcuffs, some new twist in the case. Had they changed their minds?

The doorbell rang again.

He peeked through the front window. A white Honda CR-V sat in his driveway.

Harper.

He yanked the door open.

Harper and Landon stood on the porch. Harper's eyes shimmered with tears. Landon beamed. For a long beat, no one spoke. Then Harper lunged forward and wrapped him in a tight hug, sobbing.

"I am sorry," she whispered into his shoulder.

"You don't need to apologize," Alex said, pulling back gently. "You were protecting him."

Landon looked up and launched into Alex's arms, catching him off guard., "Whoa—big man!" Alex laughed.

"I brought you a car," Landon said proudly, holding up a small red Corvette. "It goes really fast."

"I'll bet it does. I can't wait to try it out."

"Do you have any Hot Wheels here?" Landon asked, already peeking past him into the house.

"Landon!" Harper sounded mortified.

Alex grinned. "No Hot Wheels, but I've got some chocolate milk in the fridge. And coffee for your mom. You two want to come in?"

"We'd love to," Harper said, her smile soft and a little shaky.

91

The funeral for Nancy Hollins took place on a cold February morning. The sky was clear and deep blue. It was a small graveside service and sparsely attended. She barely had enough funds to cover the burial expenses. Some good Samaritan had donated a headstone. Alex had suspicions it was Emory.

Harper sat next to Alex, threading her arm through his. Despite the heavy winter coats, he could feel the reassuring warmth of her body. Landon sat beside her clutching the tattered puppy that was a permanent presence with him. Vanessa and Emory stood looking somberly on.

After his experience with Silas, Alex was done with religion, so having a funeral for his mom took some convincing. Emory reminded Alex this was for his mom, not him.

Alex agreed.

A middle-aged gentleman with a kind face stepped up to the casket. He was wearing a black shirt with a white clerical collar. He nodded towards Alex.

"Family and friends, we are here today to celebrate the life of Nancy Hollins." He pointed towards the casket. "I don't believe anyone here would argue she had an easy life. No, in fact, I think we would all agree she had quite the opposite. A life plagued by disappointment, heartache, anguish, and grief."

Alex tensed, trying not to take the comments personally. Harper pulled him tighter.

"But you wouldn't know it? She always had a smile, a word of encouragement, and a cup of coffee ready for whoever needed it. She was generous. Despite not having a lot, she gave a lot. Despite her circumstances, she persevered. Despite having every reason to be angry, she remained kind. Her quiet kindness reflected the words of our Savior in the book of Matthew where he says, 'Truly, I tell you, whatever you did for one of the least of these brothers and sisters of mine, you did for me.'"

The pastor paused, letting the words sink in. A tear ran down his cheek.

"That is a noble yardstick for all of us to be measured against. Not how we treated those who could help us in return, but how we treated those with nothing to give, no means to help us back."

"The least of these," he continued. "Nancy was a woman of great faith, and I know her faith was tested mightily at times, yet she still found it within her to do for others. I ask that as we lay her earthly body to rest, we carry her legacy of caring forward."

The pastor closed his Bible and ended the service with a prayer.

Alex walked up and placed his gloved hand on the casket, "Bye Mom. I love you." He leaned forward and gently kissed the cool metal of the casket, walked back towards Harper who was talking with Emory and Vanessa.

"Beautiful service," Emory said.

"Yes, it was a very nice testament to your mom," Vanessa said.

"Thanks," Alex replied. "I know she meant a lot to me, I guess I never really knew how far her kindness went. We may never know just how many people she touched."

There was a tug on his pants leg and Alex looked down to see Landon with his arms outstretched a tattered bear dangling by an arm.

"Lando!" Alex exclaimed, kneeling and swooping Landon up with a flood of giggles.

Harper leaned in and gave the three of them a hug. "I think you're stuck with us," she said.

"I can't think of anyone else I would rather be stuck with." Alex smiled.

Epilogue

Bay seven in the intensive care unit at Pinehurst Memorial Hospital was like the others, dimly lit and reserved for those teetering on the edge, home to the sickest of the sick. The current patient lay sedated a heavy bandage covering most of his torso. A chest tube drain sat quiet bubbling beside the bed. The patient's chest rose and fell with the rhythm of the ventilator, inflating and deflating his lungs through a tube secured in his mouth.

The intensivist had already given a grim prognosis. Between the amount of blood he lost from the gunshot wound and the prolonged hypoxia from the collapsed lung, the team doubted he would survive and if he did there was concern for significant cognitive impact. Worst case scenario he regains consciousness only to end up in a facility being fed through a tube, best case scenario he doesn't wake up.

The room this evening was quiet except for the steady beep of the monitors. Nurses scurried around outside the room tending to other patients, no one expected bay seven to wake up anytime soon. It was at shift change as the old guard was leaving and the new guard was coming on board when Silas Weston opened his eyes.

-The End-

Acknowledgements

People often asked why I wanted to write a book. The truth? I'm not sure I ever had a perfect answer, it was just something I wanted to do. I have toyed with writing stories for over fifteen years, starting and stopping more than I can count.

About five years ago I found myself in an unexpected career shift that gave me the nudge I needed. I finally sat down, focused and followed through. The pages you just finished are the result.

While writing a novel is often framed as a one-person job, it absolutely isn't. Plenty of people helped me get this story across the finish line.

To my wife and sons, thank you for supporting me, tolerating the countless hours I spent barricaded in my study, and knowing when it was time to drag me away for my own good.

To my parents, thank you for being my first fans. And to my dad in particular thank you for modeling the exact opposite of Silas. Your grace and compassion to other shaped more of this book than you realize.

Thanks to Jenny Horton and Erica Gillespie for their beta reading superpowers. They made this book cleaner, tighter and far more readable.

And to everyone else who played a role, large or small, thank you. It was long journey that I was fortunate enough not to have to walk alone.

William Price

www.ingramcontent.com/pod-product-compliance
Lightning Source LLC
Chambersburg PA
CBHW050525110726
47899CB00005B/1596